To Jon,

GW00854645

Trouble with Swords

A Temporal Detective Agency Novel

Volume Two

Best wishes

Richard Hardie

Discover us online:
www.authorsreach.co.uk

Join us on facebook:
www.facebook.com/authorsreach

To Dom who became a good friend.
To Sarah and Ben who started a journey together.
To Emma who inspired Tertia, and to Jane who was always Merlin.

The Author

Richard lives in the South of England with his wife, son and cocker spaniel. His daughter and her fiancé live nearby.

By necessity, he sells IT software, however by choice he write books for Young Adults. Twice a year, he goes to the Gower with his cocker spaniel and walks for miles along the glorious coastline. Amazingly, many plotlines arise during those trips and lots of plot logjams get freed up. It's a very cathartic time!

Richard was a Scout Leader for 15 years, during which time he wrote and helped produce five successful Gang Shows. That gave him a tremendous understanding of the humour and likes of children of all ages, and some of his characters are actually based on Scouts he knew, both girls and boys. His greatest influence (asides from the kids themselves) has been Terry Pratchett, who back in 2002 actually helped him write a scene for one of his Gang Shows and even acted in it.

Richard's first book in the The Temporal Detective Agency series, *Leap of Faith*, was a finalist in The People's Book Prize 2013/14. *Trouble with Swords* is the second book in the series.

Find Richard Hardie at **www.rhardie.com**.

The Temporal Detective Agency series:

Leap of Faith
(finalist in The People's Book Prize 2013/14)

Trouble with Swords

Trouble with Swords

A Temporal Detective Agency Novel

Volume Two

Chapter One

A Theft, a Homecoming and a Plan of Sorts

When Merlin calls, you don't make excuses like telling her you'll drop by after coffee. You leave whatever you're doing and go as fast as your little legs can carry you, because her reputation for changing people into rabbits is no idle threat. Believe me, it's a sure-fire promise.

Actually no one has ever seen her do it. But when people disappear, as they sometimes do around Camelot, and the number of bunnies multiplies ... well, everyone puts two and two together and makes five. Merl just smiles and carries on feeding carrots to her furry friends, while the rabbits carry on doing what rabbits do best.

Merl called us a couple of days after we got back from the year 1734. We'd just solved a Temporal Detective Agency case in South Wales, beating the evil Black Knight and his wrecking thugs with the help of our old friend Sir Gawain. I ended up with a nice diamond brooch, while Marlene, Merlin's younger sister, got the Mona Lisa to cover the damp patch on her office wall, and Unita (or Neets as I call her) managed to grab a Welsh boyfriend in the shape of Gawain's son Bryn. Job well done.

My name's Tertia by the way, and I suppose I got a boyfriend out of it as well, though David's more of a friend who happens to be a boy, no matter what he thinks. He's also the Black Knight's adopted son, not that I hold that against him unless I'm in a particularly nasty mood, which isn't often because luckily I have a very nice nature ... even if I say it myself. David's real parents drowned in a shipwreck on the Gower coast, but on a whim the Black Knight decided to keep David alive and adopt him, so long as he made himself useful.

The five of us were having tea and bickies in Galahad's *Olé Grill* restaurant cave when Marlene's talking cup went off in her pocket. Actually it sounded more like someone clearing their throat down a trumpet and from the urgency of the rasp it wasn't going to be a social chat. Marlene put the tin cup in the middle of the table so we could all join the conference call and as the agency's senior partner she sat nearest to it, taking charge.

"Okay, Merlin," she said, recognising her sister's cough, "we're all ears, because you don't normally phone us on the cup out of the blue, so what's up in Camelot?"

Marlene leaned back in her chair, raised its front legs and balanced on the rear ones, something she never let Neets or me do because she said it wasn't ladylike. The boys always got away with it though, because Bryn was built like a brick privy and David was just death-defyingly obstinate, like a lot of smaller people. Yeah, all right. Like me!

"Merlin, are you still there, dear?" Marlene pinged the cup with her forefinger and smiled as I stopped it from skittering off the table onto the floor. The cup started talking and after that we didn't get a word in edgeways, but that didn't matter because what Merl had to say was pretty awesome, especially the bit about she and Arthur expecting a little prince of their own.

Marlene finished the call and put the cup back in her pocket. "It looks like we're going back to Camelot, girls. The royal pair needs the Temporal Detective Agency's help and I've always found it's best not to turn down royalty."

Neets looked at her beloved Bryn and I glanced at

David because Marlene had very obviously said *girls*. Boys were not included in this trip.

"Bryn, David, I have another little case for you to solve while we're away. An old friend has sent me a message through the usual secret channels asking the TDA to look into the disappearance of the crew of a ship called the *Mary Celeste* back in 1872. He wants to see if we can find out what went on and help one of his relatives who was on board. There may be nothing to it, but see what you can do." The boys began to protest, but Marlene held up her hand. "This isn't a club, it's a detective agency. Finish your tea and get ready, please." The boys nodded meekly and even David, who had opened his mouth to argue, wisely closed it again.

Half an hour later the five us of walked through the Time Portal.

Zzzzzp.

The boys went to a ship in the middle of the Atlantic, while Neets, Marlene and I zoomed back to Camelot, leaving Galahad in charge of the *Olé Grill* restaurant and Unita's cats in charge of the Temporal Detective Agency. Safe hands and paws all round.

We walked out of the Portal into the fifth-century Camelot cave, which to Neets and me was home away from home. Okay, it was the same cave the Temporal Detective Agency operated from in the twenty-first century, but this was fifteen hundred years earlier and also happened to be close to where we were born, so every nook and cranny was familiar to us. Yet everything looked somewhat newer and more like a chaotic home without the *Olé Grill* restaurant taking up most of the space. Merl had been a fairly regular time-traveller and had an obsession with collecting souvenirs from everywhere she went, which meant her cave looked a little bit like a seaside gift shop, but without the sophistication.

Merl gave us all a quick cuddle while Marlene busied herself in the kitchen area, then we gathered round the largest and most familiar piece of furniture in Merl's rather cluttered cave. Arthur had given his wizard the task of preserving Camelot's Round Table some years earlier and Merl had insisted it could only be done in her cave if magic was to be involved. She never explained to the struggling peasants why magic couldn't be used to transport the table and they never asked for fear of increasing the rabbit population. Unfortunately, all Merl's attempts with wizardry and even chemicals proved unsuccessful, though to be honest I couldn't blame the woodworm for not leaving such a tasty bit of lunch.

I noticed that Neets took Bryn's father's seat at the place marked *Sir Gawain*, while Merl and I randomly plonked ourselves down causing minute clouds of woodworm dust to erupt like mini geysers. Marlene joined us, carrying a tray of cups filled with Merl Grey tea, and sat two places away from her sister, so that in between them the faded name of *King Arthur* was visible on the tabletop. We sipped and sighed because drinking Merl Grey in Merl's cave was the ultimate way to enjoy the brew.

"Bloody good tea, Merlin," Marlene said with feeling and a gurgle as she drained her cup. "The stuff Unita makes isn't a patch on the real thing. Shame there's no bickies though, but understandable if you and Arthur have been away. Speaking of which, where is the royal ox?"

Marlene blushed as a shadow detached itself from the wall and Arthur of the Britons stumbled forward, tripping over his scabbard, which I couldn't help noticing was minus a sword. He'd ruined his grand entrance and the detective in me started working overtime. Marlene patted the chair between herself and Merl and our once and future king sat down looking like a sorry cocker spaniel, but without the long furry ears.

"Hullo, Arthur." Marlene gave him a coy little smile and a finger wave, while Merl remained tight-lipped. "Enjoying your honeymoon on Avalon with the lovely Merlin?" Arthur mumbled something none of us quite caught, but the silly smile on his face spoke volumes because we all knew the wizard and her king were deliriously happy. This was surprising really because their relationship had hardly been the normal *boy meets girl* story.

As far as the people of Camelot were concerned, Merl was an old man with greasy grey hair, a long straggly beard and an eagle's beak for a nose. Amazingly, no one guessed her secret and even Arthur had thought his best friend and loyal adviser was a man and interested in only one thing … magic. That, of course, had been wrong in every single way because Merl had been madly in love with her king for years, even though she'd resigned herself to becoming an old and shrivelled spinster. The problem was that Arthur secretly loved her back, which was great, but very confusing for the poor guy. Things were getting complicated and a year or two earlier I'd realised it was time for Merl to come out as it were, so I grabbed the two of them one morning before Merl could put on her disguise and set the record straight.

The King of the Britons had stared at the clean-shaven Merl, whose voice must have seemed higher than he had remembered and whose body shape was somehow pleasingly different in a curvy sort of way. He gave a start when he realised everyone was waiting for him to speak, then let out a long sigh and gazed intently into Merl's eyes. "Tell me one thing, will you, Merlin?" The king had looked so uncharacteristically nervous.

"If I can, Arthur." I'd never seen Merl blush before, especially not the deeper orangey red of Marlene's hair.

"Are you … are you really a woman?" He'd mumbled the words into the ground, his fists clenching and unclenching by his sides.

Merl had cupped her ear. "I'm sorry, Arthur, I didn't quite catch that."

"I said, are you a *woman*?" This time the king had nearly shouted as he hopped from one foot to the other like a child desperate for the toilet.

The cave had fallen silent and the seconds dragged by as Merl blushed uncontrollably, this time well beyond the colour of Marlene's hair. She closed her eyes and hung her head. "Yes, Arthur," she said at last in a tiny voice, because she must have been terrified at what the king's reaction would be. "I'm a woman." Under her breath she added hopefully, "Your woman."

Arthur punched the air, skipped around like a mad thing and shouted something that sounded very much like *Yes! Yes! Yes! You little beauty!* but I couldn't really be sure. He stood in front of the beetroot-coloured wizard and kissed her gently on the forehead. "Thank you." He'd said it so quietly that only she and those nearest to them had heard. The wizard and the king had stared at each other silently, catching up on many years of misunderstandings and wishful thoughts.

I'd made the match back then and now I was going to have to save it.

"I hear from your beloved that you've been a silly boy and gone and lost your toy sword." Marlene believed in pinning the tail to the donkey.

"That is *not* what I said," Merl said indignantly.

"Excalibur has been stolen and whoever did it now possesses the most powerful talisman in the land. Without Excalibur, Camelot is as good as dead meat and so are we."

"I know, dear," said Marlene. "I was just trying to lighten the atmosphere. I told you the Temporal Detective Agency would help, and help we will. Now, whom do you suspect?"

"If I half knew who did it they'd be outside calling themselves Floppsie and munching on a carrot by now! It could be anyone with a grudge against Arthur, or an ambition to be king, which usually comes to the same thing. Right now if Arthur openly returns to Britain and can't show Excalibur, every warlord in the kingdom will descend on Camelot and there won't be very much left to chew on. It's only the magic of the sword that keeps the vultures at bay."

"I take it Excalibur disappeared while you were on Avalon enjoying your extended honeymoon?" Marlene got up and refilled her mug when Merl nodded. "Then it looks as though someone knew you were both there and that the sword was with you. That probably points to it being an inside job. Or, of course, maybe you just mislaid it, Arthur?"

The king shook his head vigorously.

"And nobody knows about Arthur and you, Merlin, except us, of course? Congratulations on the news about the future little prince by the way. Thought of a name yet?"

11

Merl smiled and went all mumsy. "If he's a boy we thought Melvyn and if she's a girl then Mildred." Her smile froze. "But if you don't find Excalibur, there won't be a little prince, or two loving parents, and probably not even an auntie."

Marlene looked appalled. "Ah, it's as serious as that?" I knew being an auntie had always quite appealed to her, but being a dead one had permanent drawbacks. "Then it's time for action, my dear. It's obvious Arthur is in danger until we get Excalibur back, so our priority is to keep him safe with a royal disappearing trick or two." She had a sparkle in her eye. "Unita, make some sandwiches. No tuna in mine as it gives me the burps, and brew some more Merl Grey and put it in a travelling flask, or whatever passes for one here. Tertia, you and I need to have a chat," she looked at Merl and Arthur, "in private if you don't mind, your highnesses."

I tried to look nonchalantly unconcerned as Marlene watched the royal pair scrape their chairs back from the Round Table and wander into a far corner where their grumbles couldn't be heard.

"Right, to business." The TDA's senior partner tapped the table with her forefinger, probably waking up a family of sleeping woodworms, but before she could say anything else I put a hand on her arm and squeezed hard. She squealed and looked hurt, but at least she stopped talking.

"What's going on?" I still held onto her arm.

"What's the point in coming all this way, not to mention back in time, and then sending Merl and her Arthur into a corner like a couple of naughty kids? I thought we were here to help them. And why send the boys after a ship and Neets off to make a picnic lunch?" I couldn't help thinking that secrecy is sometimes necessary in the temporal detecting game, but these were our closest friends, colleagues and potential clients.

Marlene let out a *sigh!* But I rather suspected it was more of a reluctant *sooo!* Because now she was not only going to have to tell me things in confidence, but she was also going to have to explain why the others in the TDA couldn't join in. Although when she finished talking I realised why she was our senior partner and why Neets and I did as we were told … sometimes. Marlene had a plan, with a capital P, and Merl and Arthur were not going to like it one little bit. Come to that, Neets wasn't going to be a happy bunny either.

All we had to do was find a reputedly magic sword, unmask whoever stole it, and keep Arthur out of sight until we'd finished. Those were the easy bits. The hard bits were what I had to do to Neets and the boys and how on earth we were going to kill Arthur without Merl objecting too much, or turning us into rabbit poo.

Marlene called back the royal pair and briefly outlined her strategy with one eye on an escape route.

She ducked just in time and dived for the nearest hiding place.

"Okay, here's the plan," she said from underneath the Round Table.

Chapter Two

A Royal Burial and an Equally Royal Holiday

Poor old Arthur.

We buried our king on the island of Avalon after pushing him through the streets of Camelot on a rickety handcart that threatened to toss him off every time we hit a rut.

The crowd cheered! Not because Arthur was dead, but in anticipation of a holiday feast and a few days off work. I wasn't really surprised because they were a typical bunch of Camelot freeloaders, but without them the scam would never work. Scam? Let's face it, most of Arthur's reign was based on one scam or another, and most of them were thought up by Merl to gain power. Now her sister was getting in on the act to keep the royal pair alive and maybe keep the power intact.

I looked up at the castle and wondered who, other than Arthur, was left to live there. Galahad was running his *Olé Grill* restaurant chain based in our TDA offices; Iolanthe, Bors and Mordred had set up a small manufacturing company; doddering old Lancelot and Guinevere had gone to North Wales together in spite of the knight's advancing age, and Gawain had become squire of a small village in South Wales. The place was pretty well empty, but it still stood head and shoulders above the people of Camelot.

Arthur's capital overlooked a large, rather murky lake that provided drinking water, washing, food, and sewage facilities for the whole community, though no one wanted to think about the last bit. Less than a quarter of a mile across the water the mystical island of Avalon was home to wildfowl, water voles and a family of badgers, but why it was mystical no one was sure any more. Its reputation, and rumours spread by Merlin, had done the rest and now nobody ever went to the island except ignorant holiday-makers on a picnic, plus of course a couple of royal honeymooners in search of peace and quiet.

Actually, that's not quite right. When we were kids some of us used to swim out to the island just to prove that we could and when we got there we stood on the shore for a few seconds and then raced back in case the ghosts got us. Neets held the record for some years and it proved handy that sunny morning when we buried our king.

We continued our rickety way through the village.

"Arthur, for God's sake keep still and stop grinning," hissed Marlene. "You'll give the whole game away. Just lie down and look like a corpse." Our small funeral procession had worked its way through the outskirts of Camelot and was now getting near its centre. People were beginning to take notice of the two girls, a woman, their very own Merlin and the trembling body. Marlene told us to mingle with the crowd and encourage the grieving with a fine bit of teenage wailing.

The rutted mud road grabbed the wheels of the wagon, making it jolt and swerve like a supermarket cart. "Slow down, dear." Marlene put a restraining hand on my shoulder when I came back to help. "You'll have the thing over and Camelot needs to see Arthur, not glimpse a bouncing blur. Smile a bit if you want, but in a sad sort of way. And, Unita, stop that dancing."

Arthur looked fantastic in the finest armour Merl had been able to grab at short notice, with a very rough replica of Excalibur clutched in his hands and its matching shield laid on his chest. He looked every inch the fallen hero. Actually the sword was mostly hidden, but everyone knew it had to be Excalibur because Arthur never let it out of his sight and many people said he wouldn't be seen dead without it.

"Wail like Marlene told you," Merl whispered to us out of the corner of her mouth. "Your King's been killed in a great battle, so mourn for his loss as loudly as you can … *No, not you, Arthur!*"

"What's happening, Merlin?" someone shouted from the sidelines. "Who's on the cart?" The crowd pushed forward and Merl quickly pointed at the royal standard draped over the body, beating Arthur by fractions of a second.

It was scam time and when we reached the lakeside I sensed the crowd's mood was perfect. Marlene gave her sister a nod and Merl slowly raised her arms, then with the authority that only the world's most famous wizard can command she called for silence.

"Good people of Camelot." Cheers came from the surrounding crowd, though I thought *good* was stretching things a bit far. "Arthur, your King of the Britons, has fought a most bloody battle defeating a terrible enemy in the process," she paused for a moment, lowering her voice an octave, "but sadly in his moment of triumph he died an honourable and heroic death in your defence." Merl sagged dramatically while we shook our heads at this terrible news. Even Arthur looked shocked. "Our king will be ready to come to our rescue in the hour of the country's greatest need. But most important of all – and I want you to make a special note of this – the Lady of the Lake will be taking care of Excalibur, our great talisman. So Arthur's magical sword, which you see here lying on his body – *stop giggling, Arthur!* – will return to the extremely deep and dark waters of the lake." She turned to Marlene and whispered. "*Going well, isn't it! I've always liked theatricals.*"

Having finished her speech, Merl gave Neets a nudge and my cousin left for a more remote part of the lake shore while I helped lay Arthur's body on a waiting barge, carefully draping his flag over him and adding a few lilies to complete the overall effect. We pushed the barge away from the jetty, jumped in at the last minute and paddled like fury into the mirror-still waters of the lake as Arthur beat time with his knuckles and muttered, "Ramming speed!"

Halfway to the island Marlene looked intently at the shore to make sure the population of Camelot was still engrossed in our bit of theatre and nodded for Merl to carry out the most important part of the scam. With her arms stretched out over the waters she started to chant in the weird sing-song voice that all us magical people use when we want to impress a gullible crowd.

"Oh, Lady of the Lake. Oh, She Who Lives Under the Water. Oh, Guardian of the Deep, I commit Excalibur, the mystical sword of Arthur, King of the

Britons, into your keeping deep down at the bottom of the lake where no one will be able to get at it, ever. Here it is … now!" As she finished the chant Merl picked up the cheap old sword Arthur had been cuddling, raised it high for everyone to see and hurled it far out into the lake.

Then, because my Merl was the best wizard in the world, the scam magic began.

As the sword disappeared, a hand and then an arm slowly rose above the surface of the waters. In itself that was pretty neat, but what really caused the *"oohs and aahs"* from the shore was the sight of the gleaming sword apparently being grabbed by the Lady of the Lake as it finished its arc through the air. Inch by inch the arm and the fake Excalibur disappeared below the waters and we all knew the scam had worked when we heard spontaneous applause, followed by loud cheers and the odd wolf whistle.

As Neets sank beneath the surface clutching the mock Excalibur – okay, no prizes for guessing she was the Lady – the rest of us rowed for all we were worth while Arthur beat time with his fists, again shouting *"Ramming speed, you landlubbers!"*, but this time at the top of his voice. Neets grabbed the tow rope Merl had thrown her and hung on for dear life, because being Lady of the Lake can be pretty tiring stuff and water skiing was out of the question.

The barge scraped on Avalon's stony shore enabling us to carry the protesting Arthur high onto the close-cropped grass, where we dumped him like a sack of protesting turnips before walking halfway round the island.

The far side of Avalon was nicely hidden from the mainland by low hanging willow trees. They also hid a small rowing boat so Arthur could get back to Merl's cave unseen while the rest of us would have to row back to Camelot and tell the whole village that Arthur was sealed in his Avalon tomb and, most important of all, that Excalibur was definitely beyond the reach of mortal men.

It was time for the second part of the scam.

I decided to swap places with Neets and go back with Arthur because she'd always been a much better wailer than me and nobody in Avalon would notice the difference. We were just *those two irritating kids* to them. I silently steered as Arthur muttered *"Crawling speed,"* probably in protest at having to do all the work for a change as he rowed us back to the shore. We landed about half a mile away from Camelot and hid the small boat among the bulrushes before creeping along the shoreline to the village. To make doubly sure we weren't seen I draped a cloak over Arthur's shoulders and adjusted the hood so that his face and curly blond hair were kept in the shadows. As for me, I was just another teenager and like I said, really of no interest to anybody, but even hidden behind some outlying buildings I still kept my face down as we watched Merl finish the funeral scam with a short speech.

Arthur and I dodged from building to building using side streets and we had no problem keeping pace with the wizard's triumphant procession out of the village. Everybody was enjoying the last of Merlin's piece of theatre, which suited me fine because it meant I could watch out for anything unusual in the diminishing mob, as any promising detective should.

Three people in what was left of the crowd caught my eye because unlike everyone else they weren't cheering. One was wringing his hands and almost crying with frustration as Merlin and the two girls swept by. His multi-coloured herald's costume left little doubt as to who he was. The other two wore hooded robes that covered their features completely, which on a warm summer's day was suspicious in itself, but there was something in the way they kept pace with my friends, but never showed the slightest bit of emotion that made me single them out for TDA attention.

"We did it, Merlin!" Neets called out excitedly as the procession passed between the houses. She skipped along waving at the faces staring from nearly every window and made several gestures that were open to interpretation when people didn't wave back. Unfortunately, Bryn wasn't around to keep her in check and I wasn't about to blow my cover.

"Don't get overconfident." Marlene quickened her

pace as they reached the outskirts of the village. "We've bought ourselves some time, but only a day or two at the most and unless we find the real Excalibur and who stole it within the next twenty-four hours, Arthur may have to stay *dead* for a very, very long time."

I could see that Merl was close to tears. Marlene sometimes had a mouth that beat her brain by a mile in the empathy stakes.

Arthur and I sprinted the last few feet to the cave's entrance, dodging from bush to tree so as not to be seen, although that probably made us even more obvious to anyone watching and took us twice as long to reach Merl's side.

"Were you seen?" the wizard asked anxiously when we arrived at the cave.

"No," I said. "We kept off the main road and then came through the woods. We didn't see a soul the whole way and I'm sure nobody caught a sniff of us."

Merl began to smile and I knew she was going to make some sarcastic comment about washing, but for once I was wrong. She shooed Neets along and watched her disappear into the cave before putting a friendly arm around Arthur's shoulder. I walked by her side as she stroked her false beard thoughtfully. "You don't seem too sure about things, Arthur." Our king looked nervous now that the exhilaration of being buried on Avalon had worn off and I could tell Merl was feeling rather sorry for her king.

"Don't worry, everything's going to be fine." She had the grace to blush. "All you need to know is that you're still king and that whoever stole your sword can't discredit you now that the whole of Camelot thinks Excalibur's at the bottom of the lake and you're dead." She gave his shoulder another squeeze and stared into his eyes. "I'm sorry, Arthur, but the thief's still a threat to both of us. Our problems are very far from over, just postponed."

Merl led the way deep into the cave and Arthur could hardly miss seeing an archway-shaped ultraviolet glow in the far corner. He looked far from amused as he stared at the throbbing Time Portal. "What did you mean when you said our problems were far from over, Merlin? Surely we're safe now that I'm technically dead and Excalibur's out of the way?" This was not a stupid question and I decided I might have to reassess my estimation of Arthur's intelligence.

I could tell from Merl's face that she was feeling an overwhelming surge of sympathy for the man she loved. "*I'm* probably safe, Arthur," she replied, "but unfortunately it's you that somebody wants to get rid of. So for your own good you'll have to disappear, at least until Marlene and the TDA find the real Excalibur."

"Go away, you mean?" He hadn't been more than a few miles from Camelot since becoming king so I could imagine how the prospect of an adventure holiday might be quite appealing. "Where to?"

"My darling Arthur, *whenever* you want."

Merl nervously moved things round the large table that dominated part of the cave and whistled tunelessly. A look of suspicion spread over Arthur's face. He put both hands on the wizard's shoulders and turned her to face him. "Do you mean *whenever*?" We all knew Arthur had heard correctly because Merl never got her words wrong.

She sighed. "We need to get you as far away as possible, Arthur," she said, reluctantly trying to take the king's hands off her shoulders, though I suspected she wanted to turn it into a cuddle, "and I'm sorry to say that hiding you somewhere in the countryside won't be good enough; you're too well known. So sending you elsewhere in Time is the only solution." Merlin looked at the downcast king as he released her and she laid a reassuring hand on his arm. "I really do hope it won't be for long."

Arthur sat down at the large and very familiar round table, tracing shapes in the dust with his finger, then looked up with a smile. "Can I choose where and when you're going to send me?" When it came to the crunch he was no fool, just a bit slow on the initial uptake, in a nice-guy sort of way. But Arthur's enthusiasm for time-travel surprised me and it looked to me as though Merl was just a wee bit upset. I could fully understand why because he hadn't even asked if she was travelling with him.

"Where do you want to go?" she asked.

"Rome," Arthur replied without hesitation. "I've always wanted to see the place and the Romans knew how to fight a good battle even in peace time! Besides, their Saturday afternoon Games in the Coliseum are legendary."

"If you're sure, Arthur, then Rome it is." Merl flicked a switch to one side of the Portal. "Approximately five hundred years ago in the reign of Emperor Domitian." She turned knobs on the other side of the gently humming archway and pressed a button. "Are you absolutely sure that's where you want to be?"

"I'll be safer there than in Camelot, Merlin," replied the king, though he looked far from certain. "Won't I?" He stood up.

"I sincerely hope so, my darling," she said quietly. "I just know you won't be safe here, but then it's all relative I suppose." As she spoke she gently walked Arthur across the cave towards the Time Portal, still hoping for a last-minute shout of *'Stop. I've found Excalibur. It was under the bed all the time!'* but none came as she knew it wouldn't. "Close your eyes, Arthur, and open them again when you feel the warmth of the sun on your face."

The king inched the final few feet towards the Portal and put in a hesitant toe. He gave a start as the gentle hum increased in volume and the glowing light became a glare, but moved forward again as Merl gently encouraged him. "Like this, Merlin?" asked the king, covering his eyes with an arm. "You're sure this won't hur—" As he disappeared through the shimmering archway, Merlin held Arthur's hand for just those few seconds longer than was necessary. Then with a…

Zzzzzp.

…our king was gone and we were left alone to find Excalibur and its thief.

Merlin cried.

Chapter Three

An Unwelcome Message and Attacked by a Hacker

"He'll be fine, Merl." Unseen, I'd joined the wizard, because I knew better than anyone what she was feeling. After all I'd been watching her and Arthur since I was six and without realising it had seen the wizard's affection for the young king grow into an impossible love. I slipped my arm through Merl's. "Arthur's always been at his best in a fight with overwhelming odds against him." I'd meant to say *almost* overwhelming, which would have sounded a lot more optimistic.

Merl gave a weak smile, patted me on the arm and

made a poor attempt at a reassuring cuddle. "I know, but I already miss the dumb ox so much." Her lips began to tremble as she turned away so nobody would notice and sat down in her favourite chair near the fire together with her sadness and an increasingly wet handkerchief.

"Get a cup of Merl's favourite." I shooed Neets into the kitchen. The wizard had discovered the hot drink on one of her trips in Time and had developed her own Merl Grey brew by adding a few secret ingredients. She sipped gratefully holding the cup in both hands until slowly the colour came back into her cheeks. By the time the cup was empty she was almost back to normal.

"That's better," Marlene said as she sat in the chair opposite her sister. "It's not like you to get depressed."

Merl gave a sheepish smile as she passed the empty cup to me. She eased herself into a more upright position and looked as though she was aware of the welcome warmth of the fire for the first time. "Don't worry. I'm not giving in yet." She sniffed the air and looked puzzled. "All right, who's eating peppermints without offering them around?" Someone else was in the cave … in *her* cave, unseen, unwelcome, but not unsmelled.

"Merlin, I want to talk to you." The owner of the voice sounded as if he was used to shouting, not because he had a naturally bellowy voice, but because otherwise nobody listened to him. As he walked nervously into the cave we all recognised him as the pompous little herald from Camelot who for years had been in charge of rituals and official announcements. He was the man I'd seen after the funeral looking so angry and frustrated. The herald didn't get far and was immediately surrounded by the Temporal Detective Agency, with Neets and me escorting him by his elbows towards our little group. Up close he was even smaller, had less hair and was quite honestly grubby, compared to the well groomed focus of attention he presumably thought he was. His official clothes were faded and threadbare and I couldn't help thinking that if this man represented the pomp of Camelot, then the place deserved to fall apart.

"Oh, it's you," Merl said eventually as the herald gave a mock bow and tried to look casual by wandering round the cave examining its contents, human and otherwise. No one tried to stop him because he posed no threat that we could see, but he spoiled the effect when he tripped over his own feet to land sprawling in Merl's lap. She looked at him as though he'd emerged from the rear end of one of her rabbits and pushed him none too gently onto the floor. "What brings you here like a bad smell?"

Neets and I helped the herald to his feet and smacked dust off his clothes, surrounding him in a mini cloud of floating specks. Neets, Marlene and I had known him since we were kids and his whingeing

Jamie Murray

Tennis

389

Paralympic Games

London 2012
Official Sticker Collection

© LOCOG 2007 · 2010

Made in Italy by Panini
S.p.A Modena

pomposity had always made our flesh crawl. But then we all knew popularity had never been his aim, he just wanted to be important by whatever means, and he was happy with just being the mouthpiece of someone powerful and sharing their spotlight.

I saw him for the first time when I was six on the day Merl pulled off the Sword in the Stone scam and made Arthur the King of the Britons. The whole event was supposed to be a highly organised spectacle with lots of knights and jousting and stuff, but Merl masterminded the whole thing, grabbed all the attention and made sure only Arthur got to have a go at pulling Excalibur out of the stone. She did all the announcing and organised the whole show, leaving the herald purple with rage and as speechless as a beetroot. He'd looked pretty much the same this afternoon down by the lake at Arthur's funeral, but somehow I didn't think he'd come all the way to the cave just to complain.

"Let him be," Merl said from her chair, as she straightened her robes and checked her false beard. "He has no weapons?"

"No," said Neets. "Tersh and I frisked him when he came into the cave." It was amazing how quickly Neets had picked up detective slang. "He's clean … except for the dirt." We were both ready to pounce on the herald given the slightest excuse, but I sensed the pompous little man was sensible enough not to give us one.

"You know me?" Marlene said to the man who cowered away from the tiny, dumpy woman with the orange flame-coloured hairstyle. "I'm sort of Merlin's business manager and I handle the royalties, especially when it comes to King Arthur." I winced at her *probably* unintended pun. "So while you still think carrots and lettuce are boring salady things tell me quickly what you want here with my client ... I mean Merlin."

The man shuffled from one foot to the other like someone desperate for a pee, then struck a nobly heraldic pose as he held up a very official looking parchment scroll. He cleared his throat and began to read. Actually it was more of a shout, but we let him continue, because like all Camelot people we love a good piece of theatre.

"*My Lords, Ladies and Gentlemen,*" he began, unnecessarily I thought as there was only one Lady (Marlene), unless he knew Merl's secret, which we were pretty sure he didn't. "*Pray listen and take heed of this important message...*"

"Blimey. A commercial break already!" muttered Marlene.

"*...which is intended for all those present here, especially for the brother and sister known as the wizards Merlin and Marlene.*" At this point he lowered the scroll and spoke in his usual voice. "I just want to point out at this point that the opinions expressed in this scroll are those of my temporary employer and not mine at all. Most certainly not. I just thought I'd better let you know because I definitely do not like carrots and I am only the messenger."

"Point taken," said Merl. "Now get on with it before I forget my manners and turn you into a vole. Firstly, who's the message from?"

"Ah, now there's the thing." The herald shuffled his feet again. "You see, I don't really know. He's rich and I know he's a man."

"*He* would be," muttered Marlene.

"But other than that…" The herald shrugged and waved the scroll. "May I continue?" Marlene and Merl nodded. "*By issue of this proclamation the wizard known as Merlin is ordered to surrender Arthur, once King of the Britons, whether living or dead for disposal as I shall deem fit* … that's him again, not me … *the wizard will then agree to eternal banishment from Britain and will not communicate by any means with persons from Camelot whether living, not yet born, or reputedly dead.*"

"Excuse us a moment," said Merl getting out of her chair and taking Marlene by the arm. "I just want to have a quick word with my sister."

I tried to overhear what was said, but the look on Merl's face was better than a dictionary. Her face was livid red with anger and I was pretty sure the rabbit population was going to reach bursting point at any moment, though Marlene managed to calm her sister down with a gentle slap.

"Okay, you can come out now." Merl toe-poked the only part of the herald not hidden under the Round Table, then sat down again trying to look calm. Deep breaths and a bit of false beard stroking helped. "I'm not going to hurt you, but please remember where you are, who you're talking to and, well, those two will do for the moment." The herald clambered out from his hiding place and stood in front of us like a naughty school boy, shuffling his feet and picking his nose. "Now, have you finished your message?"

"Yes, sir." Now that the herald had finished reading his scroll he seemed at a loss as to what he should do. "Can I, er, go back to Camelot, please? That is unless you have a message you want me to take back."

"You said you had no idea who gave you the scroll," Marlene pointed out with a very pointy finger, "or even where he might be now, so you're no further use to us." She looked at her sister who nodded. "You can go back to the castle. Tertia, make sure he leaves and watch him in case he doubles back."

He didn't and I watched him scamper down the rocky path back to the village. In the twenty-first century, of course, a tarmac road led to a well-hidden car park for the convenience of the *Olé Grill*'s customers, but this was the fifth century and the wheel was still a novelty.

Back inside the cave Merl and Marlene were both pacing up and down, missing each other by inches and trying to make sense of the past few minutes.

Neets was sitting at the Round Table staring at the wizard sisters with a look of fascination on her face and half a twenty-first century *Olé Grill* biscuit in her mouth.

"Something's not right." Merl ripped off her false beard and threw it in a corner. "Okay, none of it's right, but what was the point of sending the herald up here with that pompous message? As far as everyone's concerned we buried my Arthur this morning and gave Excalibur back to the Lady of the Lake. Whoever he is, the man has no bargaining chips left."

"Unless…" Marlene stopped pacing and stood behind Neets. "What if he knows Arthur's burial was a scam? He knows we didn't throw the real Excalibur away because he presumably still has it, so technically he could still make his demands from a position of strength. On the other hand, as he can't know you sent Arthur back to ancient Rome his only real advantage is the fact we've no idea who he is."

Merl frowned. "That sounds like a pretty big advantage to me."

"Oh, I don't know. He probably thinks he's dealing with an old wizard, his younger sister and a couple of kids. The Temporal Detective Agency will come as a nasty shock, mark my words."

"It comes as a nasty shock to most people," mumbled Merl.

I felt it was time to add my bit to the discussion. Let's face it, it's not like me to stay out of a good argument and this had all the potential to be one of the best, especially with my help. Besides, Merl and Marlene may have been older and wiser than Neets and me – well, older at least – but I reckoned they'd missed a couple of tricks and forgotten to look at the bigger picture, whatever that was. I stood between them like a referee, folded my arms and gave them the benefit of my deductive powers.

"I hate to interrupt because you're obviously enjoying yourselves," I was probably pushing my luck there, "but whoever sent the herald isn't here. *We're* here and I bet he's in Camelot having a laugh at our expense. I reckon he knows we sent Arthur on a temporal holiday, because his friend the herald will have told him by now, but hopefully he won't know where yet." I looked at the two sisters and to my surprise they were actually nodding, and not with boredom either. "The way I see it the longer we keep Arthur away from Camelot, there's more chance of Excalibur's thief taking over the country and becoming king. And now we've thrown the sword into the lake we've got to have a darn good reason for bringing it back again." More nods. I was on a roll ... probably ham on rye, hold the mayo. "We've got to find the real Excalibur and bring Arthur back within the next twenty-four hours, or our lovely king might as well learn Latin and remain a Roman. Come to that we might as well join him!" I was tempted to mention the two suspicious characters wearing cloaks and hoods I'd seen in Camelot after Arthur's funeral, but I didn't because there would only have been awkward questions as to why I hadn't said anything earlier. Besides, I couldn't see what difference it could make.

"Wow, Tersh." Neets was obviously impressed. "How'd you work that lot out without my help?" The sting was in the tail, and I could only presume she was missing Bryn, because Neets usually put the sting up front, if there was one.

"Tertia's right," said Marlene. "We took everything at face value and the Temporal Detective Agency never does that. That's why we solve cases. That's why we win."

I thought Marlene was stretching the truth a bit, but she'd got the basics right. Sitting in the cave agonising was going to solve nothing. Mind you, I wasn't sure what good leaving it would do, but it couldn't be worse than sitting on our backsides watching the woodworm eat the Round Table. The TDA was back in Camelot to do a job and hopefully this time we were going to get paid.

"There's more to all this than meets the eye, or Merlin wouldn't have called in a bunch of professionals like us." This time I thought Marlene was stretching everything to the breaking point. "So let's get down to Camelot while there's still daylight left and do some detecting." She gently patted Neets on the left shoulder and firmly pulled her to her feet by the right elbow, but it didn't take a medium to see the reluctance on my cousin's face. It was the look of *I'm missing Bryn and I don't want to move.* I gave her a look of *get off your backside or I'll kick it for you.* She got up.

The four of us prepared to leave and walk down the valley to Camelot village. Merl, Neets and I looked around the cave that had played such a big part in our lives up to a year ago and realised we no longer belonged here. One day it would become the heart of Galahad's thriving *Olé Grill* restaurant chain and eventually the office of the Temporal Detective Agency, but until then it was just a cold, empty cave. Merl didn't even bother to switch on the magic locks.

Armed with a flask of Merl Grey we walked past the rabbits and set off once again for Camelot, full of good intentions, but no real plans. We'd have probably made it too if our path hadn't been blocked a couple of miles outside the village by two cloaked and hooded figures on horseback. They carried drawn swords that looked far from being blunt and ceremonial, but rather more sharp and pointy.

One of them laughed and instinctively I knew these were not a couple of nice guys offering to escort us into town. I also knew I should have mentioned seeing them earlier in the village, but rather a lot of water had gone under that bridge. The riders walked their horses towards us and it looked as though our first royal case was going to come to a bloody and rather sudden end, especially when the leader swung his sword at Merl's neck.

The rest of us ducked and I got ready to catch the wizard's head as she stood there waiting for the inevitable. I closed my eyes and listened to the savage *swish* of the sword stroke.

Chapter Four

Merlin Takes it on the Chin and a Trip is Planned

I winced as I heard Merl give a strangled cry, but after a few seconds of failing to catch a single falling head I dared to open my eyes. I stared in amazement at the wizard as she stood in front of the hooded figure, anger spilling from every pore of her body. The sword was still pointing at her throat, but instead of blood dripping off its end, Merl's false beard dangled like a dead rat.

"You *are* a woman." The man laughed again. "I always suspected as much." He turned to his companion, flicked his sword so the beard landed on the other horse's neck. "Put this rag somewhere to remind us what a fraud Merlin, the world's greatest wizard, really is."

None of us moved. With two mounted swordsmen confronting us there didn't seem much point in doing anything except wait for their next move. Somehow I didn't think we'd have to complain of boredom, but for a few moments I took the chance to look closer at our attackers, at least at what little wasn't hidden by their hoods. The leader was tall from the way he sat on his horse, clean-shaven and with long dark hair. Much of his face was in shadow and even though I couldn't see his eyes clearly, the menace from them was all too obvious. His companion was shorter and kept his hood as low as possible so that none of his face was visible. His hands were small, almost delicate, and he left all the talking to his leader.

"I congratulate you on this morning's piece of theatre, Merlin. The gullible folk of Camelot were very impressed and throwing an old sword into the lake was clever enough to wipe out the fact I'd already stolen Excalibur. You're good, but not that good. I know you've sent Arthur somewhere out of my reach, or so you think, but I now have other plans for the royal fool. I intend he should have an elegant death and in fact I plan to literally eliminate him. And I mean *literally*. On that note I'll bid you good day." He turned his horse to ride off, then as an afterthought looked over his shoulder at Merl. "Oh, and remember, wizard, that I have your beard. You are now a woman." He laughed. It sounded a bit false in an evil sort of way, but it was something he seemed to like doing at other people's expense.

"Who are you?" Merl shouted. "At least tell me that. I seem to know you, but I'm certain I've never seen you before."

"Oh, we've met, Merlin, a number of times in fact, and doubtless we'll meet again. Only then will you realise you know me for sure and understand how powerless you've been to save your precious Arthur." Evil laugh. Before Merl could open her mouth he cantered into the woods to the side of the track followed by his silent companion. The whole thing took no more than three minutes and our best laid plans, such as they were, lay in tatters along with Merl's beard.

"It's a good job I always carry a spare." Merl fished in her pocket, took out her second-best sheep's wool beard and adjusted it with the familiar skill of many years disguising. I wasn't sure, but for a moment I was certain she was grinning and if she was, she was the only one of us doing so. Marlene looked at a loss as to what to do next while Neets sat at the side of the road looking glum and mumbling something about how Bryn could have sorted it. I just felt depressed, although the nonchalant way Merl dealt with the loss of her favourite false beard made me feel better.

"Did anyone recognise either of those thieving ... people?" Merl tried never to swear unless it was darn well necessary. "The tall one, the leader, looked vaguely familiar, though I can't place him. There was something about the other one that seemed really strange, but again I can't put my finger on it." She looked at us for agreement, support ... anything, but only got glum shrugs in return.

"Oh, come on!" Merl was not impressed. "Call yourselves detectives? We learned loads just now and you missed the lot. Think about it. Those two didn't need to stop us and they unearthed nothing of any worth, other than the fact I'm a woman. But they seemed to already know that. What they *did* do was talk."

Even I couldn't see where we'd gained anything and I'm the one in the Agency with amazing deductive powers. Merl had been unmasked, or unbearded at least, and our attackers had shown they knew exactly where we were and what we were going to do. Still, I'd discovered over the few years I'd been Merl's apprentice that she was as sharp as a bucket of razor blades, and if she said we'd learned something to our advantage, then you could bet your boots we had.

"It's going to be dark soon," I said, mainly to Marlene and Neets, "and if we want to get to Camelot before the sun goes down then I suggest we start walking while Merl talks. Okay with you, boss?"

Merl nodded and set off at a reasonable pace, but

not so fast that her more dumpy sister couldn't keep up. Neets walked beside me and I couldn't help thinking all this was about men. Merl and her beloved Arthur, Neets and her adored Bryn, me I suppose and the deluded David, and Marlene ... well, we all reckoned Marlene was still hankering after the famous Chief Inspector Smollett from our adventure with Gawain and the Black Knight. Then there were the Excalibur thieves who were also presumably our attackers. Not a woman in sight. Merl was now setting a cracking pace.

"So what did we learn?" she said. "We know now that the leader is a tall, beardless man used to giving orders and his companion is small and quite possibly a boy, which is probably why he remained silent. They know Arthur's alive and that we've sent him somewhere beyond their influence. We also know that they intend killing Arthur, but what on earth does *elegantly* mean? What's more, *literally eliminate him* is a very strange thing to say when they've already told us they'll kill him, unless eliminating Arthur means something more than just get rid of him. I have a horrible feeling I'm beginning to understand what they intend doing and we've got to stop it. You said we had twenty-four hours to get everything sorted, Tertia, but I rather think we have a lot less than that." Merl quickened her pace and Marlene started to puff.

By now the sun was fast approaching the horizon and we were about to enter Camelot village for the second time that day. On this occasion, though, Merl insisted we make straight for the castle and that nipping into Galahad's original *Olé Grill* Spanish-themed restaurant for a quick snack was definitely not going to be allowed. Shame really, because Galahad's first restaurant based in Camelot was still his favourite and was where he liked to occasionally pop in unannounced to cook food to die for. I put it down to the wild mushrooms!

The village seemed almost deserted, although I put that down to too much partying after Arthur's funeral. It also occurred to me that it was just possible that the good people of Camelot had begun to realise that Arthur was really dead and that the peace brought by the reigns of Uther Pendragon and his son was over. The chances of another good king sitting on the throne were slim to say the least and the likelihood of an evil tyrant coming to power was odds on favourite enough to give anyone a headache.

Merl led us through the windy streets until we came to the steep track that took us to the gates of Camelot castle. She knocked on the giant wooden gate and when after two minutes no one opened up, I turned the handle and swung the doors open far enough for all to head inside and look at the empty and incredibly silent courtyard. We'd expected the normal bustle of a busy castle, coupled with the urgency of preparing for a coronation, or after our confrontation in the woods with Excalibur's thieves, maybe an aggressive welcoming committee. But nothing, and a deserted nothing at that, threw us completely.

"Hello. Is there anybody here?" It was a fair enough shout from Merl, but it occurred to me that anyone friendly would have already come to us with open arms, and if they didn't want to be seen they'd remain silent and hidden until we found them. Still, someone had to break the silence and Merl had the voice for it. No one answered and Merl didn't waste her breath on a second shout.

I put my ear to the cobbles and was sure I could hear a faint noise coming from under the courtyard, but as Arthur had converted the dungeons into store rooms it was unlikely to be screaming prisoners. I ran across the yard followed by Neets and opened the main castle door leading to a long corridor that gave access to every stairway, room and recess on the ground floor. At the far end we could hear what sounded like a hundred people all shouting at the same time, but not necessarily at anybody in particular. "It's the kitchens, Neets." I moved to the top of the stairs leading down to where the castle's head cook was king, rather than Arthur. "The place is full of people, but why here when the rest of the castle is empty. This is worth investigating."

We crept down the stairs, though we needn't have worried because no one would have heard us above the noise of cooking and quite possibly nobody would have taken a blind bit of notice anyway. We were just two girls, which when you're temporal detectives is a great disguise.

The kitchens were vast with row after row of ovens, cooking hobs, spits and griddles while pots and pans of all shapes and sizes hung from hooks side by side with ladles, tasting spoons and weird devices for scraping, grinding, crushing and generally preparing meats, vegetables, fruits and sauces. The most amazing thing, aside from the noise, was that everything was spotless. Everything gleamed as though it was brand spanking new, while the wooden preparation surfaces were scrubbed and immaculate. Then I saw the reason why.

Galahad stood in the middle of the kitchen area, calmly controlling the chaos.

I'd forgotten that none of the *Olé Grill* restaurants down the ages had their own kitchens, although not one of Galahad's clients ever guessed and the food inspectors never seemed to worry for some reason. All food orders were taken in the *Olé Grill* in the respective centuries and then sent through the Time Portal back to Merl's old cave in Camelot times, before being forwarded to the castle kitchens through a small local Portal. When the food was ready for serving, the process was reversed. It involved time travel, so it didn't matter how long it took to cook, or how difficult the ingredients were to find because Galahad just set the Portal dials for twenty minutes after the order was placed and it worked a treat.

One thing had always puzzled me though. In a place where coal was a rarity, electricity didn't exist and the dried cow dung used by the average villager would have added a certain something to the taste of Galahad's cooking ... what powered the great ovens and hobs in the castle kitchens? Under the threat of me disclosing that the right eyeball of Nelson's statue was actually a hardboiled egg, Galahad eventually told me he'd installed twenty-first century solar panels all over the castle roof and tower. That sort of gave me half an answer, but under even greater pressure from Neets, who whispered something I didn't quite catch, he admitted that on cloudy days and at night he wired up the kitchens to the Temporal Portal and used their magic reserves to power the stoves and ranges. This was definitely something Merl would not have appreciated if she'd found out and it was only because I managed to persuade Neets that the knight was being environmentally friendly and totally *green* that my cousin agreed we should keep quiet. Neets is a bit like that at times. After that I noticed Galahad hid any tell-tale cables and odd junction boxes until the sun disappeared and only reconnected everything when he was sure Merl was well away and there was no chance of a bunny-like punishment.

Galahad was the ultimate celebrity chef and aside from Neets he was my best mate, not least because we shared what was left of the Koh-i-noor diamond. He had a tie pin and cufflinks, while I had a very nice pendant that I kept safely under lock and key.

Neets and I went over to the small area of calm that surrounded the knight, but our intended chat lasted no more than three minutes.

"Galahad, over here!" Marlene was standing right behind us and nearly deafened me. "And you two as well. Merlin and I need you all in the archive room right now." She turned and marched up the stairs, giving us no chance to argue.

"Cooking's over, guys," Galahad called out eventually as he followed Neets and me after a fast disappearing Marlene. "Take five. In fact take as many as you want and don't even bring them back."

The castle didn't actually have an archivist as such, because nobody thought there was much need for one. It was where people could go and make diary notes in peace and quiet and over the many years several hundred people had scrawled their notes on parchment, vellum, paper or whatever came to hand. Once in a while the castle's scribe would copy everything decipherable into a clear, copperplate history of castle life.

The archive room was at the top of Camelot's East Tower. Actually it was Camelot's only tower, so I supposed it was the South, North and West one as well, but for some reason it was called the East. It had four windows that didn't point in any particular direction and a domed ceiling that looked as though it was covered in mystic diagrams, but it was actually where the plaster had cracked over the years into a thousand shivering lines. On a small table in the middle of the room was a large leather-bound book, a candle in an ornate silver holder and Merl. Actually she wasn't on the table, but she might as well have been the way she was poring over the book. The one chair in the room, intended for the reader, was ignored, which I reckoned meant Merl was on to something.

"*Kill elegantly* and *literally eliminate* Arthur." Merl stabbed the open archive book with a forefinger. "I'm certain the answer's in here somewhere and I don't know why, but I can't help feeling our friendly villain meant every word. I don't think he meant he would kill Arthur, or even have him assassinated, especially now he's out of harm's way in ancient Rome. He meant eliminate Arthur as in wipe him out completely." She slammed the book shut. "Marlene, I want to try something on you. I've already tried it on myself with very disturbing results. Sit in the chair and close your eyes."

Being a gentleman and a restaurant owner, Galahad pulled the chair round to Marlene's side of the desk and with a slight bow placed the chair directly behind her so she could sit straight down. Marlene looked suspiciously at her sister, then sat back and closed her eyes. "Now what do you want me to do, Merlin."

"You have the same psychic wizarding abilities as

me, now I want you to empty your mind of all past thoughts and experiences. Done that?" Marlene nodded. "Now tell me the first thing that comes into your mind after I ask you each question."

Being a detective I quite like riddles, but this sounded like a pointless waste of time. Nevertheless, as it was Merl I was prepared to keep my mouth shut.

"Arthur is in front of you, Marlene," Merl paused for a moment. "What does he look like. First impressions now. No thinking about it."

"He's quite short, a bit overweight – actually a lot overweight – and he's going bald. He giggles a lot."

"Do you fancy him … even a little bit?"

"No way! He's gross!"

"Okay, you can open your eyes now." Merl sat on the edge of the desk and I could have sworn a tear ran down her cheek. Just one.

"Blimey, Merlin, that was Arthur? But we know he's nothing like that slob. What's happened?"

"I believe what you and I saw was the potential future. I think our villainous friends intend eliminating Arthur from history itself and that can only mean they plan on going back in time to stop Arthur from being born."

"A leap in the dark, isn't it, Merl?" It's usually me that jumps to conclusions, certainly not the great wizard.

"Not really, Tertia, look at it this way. The leader seemed familiar for some reason, so he must be local."

She started pacing round the room, which wasn't easy considering how many of us were crammed in such a small space. "He seems to know his way around and had enough knowledge of Camelot to get the herald to deliver his message for him. When he stopped us outside the village he came over as someone accustomed to giving orders and he certainly knew how to use a sword. As to knowing I'm a woman, that would make him part of the inner Camelot circle, and even then there's only two or three people who know my secret. The little mental test with Marlene proved I'm right. What we saw was very definitely a future that is being built because of changes being made in the past." She stopped at the desk.

"But if they stop Arthur from being born, how come you and Marlene saw anything of Arthur at all?"

"Because you can't change history, Tertia, in spite of what people think. History will always happen the way it wants to. It may have to bend a bit and make some alterations here and there, but in the end the result will be the same. There will be a king called Arthur. He just won't be *my* Arthur ... he won't be anything like him in fact."

"You're saying they must have access to a Time Portal, Merlin." Neets was making her first contribution. "Surely that's not possible. We have them all."

"Not all, Neets." I said. "Galahad has one in the castle kitchens and, of course, Merl's is unattended in her old home at the moment."

"Damn, and I didn't set the cave's magic locks either. I am a fool!" It was most unusual for Merl to admit the obvious.

"Are there any others?" asked Marlene. It was a good question.

"There could be one, or two … actually three … in my old laboratory at the top of this tower. The same portable prototypes that Gawain and the Black Knight used to escape to South Wales, but they're safely under lock and key. I'm sure of that at least."

"By the sound of it they won't need your old ones upstairs," said Marlene. "There's enough lying around in the Camelot area just waiting to be had."

"They may not, but we will. Girls, I want you to go on a little errand for me."

"Sure thing, Merl," I said without thinking. "What do you want us to do?"

"I want you to go to Elizabeth the First's time and meet up with three old friends of ours. At the moment they're working for someone called William Shakespeare, but at one time they knew Arthur better than anyone when he invaded Scotland by mistake. I want you to find out what they know about his past and especially about his ancestors. There has to be something we're not aware of and if anyone knows what it is, they will. I also want you to give them this," Merl handed me a folded and sealed sheet of parchment paper. "In return I've asked them to give you a package. Please bring it back safely. The past, present and possibly all our futures depend on you."

There's nothing like a nice bit of pressure, I thought, and this was several tons of the stuff in a barrel. Mind you, Neets and I nodded happily, because this was meat and drink to the TDA and Merl's Girls.

"Galahad, take the girls to the castle kitchens and set the controls for these coordinates." Merl handed the knight a piece of paper. "I'd be grateful if you could stop using the Portal for *Olé Grill* purposes until this is finished, or Tertia and Unita may not be able to get back and that would be a shame."

I could think of worse shames, but not many, and from the look on Neets's face never seeing Bryn again was featuring very high in her thoughts. Visions of David never crossed my mind. Honest! On the other hand, as we followed Galahad to the kitchens I did fleetingly wonder if he was thinking of me.

We walked into history.

Zzzzzp.

Chapter Five

When Shall We Five Meet Again?

I knew we should have changed our clothes before leaving Camelot.

I looked at our wizard robes covered in mystic symbols and realised from the crowd's murmuring that we were causing a fair amount of unwelcome interest. What's more I already knew from Merl that performing magic was almost certainly illegal in Elizabethan times on pain of an exceptionally warm death. I decided not to panic and behaved as though the robes were the latest in Camelot fashion, giving a little catwalk twirl and an arrogant smile. Neets did the same, although the arrogant smile came naturally to her. As a result, nobody challenged us and a few actually started to admire our costumes, though mostly from a hesitant distance.

People generally hate being turned into rabbits and everybody deep down knows that unspeakable things happen when you mess around with a wizard. As a result our walk towards Shakespeare's Globe Theatre was well observed, but otherwise went without a hitch.

I looked at the watery blue sky, judging the time to be somewhere around mid-afternoon and because the sun was fairly low and approaching the horizon I reckoned it was probably late September, though for the same reasons it could have been March. Knowing the Globe lay on the South Bank of the River Thames we made for the nearest bridge, pausing midway across to admire the Elizabethan shops and houses that not only lined the river, but also the bridge itself. We were reasonably impressed but not overly, because we'd been shopping in Salisbury with Marlene in the twenty-first century and that was a *real* town. We reached the southern bank and to our left we saw a large, round building about half a mile away that roughly matched Merl's description in that it was round, large and wooden, though if I wanted to be really catty I could say that maybe Merl had been talking about her beloved Arthur in one of his stubborn moods.

I knew we'd reached the right place when a scrawny hand grabbed my shoulder and I was even more certain when a toothless voice cackled in my ear ... and swore.

"Bleedin' Tertia! Of all the bleedin' devils, what are *you* doing 'ere?" I shook off Rosie's hand and brought my heartbeat back to only twice its normal speed. I stood and looked at the witch. There was something different about her, especially in the wart department. In Camelot I remembered she'd had two or three good-sized ones, but she now had several strategic growths on her nose, forehead and chin, emphasised by the thick theatrical makeup covering her face.

Rosie was the chief of the three witches that Merl had sent us to see and I greeted her like an old friend, because that's what she was. There wasn't a nasty bone in Rosie's body (rumour had it she used other people's nasty bones), and although she would never admit it she was a sucker for helping any lame duck. Neets and I first met the three witches (Rosie, Petal and Jennie) when Arthur brought them down from Scotland because things were getting a bit hot for them after the Macbeth episode. Actually Arthur shouldn't have been there either, but he misread the map and it wasn't until one of his knights pointed out that they were not in Devon that he apologised to the confused survivors and came back to Camelot. After that the witches became Camelot favourites and spent their time curdling milk and cackling, but doing nobody any real harm.

Then one day they disappeared leaving a note for Merl explaining that they'd discovered this little device thing in the wizard's tower laboratory – they just happened to be passing and the locked door was slightly ajar – and found themselves in Shakespeare's time where they'd caught the acting bug and were busy advising the famous bard on some of his plays. They were sorely missed by everyone in Camelot for their sense of humour and tuneless whistling, due mostly to a severe lack of teeth.

"I might ask you the same thing," I said at last. "Personally we're here to save Arthur and probably the world from an evil genius." I didn't mind exaggerating. "And you?"

"We're actors!" said Petal with smug pride. "We do acting in this place for Mr W Shakespeare." I hadn't noticed the other witches until they stepped out of the late-afternoon shadows into the sunlight. All three had makeup covering every inch of their faces and whereas before they'd always been witchlike, now their clawed hands, noses that nearly met their chins and hunched backs looked totally exaggerated.

"We're getting a bit bloody typecast," added Jennie. "Ever since we suggested having three witches in one of his stories, that's all we ever get to bleedin' well play. Mind you we're bleedin' good and the audiences love us."

"We've been doing it for some time now using Merlin's spare Portal," cackled Rosie, "and we're quite well known right up and down the bleedin' centuries as the must-have *when shall we three meet again* type witches."

"Word has it we're up for an Oscar Lifetime Achievement Award soon," said Petal proudly, "if we can cut the bleedin' swearing down a bit, that is." She blushed gracefully and not even theatrical makeup could hide it. "What's more, it's like Jennie said, the audiences love us, especially me 'cos I'm the pretty one." She grinned and her one remaining tooth glinted in the late afternoon sun.

It was time to strike a deal.

"Ladies, come over here." I pointed to a bench that surrounded the trunk of a nearby chestnut tree. I walked over to it, sat down and stretched my legs out in front of me with a grateful sigh. It had been a long day. Neets sat down next to me on the basis that the word *ladies* had probably included her. The witches joined us, but remained standing, partly out of respect for the fact we were Camelot elite, but mostly because the rest of the bench was covered in bird poo.

"I don't want to hold up your acting," I continued, "but Camelot's got major problems and to top it all we need you to give us a hand to find Excalibur." I spent as little time as possible telling them about the sword's theft, Arthur's burial, his departure for Rome, the two potential assassins and the threat to eliminate him – possibly from history itself, if Merl was right. I spent a little more time on Merl's suspicions and especially her embarrassment at having to ask for help. The witches loved the last bit, as I knew they would, and gave little cackles of glee.

"So, Merlin wants our 'elp," muttered Rosie as she traced a random pattern in the dusty earth with her toe.

"Very wise of her," cackled Jennie as she rubbed out Rosie's patterns, which may not have been so random after all.

"Highly understandable in the circumstances," agreed Petal.

"What circumstances?" asked Neets. "You couldn't know anything except what we've just told you." This was the Neets of old. The pre-Bryn Neets with a brain like a knife … well, okay, like a hammer.

Rosie blushed under the greasepaint and shuffled her feet, while Petal and Jennie looked at her for a lead, but they just got a deeper blush, which probably spoke volumes. Unfortunately I didn't speak the language of blush.

"You already knew about the two men trying to eliminate Arthur before we came here," Neets continued, proving she wasn't just a pretty face. Her words, not mine. "I'll bet you know who they are, too!"

"No, we don't, honest!" protested Jennie.

"Er … we do. A bit," admitted Rosie, making more

patterns with her foot.

"Only a little bit," added Petal, holding up an index finger and thumb with a tiny space between them.

"Do we?" Jennie looked genuinely surprised. "Blimey! Well, you live and learn."

The witches were looking most uncomfortable and it was time to get some straight answers while they were wrong-footed and before they went back to their normal trick of speaking in riddles with silly hag voices. After all, that's what they'd done for poor old Macbeth, with all their talk of kingships, putting out dogs called Spot and walking forests.

"Who are they, and how come you know them?" I said and they seemed good questions to me.

"The main one was already 'ere when we arrived, Tertia," Rosie said with a shrug. "'E's sort of Mister W Shakespeare's Leading Man, but we don't see much of 'im, except when 'e's on stage."

"You mean he's an actor?"

"Yup, and I suppose he's quite good too in an amateurish sort of way," said Petal. "Not as good as us though, if you see what I mean." The other two nodded in agreement. "But with a bit of coaching he could be reasonably good." She blushed again and gave a silly simpering smile. "I've offered."

"Keep to the point," I said sternly, hoping they weren't about to go into riddle mode. Witches have a tendency to do that on the spur of the moment. "Petal, you've got the most teeth ... well, you have a tooth anyway … so tell me in words I can understand without too much spittle all you know about this man, what he's doing here and what he intends doing to Arthur. I appreciate some of it may be guesswork, but do what you can."

Petal looked at Jennie, but more particularly at Rosie for approval, and got a nod to proceed. Being the youngest, and because she could, Petal sat on the ground and began her story.

"It's like this," I realised it wasn't going to be quick when Jennie and Rosie slowly lowered their aching bones to the ground and sat next to Petal. "We got the acting bug when we put on those little play things for Arthur's court and the thrill of being applauded by a packed crowd of almost twenty people was something you need to experience to understand." Neets nodded in agreement, but then I'd always had her down as a bit of a drama queen. "Then one day we sort of got lost in the East Tower, somehow found ourselves in Merlin's old workshop with the dodgy lock and had a good look around to sort of check that nothing was missing, you understand."

Rosie took up the story. "This device thing sort of came into my hands and before you could say *I wonder what happens when you press this button* I'd pressed this button and we heard a noise like *Zzzzzp* and found ourselves here."

Weird, I thought, all Merl's remote Time Portals have dials for setting time coordinates and the one the witches found would have been no different. Strange it should have been set for the Globe Theatre in Elizabethan England. It wasn't something Merl had ever shown any interest in, but I supposed it had to be set for somewhere.

I looked at them in disbelief. "Are you saying that with all the things you could have done with Merl's old Time Portal – all the good, as well as, I suppose, all the harm – you chose to zip around Time playing yourselves on stage? I am not impressed!" I put on my best school mistress voice and crossed my arms *á la Merl*. At least I wasn't tapping my foot, which was a relatively good sign.

Jennie looked deflated. "We only wanted to have some bleedin' fun, Tertia," she whined. "After all, being cooped up in a cold and draughty cave with the odd newt's eye for bloody dinner is no joke. Especially when you can do the same thing on a warm stage, be given three meals a day and bleedin' well get paid for it. Blimey, it's a no brainer!"

"What's more, it's like Jennie said, the audiences love us!" added Petal. "Especially me 'cos I'm the pretty one, as I may have said." She grinned and her one remaining tooth gleamed.

"We watched a couple of plays by this guy Mister W Shakespeare," continued Rosie, "and knew we'd come here for a purpose, whether Mister S liked it or not. 'E took a bit of persuading and Petal had to do most of it because she's the pretty one, but eventually 'e agreed to write us into his version of Macbeth and we ain't looked back."

Jennie finished off. "So anyway, he's doing Julius Caesar and Cleopatra at the moment and with our in-depth knowledge of what they got up to we helped him write that one."

"What in-depth knowledge?" asked Neets.

"We went on 'oliday to Egypt a couple of times," said Rosie, "because this acting lark is dead tiring and after a bit of trial and error we worked out how to set the Portal controls for wherever we wanted to go."

"What made you choose Egypt?" I asked. "It's just hot sand and weird shaped buildings with no windows." Somehow I found it difficult to see the three hags sunbathing on the shores of the Red Sea, but spying on Cleopatra and wandering around inside the pyramids, cackling at the mummies … that I could definitely see. I was about to lay into them verbally for misusing Merl's property when Petal came out with an *Oh, by the way* that was probably the answer to the whole riddle, if only we'd known what the whole riddle was.

"Well, it's strange," Petal said before Rosie could interrupt, "but Mister S's Leading Man asked us lots of questions about it and we managed to give him lots of answers from a sort of history book we found in the room above Merlin's workshop. He must have told Mister S because the next thing we know is this play coming out about Egypt."

"And we're not even in it," moaned Rosie.

"The book in the castle archives?" Neets turned to me. "Why would it mention Egypt, Tersh?"

"Oh, that's simple," said Petal, shooting her hand up as though she'd just seen the easy question in a hard test. "Somehow Arthur's dad was related to Cleopatra, so of course it's all in their family tree. We spotted that."

"Blimey! Arthur's an Egyptian!" exclaimed Neets, and I had to admit it looked that way, but then I'd read somewhere that everyone is related to everyone else in the world somehow if you went back in time far enough. "And we thought Merlin was going to be the mummy!"

"That's all we know though, Tertia. Honest," said Jennie. "I mean we didn't want to read any more of the book because that would have been nosey and as you know we never stick our noses into other people's business. Everybody knows that. The whole world knows it!" She must have been working on the basis that if you tell a lie enough times, lots of people will believe it. It's like shouting at foreigners so they'll understand you.

"Besides, it was bleedin' difficult to read some of the older stuff," added Petal, blowing the lie apart. "It was all sort of in blurry writing."

With all these semi-facts and hints, my brain was racing, which may sound good, but it sometimes has a habit of coming second. I could almost accept that

Merl's prototype Portal had been set for Shakespeare's time – it had to be set for some point in time and maybe Merl had actually visited the place, which would explain it. But if that was the case, why didn't the Portal dump its travellers closer to the Globe Theatre? The witches' love of being on the stage explained the Globe, but not really why they thought Mr Shakespeare's leading actor was our leading villain. After all he'd just shown an interest in history as far as I could see. There were two ways to be certain. Get verbal proof from the three witches (probably in a riddle), and get to see the man face to face, which might be a little bit more dangerous given his skill with the sword and a beard if it was the same guy. That was a chance Neets and I as detectives would have to take.

"Right, here's the deal," I said, because witches like a deal. "You take us inside the theatre so we can have a look at this Leading Man of yours and we'll soon be able to tell if he's our guy or not. Secondly, introduce us to Mister Shakespeare. Thirdly, Merl asked me to give you this." I passed over the sealed parchment paper the wizard had handed me just before we left Camelot. Rosie opened the paper and read its contents before nodding and showing it to the other two. "She wants you to do some sort of favour for her. It's all in there apparently. If you do all that then we won't tell Merl how you got here, or how you've been helping the man who wants to eliminate Arthur.

Deal?"

"Deal!" agreed the witches in unison, without even the sniff of a cackle or swear word. To seal the bargain the three hags spat and shook hands with me and then with Neets. We both wiped our hands on our robes and shoved them in our pockets, wishing the witches had spat on their own hands instead of ours.

Neets and I followed the witches through the Globe's main entrance and looked at the circular theatre with its three areas for the audience. Those who could afford it had seats high up in the balconies, lower down there were tiered seats in what were really the stalls and at ground level much of the theatre was given over to standing room that surrounded the stage on three sides. We heard dramatic voices coming from the stage ahead and stopped to admire Shakespeare's latest epic rehearsal.

"Nice words. Good rhythm," I said, "but I'm sure a good tune you could sing on the way home would help." To illustrate my point I started to hum but gave up after I missed the second note. I'm no singer.

"Good idea," said Rosie, "and the Leading Man'll like it too if 'e gets to do the singing. 'e's a bit of a pompous megalomaniac if you gets my meaning." She clamped her hand over her mouth to stop herself from saying anything more.

Shakespeare was enthusiastically shouting at his actors, though not many were paying any attention while they were on a tea break. "Give it a few more days and the punters will be in here in their hundreds," he paused, "...in their tens to see *The Three Witches from Scotland and a Dog Called Spot Who Won't Go Out*, you'll see, my darlings."

"He can write bleedin' fantastic plays, 'onest." Rosie obviously felt someone needed to stand up for the bard. "But 'e's a complete bleedin' bozo at titles. We keep telling 'im the punters like a good, snappy title, but 'e won't listen."

Shakespeare turned, stopping in mid rant as Rosie tapped him on the shoulder and with a look of annoyance listened to what she had to say. He glanced at me and Neets, then beckoned us over like a king granting an audience. I counter-beckoned him and to Shakespeare's surprise he walked to where I calmly waited with my arms folded.

"Mister Shakespeare, a great pleasure!" I lied. "I love all your plays. They're so ... so long," I finished lamely.

William Shakespeare had the grace to blush, but still had enough of the author's instinct to pull out a quill pen and offer to sign a folio of his works for me. "So, you're a fan then?" said the playwright when the signing options had run out. "Sweetie, I'm very popular you know," he added proudly.

"That's nice," I said. "It's amazing that so few people come to see your plays then, isn't it. But I'm sure this one will have them rolling in the aisles."

"Darling, *Macbeth* is a tragedy!" Shakespeare said

with artistic indignation.

I looked at the witches because we all knew Macbeth was a right royal comedian, full of practical jokes. But then what did it matter a thousand years later. I turned back to the playwright. "You're absolutely right. Your play is a complete and utter tragedy. Now down to business. I would like to meet your Leading Man, please."

"All my men are Leading Men," Will Shakespeare said sweetly, emphasising the capital letters with one hand on his hip and the other extended like a teapot. "We have lots here, love, so who is it you want to see?"

I had some of my story prepared, even though it was a pretty pathetic one. "A friend of mine collects autographs and she once saw one of your plays, but was too late to get the man who played the main part to sign anything. So she asked me to pop in if I was ever in the area." I added hopefully, "I take it you keep using the same actors in your plays, Mister Shakespeare?"

Shakespeare threw up his hands. "With the price of auditioning new actors these days?"

"Excellent, so would it be okay if I had a little look round to see whether I can find my friend's favourite Leading Man?"

Shakespeare shrugged, "William Shakespeare's acting company is at your disposal, sweetie. Now if you'll excuse me I have things to do." He disappeared behind the scenery as I carefully climbed the rickety steps onto the stage and stared at those actors already in front of me, as more came in from the wings. Neets and I mingled amongst them pausing when one of the actors looked vaguely familiar, though with all the greasepaint it was impossible to tell for sure. He was the right height and weight, had the right air of arrogance, and winked at me. It wasn't a nice wink, it was one of those winks that says *you think you're in charge, well forget it, pal, because you're dancing to my tune. I'm pulling the strings and you're my puppet.* It was quite a long wink, but I didn't wait around for the eye to open again. Neets and I jumped off the stage into the audience pit.

"Is this a Tertia I see before me?" the assassin called out in his best actor's voice and pointed dramatically at me. "Alas, poor Unita, I knew her well." He was mixing up his Shakespearean plays, but nobody seemed to notice and as far as I knew they hadn't actually been written yet. "Now is the winter of my discontent made glorious summer by these daughters of Camelot!" This was good stuff and if I was Shakespeare I'd be making feverish notes. I looked around … wherever he was.

We stood, mesmerised as much by the assassin's speech as by his hypnotic eyes. I watched as he walked to the front of the stage and then down into the audience pit, sword in one hand and dagger in the other. I'm pretty sure Macbeth only ever had a dagger, because his wife would never have let him loose with something as dangerous as a sword. He'd have only cut himself.

The man's eyes never left mine for a second until he stood in front of me. He sneered and totally ignored Neets, which is a silly mistake. The small crowd of critics and advance ticket holders loved it because there was nothing they liked more than good old-fashioned audience participation.

"So, you've found me, Tertia." The man strutted round the audience pit and milked his fans' adoration with the grateful smile of a celebrity, but his eyes were as cold and piercing as sharpened icicles. "I anticipated that if the witches could get here, then you might follow them. Though much good may it do you and your friend. I've already set in motion events that will alter history, and after that the beloved Arthur won't even be a memory. I rather think Merlin may already have sensed the change and you two snivelling little brats can do nothing."

I resented being called little.

"We had no idea you'd be hiding here," I admitted. "We came here to ask the witches a favour and to get the benefit of their knowledge. You didn't need to reveal yourself, even though Rosie hinted you might be here. We weren't expecting you in London and we have other, much more permanent plans on how to deal with you." I can't half tell a lie when I need to.

The audience gasped and for a fleeting moment a

look of uncertainty crossed the man's face, but it was replaced by scorn and the icy steel returned to his eyes. "Tertia, your words say one thing and I know you mean the opposite." Contempt and hatred dripped from his voice. "Everything you do is a lie, just like your Merlin. She pretended to be a man so she could become a wizard and you've all been lying to your king for years to make the fool your mindless puppet. You're all frauds."

The audience cheered and from their reaction this had to be one of Shakespeare's best attempts because everyone eagerly turned to Neets and me to see what our next line would be. I had no intention of disappointing them.

"Merl wore a false beard so she could work for the good of everyone and because as a woman she'd have spent the rest of her life washing clothes and dishes. That went for Neets and me too." I paused and the audience applauded. At least all the women did. "Merl would never hurt a soul, especially her Arthur, but she'd kill anyone who threatened him and you know that." I went for the throat. "I'd worry if I was you, because she knows what you're doing, where you are and your real identity." The audience gasped. They loved soap operas just as much as Neets and I did.

"Oh, I'm here all right, but I don't believe Merlin knows my plans for Arthur any more than you do." The man's lips curled in a snarl and the crowd whooped.

"It's Caesar and Cleopatra," whispered Rosie. "You mark my words."

"And as to who I am, you have no idea of my identity, and yet I assure you that you all know my real name."

The critics went delirious and made furious notes with their quills. People standing in the audience pit stared, hardly breathing and seemed in two minds as to what to do, so some clapped and others booed. Neets and I looked at each other and shook our heads.

The man laughed. "You mean you haven't guessed?" He almost spat the words. "And yet we know each other so well, Tertia. I've had fun watching you and your little friends racing around, always playing the game to my rules, but I'm afraid my patience is exhausted and it's time for Arthur to be eliminated."

"But you don't know where we've hidden him," I said with a reasonable degree of confidence, "or even when. If you did, he would already be dead."

The man looked at me in mock surprise and began to circle us like a lion stalking two tethered lambs. "Do you really believe that?" He smiled almost sweetly. "Do you honestly think that if I can arrange all this that I can't do a tiny thing like find out where you put your royal thug? You both disappoint me! I have so enjoyed making an elegant game of things." He scowled and stood still. "Now it's time for action."

The man walked through his adoring fans signing

autographs as he went before he climbed the rickety steps back onto the stage. He stood next to a mock castle doorway and I knew it meant he'd almost won, because the doorway had a slight ultraviolet glow and hummed quietly. "Ah, yes. I forgot to mention I took another of Merlin's spare Portals. So I'll bid you farewell and promise that when we do meet again it'll be to see the final minutes of Arthur's life!" He laughed like the bad pantomime villain Marlene had taken us to see in Salisbury, then suddenly turned and raised a hand to throw his killing knife at Neets.

At less than twenty feet I knew he could hardly miss and with a cry I shoved my cousin as hard as I could to one side leaving myself as the target. I scrunched up my eyes and tried to shrink as much as possible knowing I was about to die, but instead of feeling the deadly thump of razor sharp metal, I heard the man cry out. I opened one eye and stared in disbelief at the small crossbow arrow sticking out of his hand and looked around for the archer who'd saved my life. The man retreated towards the Portal, snarling in pain as he snapped off the arrow's head and pulled the shaft through the palm of his hand.

"You're going to die, Tertia. You're all going to die. *Ow, that hurt!*" He disappeared.

Zzzzzp!

Rosie lowered the small crossbow and slipped it into one of her massive pockets. "I never liked him and I've never trusted any man who wears makeup to pretend to be somebody else."

"What about women?" I asked. "Merl wore makeup so everyone would think she was a man and you three are plastered in the stuff. Is that all so different?" I was joking, but Jennie bristled with indignation.

"We are three witches who happen to wear makeup so people will know we are three witches." Her voice trailed off. "We're pretending to be ourselves, that's all. That man was pretending to be something on stage that he wasn't."

Neets had been very quiet up to now, which considering she didn't have Bryn to lead around by the nose was surprising. My cousin was not usually a shrinking violet and on occasions could sometimes seem quite clever, like now.

"We've only seen him here as the Leading Man and as Arthur's potential killer back in Camelot," Neets said thoughtfully, "and we assumed what we saw in Camelot was what he really looked like. What if that was a disguise too? What if he's someone else altogether?"

I took up the thread. "You could be right. He said we'd known him for a long time, but none of the disguises we've seen him in so far rings a bell. It looks as though we've yet to meet him in his true identity."

Petal sidled up and handed Rosie a long cloth-wrapped package, which the leader of the witches passed on to me. "This is the favour Merlin asked of us, Tertia. You're to take this back to 'er when you return to Camelot."

I hefted the surprisingly heavy package and turned it over, trying to get a hint as to what was inside. Opening it was not an option because of the seal that covered the ends of the twine surrounding the cloth and from the grin she gave me Rosie wasn't about to let it slip.

"There's nothing more we can do here," I said and my cousin nodded in agreement. "Let's get back to Merl and Marlene. It's a shame the Leading Man took the portable Portal with him, because now we'll have to walk a mile or so to get back to ours." I turned to Rosie. "And that's a point. Could you ask Mister Shakespeare if we could borrow a change of clothes? Ours stand out a bit with all the wizard symbols."

Rosie looked around, but the great man was nowhere to be seen. "Looks like he's wandered off somewhere, but I'm sure he won't mind if you borrow a couple of things. Go with Petal and she'll take you to the costume store."

Ten minutes later we were walking across London Bridge dressed as Shakespeare's Two Gentlemen from Verona and attracting just as much interest from the crowds, but at least it was for a different and probably much safer reason. Nevertheless I hurried to the Portal carrying Merl's mysterious parcel and some dynamite information for Marlene.

Zzzzzp.

Chapter Six

A Forger, to Coin a Phrase

We burst through the Camelot portal and Galahad immediately clapped his hands for silence. A hundred kitchen staff sprang to attention, because there was a mounting pile of orders to get through and a celebrity reputation to maintain throughout the centuries.

Marlene was also waiting for us and wasted no time in shooing us up the stairs leading to the East Tower and Merl's old workshop. "Hurry up. We all want to know what happened to you," she said as she gave Neets a gentle shove. When she turned to me I gave

Marlene a warning look. Nobody pushes Tertia around!

"Didn't you see us on PortalVision?" asked Neets, which I thought was a pretty intelligent question, until I remembered we'd been about half a mile from the Portal and way out of sight of anyone back in Camelot. After that it became a dumb question and I exchanged a tut-tut look of *cousins, huh!* with Marlene as we trotted up the spiral stairs of the East Tower. To be fair, Marlene wheezed her way up, while Neets and I waited at each landing for her to arrive. I opened the door of Merl's old workshop, but Marlene grabbed my arm and pulled me slowly up the next flight of stairs to the archive room.

"Old friend ... here to see you both," she puffed as I looked through the open door. Merlin was still crouching over the table like a predatory librarian, while seated in the only chair was the last person I expected to see. Lancelot slowly got to his feet, helped by the stick he used for walking and the edge of the desk. Even so he nearly stumbled and Neets and I rushed forward to steady our old friend. He didn't look a day older than when we last saw him, but then he'd looked about ninety back then. Even with our support his knees knocked and he leaned forward from his waist so that the top of his head only reached our shoulders. His long white hair framed a face with so many lines that no amount of creams, or even ironing, could have smoothed it. Not that we'd have wanted to, because old age was part of his charm and we'd never known him to look any different. He was Lancelot and he was our old, bent, rickety mate.

"Good to see you, girls," he quavered. "Keeping well, I hope?"

It was great to see Lancelot again, but as far as I knew he'd gone off to Wales following Guinevere and, provided he remembered why he'd gone there and who he was, he'd intended spending the rest of his life in the place. And yet here he was back in Camelot alone and looking reasonably cheerful. I doubted that he just happened to be passing by and dropped in for a chat and a cup of Merl Grey.

Merlin looked up from the book she'd been studying. "Lancelot has some rather disturbing news for us. Oh, and in case you were wondering, which I'm sure you were, being detectives and all, he heard that Arthur had died and rushed ... well, tottered ... here as fast as he could for the funeral, but of course he was far too late."

"What disturbing news, Merl?" I knew I'd get an answer quicker from her than from my old friend. Nevertheless, before Merl could say anything Lancelot wagged a finger in my face.

"Bad news, girl," he mumbled in a voice laden with doom. "Bad as bad can be, and that's ... very, very bad." Lancelot had never been overburdened in the word department. I looked at his wagging finger and noticed for the first time the ornate pair of soft velvet gloves he was wearing. Everything else he wore was old and threadbare and yet the scarlet glove being waggled looked brand new and had a complicated letter L embroidered on it. I half wondered if the other one had the letter R. Lancelot quickly lowered his hand and mumbled that they were a present from Guinevere and that she insisted he wore them to remind him of her and keep the chill off his ancient hands.

"When Lancelot came through Camelot village, he noticed, like us, that there was no one around. Unlike us, though, he didn't come to the castle, he went to the meeting hall and inside he found nearly all the villagers listening to a tall man giving a speech. More than that, he was rabble rousing. Worse than that, he was rousing them against *me*!" Merl hit the table with her fist, making poor old Lancelot jump higher than he had done for years. "Apparently I was being accused of murdering Arthur, manipulating his entire life, conniving to make him king and am now intent on taking over the country…"

I couldn't help thinking they were fifty-percent right. At least it was the nice fifty- percent.

"…imagine, *me*! After everything I've done for them all these years. I've given them peace, a king worthy of the name, cured their ailments and taught their kids. This is the thanks I get. One rabble-rouser and they're all against me. Isn't that right, Lancelot?"

The knight looked confused for a second. "Bad.

Very bad," he said, then shook his head sadly.

"Yeeesss," drawled Marlene as she gave the old knight a look of sympathy mixed with suspicion. "Tertia, we'd like you and Unita to go down to Camelot and check things out. I'm sure Lancelot believes what he saw, but we'd like a second opinion just to be on the safe side. Be careful, though, because if he's right then the crowd is as likely to go for you two as for Merlin … and probably me." She gave a little shudder and her normally flaming ginger hair seemed to dim. "From Lancelot's description this could be our friendly assassin, so be very careful."

Neets and I ran down the spiral stairs taking them two at a time and sprinted through the hallway into the courtyard. We listened for any sound, but just as when we had entered the castle there was only the background murmur of kitchen activity coming from beneath the cobbles. The large wooden gates were still wide open, but with Arthur gone no one probably thought it necessary to close them, including me. Neets on the other hand was more security minded and pulled the heavy door so that it slammed into its frame; the last sound was the locking bar falling into place. The castle was secure once again and everyone on the inside was safe. Unfortunately we were on the outside and on our way to the village. Oh well!

The road to Camelot was deserted, as was the village itself, though the locals liked to think of it as a small town because that was posher. Neets and I walked from house to house, looking through windows, and where doors were open, peering inside from natural curiosity, but even Galahad's *Olé Grill* was empty, which for a feast day was utterly unheard of. We did take the opportunity to grab a couple of the celebrity chef's special cream cakes before going through the *Grill*'s rear entrance and making our way along the back alleyways to the village meeting hall.

The main door to the building was closed and presumably locked from the inside, because no matter how much we rattled the latch it wouldn't budge an inch. We walked down a side alley and eased open one of the slatted windows just enough so we could hear some of what was being said (though I suppose *shouted* would have been more accurate), and catch a glimpse of a tiny part of the main hall.

The whole village must have been packed in there, because they certainly weren't outside, and far from being a well-organised civic debate there was rather a lot of loud bellowing going on as well as what sounded like a right royal punch-up. This would have been quite normal on a Saturday night in Camelot's taverns, except this was a Thursday and only just past sunset. Okay, I could understand a feast day following Arthur's funeral, but there was no sign of any food, let alone any drink, and Camelot people knew how to party.

We closed the window and found another one farther round the building. I knew that it led to a small storeroom that opened into the main hall and that forcing the flimsy window open and then climbing inside was dead easy, because security had never been high on the Camelot list of priorities. Besides, Neets and I are natural burglars … but only in the interest of detecting, of course. We dropped onto the storeroom floor and felt our way to the door through the rubbish that always ends up in places like this. I slipped the catch and opened it enough for us to hear clearly what all the fuss was about. It took less than a minute to realise that Lancelot had been right all along. The rabble-rouser had done his work well and the mob was out for blood and ours would do for starters.

I grabbed my cousin's arm. "Let's get back to the castle. We've seen everything we need to here." It was then that Neets's supposed intelligence and superior wisdom as my older cousin completely deserted her. She flung the door wide open and marched into the hall, then stood in front of the village crowd with her hands on her hips and feet wide apart, which given her audience, was probably not a good move.

"You stupid, stupid people," she shouted as the room fell silent, not I suspected out of respect but out of momentary shock. "How could you believe such lies about Merlin? How could you think that she, I mean *he*, would kill Arthur? If you only knew half the truth … well, you'd be very surprised!" She was right there.

As Neets continued her rant, I noticed our little friend the herald cringing on one side of the hall and looking as though he was trying to merge into the wall. It was no great shock to see him, given that he seemed to be working for the Leading Man, but I was surprised by the coins stacked in neat piles on the small table next to him. He wasn't selling drinks, snacks and souvenirs and when he saw me looking at the money he scooped up as much as he could into a small bag and ran to the rear of the hall and the locked main door. I walked over to the table and picked up one of the coins. It was quite heavy and beautifully cast, unlike our Camelot money, which tends to have a stick-man etching of Arthur on one side and whatever takes your fancy on the other. This one had a man's head in profile, with his name and the date round the edge. I whistled in astonishment, because Roman Julius Caesar coins minted more than five hundred years earlier are rare to say the least ... especially when they look brand new.

The villagers were getting restless. Actually they looked more like the crowd from one of those Frankincense horror movies, although at least they didn't have pitchforks and flaming torches. Neets was too wrapped up in what she was saying to notice how her audience was slowly moving towards her with words like *it's 'er she be one of 'em* and *kill the wench before she casts a spell on us. Tis said she can turn people into chickens.* I snatched a few more coins (it seemed a shame to leave them lying around), then grabbed Neets round the waist and dragged her back into the storeroom and the only way out of the building that I knew was open. She was still in speech mode and in the face of great odds was continuing to lecture the mob, even though they were ... well, a mob! I slammed the storeroom door and continued to drag Neets shouting and spitting to the window. The occasional kick in the shins brought her to her senses as we tumbled over whatever it was that filled the room and dived through the window into the alley.

As we ran into the main road, the front door of the village hall burst open and a howling mob streamed out carrying pitchforks and flaming torches, though where they'd got them from was a complete mystery. I half suspected that as they went inside someone had told them to put farm implements in the room to the left and anything of a fiery nature to the right. *Collect as you leave.* They had and they were after us, so we ran.

Just past the *Olé Grill* I pulled Neets into a doorway that hid us from the street and watched the bulk of the villagers go racing past in pursuit of whatever those in front were chasing. Camelot people love doing things in crowds, a bit like lemmings do.

"Seen one of these before?" I held up one of the Roman coins so the gold glinted in the torchlight of a village mob straggler. "If you have, you're older than you let on."

Neets took the coin. "Wow, gold!"

"Well spotted, but whose face is on the front?"

"Blimey, Tersh, it's Julius Caesar!"

"Exactly. The man himself. He seems to be cropping up everywhere these days. He's Arthur's ancestor according to the archives, Mister Shakespeare's written a play about him with our old friend the Leading Man playing the main part and the witches insisted the threat to eliminate Arthur was wrapped up with Caesar and Cleopatra. Now it looks like he's turned up on a load of brand new coins that haven't been seen for centuries. Could there be a connection, I ask myself? If there is one, I'm damned if I know what it is. We've got to get back to Merl right now."

I looked up and down the street for any rabble late-comers, but the whole place was empty again and the main pitchfork and burning brand brigade had disappeared. Using the back alleys, Neets and I ran as fast as we dared, without drawing attention to ourselves, and zigzagged our way towards the castle hill, where we came to a grinding halt.

The village mob was standing in front of the massive wooden gates, pitchforks at the ready, and listening to our favourite rabble-rouser's latest lies about Merl. The man was good, too. He walked among the crowd never talking to the person next to him, but rather to his entire audience so that no one was left out, but everyone felt special. Whether he was in the Globe Theatre, or here in Camelot, the man was a brilliant actor and I even thought I heard a few lines of Shakespeare pop up in there somewhere. More to the point, it was darn good job that Neets had closed the gate, though it did mean we'd have to look for another way into the castle.

We sheltered behind a rock and watched the Leading Man organise the village mob into a siege force of sorts. Most of them wandered around like angry sheep, presumably still clutching their Roman gold coins, but there were enough of them to stop anyone opening the gate and sneaking out. Okay, so the man had the castle surrounded and nobody inside could leave that way, but for the life of me I couldn't see what he'd gained. Arthur had made sure there were enough secret ways in and out of Camelot castle to withstand any number of sieges.

Neets sighed. "Bryn would have stormed the gates and got us in through the front door, wherever he is." I sighed and thought he'd have got us pitch-forked in the process.

As we made our way over the rock and grassy slope to the other side of Camelot hill, I noticed the young man we'd been ambushed by on the road between Merl's cave and the castle. His hood was still over his eyes so that his face was completely hidden and he didn't seem to be saying anything, however, he had an air of authority about him that didn't need to be expressed in words. Besides, right next to him he had a servant to do his work. And next to the servant was the pompous little herald strutting around like a faded peacock and giving instructions that no one listened to, probably because he had no gold coins left with which to bribe people.

Still within sight of the road, but far enough away from it that we weren't noticed in the dark, was a large bush, thorny enough to put most people off, but I knew that if I was careful I could pull it to one side and reveal the mouth of a cave, large enough for even the fattest of knights to wriggle through. Neets went first and cracked her head on the low roof just as I warned her that without torches she needed to be careful. Typical! Though it did prove she'd learned some new words from her beloved Bryn. I followed her after pulling the bush back into place and, being a few inches shorter than Neets, used fewer words of an unsavory nature, though the ones I did use were probably more powerful.

It took us no more than ten minutes and several head bangs to reach the rear of a tapestry in the main hall of the castle and another two minutes to join up with everyone in the archive room. *Everyone,* being Marlene and Merl, because Galahad was still in the kitchens catching up on outstanding orders and Lancelot had apparently left the castle and tottered off to meet up with Guinevere soon after we left for the village. Being older than me and less able to stand the pace, I let Neets plonk herself in the one archive room chair while I perched on the side of the table and swung my legs. I knew it irritated Marlene, but as a senior member of the TDA I didn't really care, so I dangled.

"Lancelot was right," I said. "Bill Shakespeare's Leading Man and Arthur's would-be assassin are one and the same guy. Not only that, Merl, he was down in the village whipping up the mob with gold coins and lies about you and Arthur."

"No surprises there then," replied Merl, and Marlene nodded. "So he's got the fickle Camelot crowd on his side and us bottled up in the castle, except for the fifteen-odd secret passages Arthur and his father made. Lancelot was lucky to get out when he did, or he'd have met the mob head on and there's no way he could have made it along one of the escape tunnels."

Merl was right. The old knight was so bent with arthritis there was no way he could have used one of the escape routes. In fact it was a marvel he still managed to climb on that old grey mare of his and trot up and down the castle hill. I supposed he had Guinevere as an incentive.

Merl carefully examined the gold coin I'd given her. I didn't think she'd be interested in the few I'd kept in my pockets, one of which I'd earmarked for Galahad as a trinket partner for his Koh-i-noor diamond cufflinks and tiepin set.

"This is bad news for Arthur," Merl said as she

tossed the coin in the air. We all watched with our mouths open as the coin glinted in the candlelight. The wizard caught it deftly and put it on the table. "Of course, it's a forgery."

"Why, Merl?" said poor innocent Neets, but then someone was bound to ask and another couple of seconds it would have been me.

"Because the date on this coin is 50 BC and Roman coins before the birth of Christ couldn't have a date on them, especially one saying BC. Think about it. They often had the number of years the emperor had been in charge round the edge, but never a date."

She's a clever old wizard is our Merl and when it comes to money is definitely no slouch.

"And yet this coin is made from gold, which seems strange for a forgery." Marlene had picked it up and tried to bite it. I knew that contrary to popular belief if you bite a gold coin it won't mark. It's the tin and lead forgeries that are chewable, though it's not recommended.

"What's even stranger is that real Roman coins were mostly made from bronze. Gold would have been far too expensive, so why did our Leading Man go to all the trouble to make forgeries of five-hundred-year-old coins in a valuable metal, with an obvious date mistake. He must have known I'd spot what he'd done, just as he must have known I'd send you two to the village to see what was going on." She gave Neets a shove and sat heavily in the chair recently vacated by Lancelot. "Think, woman, think! Marlene, you think too."

"What if he used gold because he could get lots of it from somewhere?" I said, almost as a way of breaking the silence. "And maybe he wanted to attract our attention."

"Or maybe he wanted to divert it," said Neets, filling her bit of the silence. "Besides, how do we know all the coins were gold? Maybe only the ones Tersh grabbed were gold and the rest were made of bronze or something."

Marlene looked at me and her eyes narrowed. "How many of the things did you take?" She held out her hand. "Come on, give. You know we pool everything."

Reluctantly I emptied my pockets and put the small pile of coins on the table. There was no way I was handing them straight to Marlene, whatever she said, or we'd never see them again and she'd end up with a heavy new necklace with matching bracelet.

"Unita could be right," Merl said thoughtfully. "What if he intended you both to go to the village hall and meet the mob, which would possibly tear you to pieces, but I doubt if he wanted that. I think he wanted you to find the coins, see they were new, had Julius Caesar's head on them and were very valuable. As good detectives you would then believe our Leading Man had been to ancient Rome in Caesar's time, especially as we know he has one of my Time Portals. Very clever."

"Blimey!" Neets was quite excited because after all she'd started this chain of thought. "Does that mean he knows you sent Arthur back to ancient Rome?"

"He may, but Rome is a very big place and Arthur will have the sense to keep a low profile." Neets, Marlene and I exchanged looks of disbelief. "On the other hand I think it could be a coincidence. Remember what the witches said about Caesar and Cleopatra being the keys to the whole thing? Well, while you were in the village I unwrapped the parcel Rosie gave you and inside was a sheet of paper parchment."

"The bill for services rendered?" I asked cynically.

"No it was a little rhyme. A sort of riddle. I'll read it…

If Cleo and her Jules meet up
They may produce a charming pup
Then Arthur's future is secure
But if they don't, he's dead for sure.

It's the typical witches' drivel they all eventually spew, but coupled with the fact that the archive book says that somehow Arthur is descended from Caesar and Cleopatra, the witches may have been talking sense for once."

"But if the coins are forgeries and he wants us to

believe Caesar is wrapped up in all this," Neets said triumphantly, "we now know that he isn't. It was all an elaborate con!"

"Don't underestimate him. This man is clever." Merl got up from her chair and gazed out the window. "I think he was trying to lead us on a wild goose chase that always pointed to Caesar, until of course we discovered the coin forgeries and then we'd know it couldn't possibly have anything to do with the Roman emperor. A great way of getting us off his back and tying us in mental knots." Merl turned and faced us. "No, it's Rome, but the question is why and how are we going to stop him?"

"So where does Cleopatra fit in, Merl?" I knew the Queen of Egypt and Caesar were an ancient item, but so far she hadn't featured much.

"She has to meet Julius Caesar and they have to fall in love. That's all." Merl sat down again. "That's it!" she shouted, leaping out of her chair. "The Leading Man is going to stop them ever meeting and he's going to do it in Rome before Caesar decides to attack Egypt. We have to stop him, or we say goodbye to Arthur." She turned to Marlene. "Do what you did before. Close your eyes and think of my Arthur and tell me what you see."

Marlene did as she was told, then opened her eyes with a look of horror. "Blimey, he's even fatter, balder and looks even more stupid than normal. Sorry, Merlin, I mean than he did in my last vision, not that he always looked stupid, well maybe just a bit ... slightly ... occasionally ... once. Oh bother!"

Merl ignored her sister's backtracking as it came to a stuttering halt. "I was afraid of that. Time is getting ready to change the Arthur we know into someone else. We need to act fast and that means we need to be in Rome. Girls, it's time for action. Please go to Caesar, save my Arthur and remember to take a couple of bed sheets with you. We'll be watching on PortalVision as much as possible and if it looks as though you need help we'll do what we can from this end. Now go."

We sped down to the kitchens, grabbed two linen sheets, a couple of chicken legs originally destined for the eighteenth-century *Olé Grill* and jumped through the Time Portal.

They say all Portals lead to Rome ... if you set the coordinates correctly.

Zzzzzp.

Chapter Seven

Ancient Rome, Real Gold and a Possible Conspiracy

Personally, as a time traveller from Camelot, I try to be inconspicuous when I pop out of the Portal, while Neets tries to look her best. Unfortunately, we both normally make a complete pig's ear of things. I usually fall over and Neets's fashion sense covers loads of centuries, all at the same time.

So this was Rome. Busy place and very ... Roman, if you go for that sort of thing. Neets and I wrapped our sheets round ourselves in the complicated way the Romans seemed to like and merged into the crowd.

Just for once, no one took any notice of us, possibly because they thought that two girls dressed in bed linen, appearing out of a shimmering archway, spells potential trouble and are best ignored. Or maybe just for a change, our disguises were spot on. We barged our way through the throng of people, dodging the serious-looking soldiers that seemed to make up a quarter of the population. They all had spears and short stabbing swords, but not a smile from any of them, which considering they were made to wear skirts wasn't surprising, I suppose. They looked alert, and the sight of two strangers dressed in sheets and running through the main Roman Forum must have been the answer to a soldier's prayer on a hot summer's day, as boredom and stiffness set in.

We sprinted between the market stalls that filled the area, knocking fruit, leather goods and takeaway foods onto the ground where local kids grabbed what they could before the stall-holders and military could stop them. The crowd chasing us was growing larger and we hadn't even done anything yet. I couldn't help thinking that the Frankincense mob in Camelot and this bunch were pretty much interchangeable, though at least the Romans didn't have flaming torches and pitchforks – just swords and spears. I stopped for a second to look around as Neets cannoned into the back of me. I couldn't believe that even *Merl's Girls* had managed to get half of Rome chasing us within a minute of arriving in the city. It usually took at least an hour or two. Of course, we could have been set up, but this was no time to look for excuses. We needed higher ground and anywhere was higher than here in the middle of the Forum market.

I untangled myself from a sprawling Neets and pointed towards a line of buildings that offered potential safety. Actually the whole of the Forum was in a sort of shallow valley, so it was mostly surrounded by higher ground whichever way we went, but I pointed in the opposite direction to the mob, because I'm no fool. We ran up the steps of the nearest building, which looked like a temple of some sort, though to be honest as far as we could see just about every building seemed to be a temple. Romans certainly knew how to hedge their religious bets!

They knew how to protect them too. Within seconds Neets and I were surrounded by a group of Roman soldiers with very sharp stabbing swords and equally vicious looking spears, all pointing in our direction. The legionnaire with the fanciest armour, the longest cloak, the biggest helmet and the sharpest sword seemed to be in command, which made logical sense to Neets and me. Everything about him said *fashion statement* and *Mr Cool*, but everything about the way he used his sword said *professional*. Personally I hate being prodded, but it's difficult to object when two feet of the best steel is being wielded by an enthusiast who knows his job and probably prods for fun.

The few words he shouted made no sense at all to me and they could have been Greek for all I knew, though I assumed they were Latin. On the other hand Neets and I were in no doubt we were being told to enter the building at the top of the steps, without delay and without asking any questions like *why?* and *can I see your identification, please?* We climbed the rest of the steps until we came to a marble platform in front of the temple entrance, where the soldiers seemed happy enough for us to stop and catch our breath. The prodding may have stopped, but the commander fired Latin questions at us and waited for answers that he was never going to get in a million years.

"We got the clothes right, Neets. It's just a crying shame we don't speak the language." I looked at my cousin, but she didn't seem to be paying much attention to me, or to the commander, which considering his Italian good looks and golden tan, was staggering. On the other hand she was still too preoccupied with her beloved Bryn to think of other male hunks. "You okay, kid?" I expected some sort of reaction but not lots of fiddling about in one of the pockets deep underneath her sheet, followed by a huge wink.

"Shore, and if youse two young ladies would koindly let me into the secret as to what yor doin' trying to break into the treasury, oi'd be a happy little chappie. Shore, and oi would, begorrah!" I nearly jumped out of my skin. The commander was suddenly speaking broad Irish from the Dublin Bay region.

"That's better, Tersh," said a grinning Neets. "I'd forgotten that Merlin's prototype controllers all had some sort of translator. It lets us understand the Romans even though they're speaking Latin and they can understand us even though we're talking nonsense."

"We could take them down the frog and toad, 'guv," said a second soldier, "and get the trouble and strife to make a nice pot of rosie lee down the rub-a-dub. They'll rabbit fit to burst over a cuppa."

"Bother!" Neets whispered as she tapped the remote control. "It's got him talking in Cockney Slang now. I'll have to fiddle with the darn thing. Keep them occupied while I sort it out." She started fiddling. "By the way, for some reason he was suggesting that to get us to talk they take us to the nearest bar where his wife works and get a cup of tea."

"Strange ideas these Romans have, Neets. I know I often say I'll kill for a cup of Merl Grey, but talk … never!" I turned to the soldiers. "Guys, if I may call you that when you're wearing skirts, we're sort of strangers in town and need a helping hand by way of directions."

I gave my most winning smile and rewarded with a soldierly barrage in a variety of dialects and languages that sounded to me like Welsh, French,

American and even Chinese. Some of what they said I didn't understand at all, which is probably just as well; on the other hand Neets, who was desperately banging the Portal remote on the ground, was using words that even made the soldiers blush.

"That's fixed the little..." She looked up. "Oh, hello!" The legionnaires were concentrating on her, rather than me, but at least when they spoke we knew the device was working properly, after a fashion. The soldiers were speaking the same language, even if it was nineteenth-century American cowboy, mixed with a bit of hillbilly.

"Hi, y'all," drawled the commander. "If you two li'l old gals wouldn't mind moseying down to the sheriff's lockup, I got a nice big room with bars reserved just for you perdy ladies." The soldier looked confused at the translated drivel, because I'm sure what he really said was something like *move your backsides and get down those steps in double quick time ... hut! hut! hut!* Neets gave the remote one last whack and stuffed it in her pocket while the soldiers carrying spears used them to give us an encouraging prod.

I felt it was time to put my foot down. "Wait, guys, we only came up here to get out of the crowd and have a better view." Being locked up wasn't my idea of the way to start our detecting work in Rome. It was time to be inventive. I fished deep in my pocket and pulled out the few Roman coins Marlene hadn't managed to keep and held one up so the military could see it. I flicked it into the air and watched their eyes follow the gold as it spun, glinting in the late-afternoon sunlight and fell slowly back into my hand. I had their attention, or rather the coin did, which I have to admit was probably more attractive than me in their eyes. I dropped the rest of the coins on the ground, where the soldiers watched them rolling slowly towards the steps. A couple of them whimpered as they scrambled after the fast disappearing money, but the rest just stood at attention and cried. Let's face it, they were normally paid in salt (dead true, hence the word salary) and seeing gold coins worth several months' pay tossed in the air with gay abandon by a teenage girl must have been heart-breaking. On the other hand, no pain for them, no gain for me.

"Gentlemen," I said, "you're welcome to keep what you can grab," my problem would have been trying to stop them. "However, if you'd care to look at the face of the guy on the coin, we'd love to know where we can find him." I paused. "Come to that, we'd like to know whereabouts in Rome we are."

"Assuming we actually are in Rome," Neets muttered, unnecessarily I thought, "and not on some movie set in Hollywood."

"Do you see any extras wearing wrist watches?" I asked.

"No."

"Anyone shouting *Action, Cut* or *It's a wrap*?"

101

"No."

"Anyone selling popcorn, candy and huge drinks?"

"No."

"So this is the real thing. Trust me on this, Neets. We're in ancient Rome."

A couple of the soldiers nodded in agreement, though one did mutter something about not being all that ancient, *thank you very much*, as he chased a rolling coin.

"Stop!" I turned at the sound of a fast approaching high-pitched, reedy voice and flapping sandals. "Stop this sacrilege at once." A short, bald-headed man wearing the most fussy toga I'd ever seen, had run out of the temple building and was bearing down on us like a ship with its sails full and an inability to stop in anything less than a mile. He ignored me and Neets, cannoned into the centurion and rebounded like a billiard ball, knocking over two of the soldiers who'd been too busy counting their new gold coins to notice him. He tripped over the hem of his toga and almost somersaulted down the steps, but managed to grab a passing legionnaire by the elbow and rescue some of his fading dignity. He also rescued a gold coin.

He held it up, slowly turning it from side to side with a look of astonishment. "Where did you get this?" he asked, of no one in particular, but I suspected he meant the legionnaires, because we were just irrelevant girlies. In unison the soldiers pointed in my direction, keeping any coins they'd picked up well hidden, and like all military volunteers they took one step back, leaving Neets and me standing out like two sore thumbs in a sledge hammer factory. I got the impression that this guy was important, partly because his toga could have covered the world's largest bed, but mostly because he obviously thought he was the bee's knees and half its body, especially the bit with the sting in it. He turned to me. "You?" he laughed and I couldn't really blame him. "What would a silly little girl like you be doing with this incredibly valuable gold coin?"

I hate being called little, especially by pompous, self-important toads like this guy, and it was only a warning prod from Neets that stopped me helping the fool demonstrate a swallow dive down the steps of his beloved temple. I gave a very forced little girlie smile.

"Please, sir," a good bit of polite grovelling is always the best way to start when barefaced lies are about to be told, "my friend and I are two girlies just up from the country…"

"Ah, that'll account for your strange accents," the little man said smugly.

"…er, yes, it probably does." *Wish I'd thought of that.* "And we were so impressed with everything we've seen that we got lost and wandered up your temple steps so that we could see where we were. These nice soldier gentlemen were just showing us the sites when you came along to help." *Go on, prove me wrong*, I smiled winningly … and lost.

"And the coin? Where did you get the coin?"

"That little old thing?" I racked my brains and decided to tell the truth … Tertia style. The soldiers were busy, urgently hiding the coins they'd picked up. "I was given it by a funny little guy in strange colourful clothes, who I think got it from a tall, clean-shaven man who's very good with a sword. My auntie Marlene told us to look for the person on the front of the coin when we reached Rome. And here we are … lost." I must admit, I was rather proud, because there wasn't a word of a lie amongst my fibs. "Can you help us, mister?" I even fluttered my eyelids, but from the way Neets winced it probably looked more like hay fever.

The man smiled, tossed the end of his toga over his left arm and walked to the soldiers with the air of someone who considers himself much more important than mere military. "Centurion, you and your men may leave us." He gave a fussy little wave of dismissal. "I don't believe these two girls pose me any great threat and as visitors to our beautiful city I think they deserve our hospitality. So I'll take over from here. I suggest you all have the rest of the afternoon off, go to the market and spend the coins you picked up … if anyone will take them." He walked back to Neets and me and I had the definite feeling we were losing control of the situation, if we ever had it in the first place. "You two are called Tertia and Unita?" We nodded. "Then follow me please. I want to show you something."

"What?" I asked. Neets made to follow the man, but one look from me and a minor kick on the shins stopped her. We both stood still, hands on hips. "We go nowhere until you tell us who you are and what it is you want us to see. No one here knows we're in Rome, and we're not about to follow some guy in a fancy tablecloth and floppy sandals just because he says so. We're Merl's Girls and we don't take orders from anybody … except from Merl herself, of course, and occasionally Marlene, but other than that we do what we want." My curiosity got the better of me. "Er … exactly what *do* you want us to see?"

"Follow me." The man refused to reveal anything more so we turned and followed him into the large round building, ducking under a ridiculously low doorway. I glanced at the words carved into the stone blocks above the entrance and muttered them into the Time Portal remote controller, "*Aerarium Pecuniae.*" My Latin pronunciation was probably a bit off, but Merl's device echoed back a reasonable translation, "*Financial Treasury.*" Neets and I ducked through the entrance, although in my case it was more of a slight nod.

We found ourselves in a circular room, lit by strategically placed oil lamps that cast a flickering light making the place seem more eerie and important than it probably was. On the other hand as far as creating first impressions went, it was pretty effective.

The walls were covered in colourful paintings, most of which were about money and people showing a great deal of pleasure in holding it. The roof was a dome giving the illusion of great height and power, though I've heard it's easier to build a dome rather than a flat roof and that they tend to stay up longer. Other than this, the room was empty, except, of course, for the man in the colourful tablecloth who pointed silently at a spiral staircase leading to whatever lay below. We took the hint, and because we'd only have looked silly otherwise, walked down the stairs into a smaller room that was much better lit and as empty as the one upstairs, with the exception of two open chests.

"Tersh, there's no way out of this place except up again." Neets had done a quick scan of the room, which to be honest, even for her hadn't taken long. "It's a trap."

"No, it's the strong room." The tablecloth man had followed us and now stood on the bottom step, blocking any escape, except one that involved a rugby tackle. Bryn would have been up for it. "This is where the consuls in charge of Rome store their most valuable items. Usually money and gold, though both are sadly absent at the moment."

"Strong room?" I loved the description except for one thing. "But there's no door."

"Ah, but there are permanent guards posted outside the treasury and at the top of the stairs."

"There's none up there now," Neets pointed out.

"There's nothing left down here to protect," the man said sadly.

As I walked over to the chests in my capacity as a member of the TDA I handed the man one of my carefully crafted business cards. He read it with a puzzled frown. "Inquisitor Temporalium Societatis?" It was the nearest Marlene could get to the Temporal Detective Agency, but it was better than nothing.

"We're detectives," I explained. "Sort of private police and we were sent here to sort this out."

"You were? Who by?"

I gave a half smile and tapped the side of my nose. His eyes shot up and I wondered who he thought I meant, though I just hoped whoever it was was a good payer and not a tall Shakespearean actor with a nasty taste in swords.

Both chests were open and it didn't take much detective work to see that they were completely empty. Right now Rome looked pretty badly off to me and I agreed with the man that neither chest contained a single coin, let alone the minutest grain of gold. I felt like a member of the audience helping a conjurer, except that I had a feeling this guy wasn't going to magic them full again.

"Two days ago these chests contained over two thousand gold coins," he said and his voice had a slight tremble, "all with the head of Caesar on one side and a birthday message on the other. Yesterday they all vanished into thin air and today you appear right outside the treasury with a number of the missing coins, trying to bribe the military." He raised his eyebrows and looked sternly at us, which was probably meant to make us girlies burst into tears and tell him everything. I laughed and Neets giggled.

"You can't be serious! You suspect Neets and me? We're the detectives!" I paused as something he'd said struck me. "You mean to say the coins were legal? They weren't fakes?"

"Of course not. They were intended to celebrate Caesar's fiftieth birthday and he was going to distribute them to the poor, although there aren't that many poor people in Rome so they'd have gone to the moderately well-off, which means they would have probably been given back to Caesar as a token of the people's respect and their desire to remain well-off, as well as alive. Consider them to be Caesar's. And of course I don't suspect you, or I wouldn't have sent the soldiers away, nor would I be down here alone with you."

His last comment made me feel dangerous, though considering I'd already defeated the Black Knight single-handed (well almost), perhaps I had every right to feel like I did. It also struck me I'd just given the military a golden bonus, and considering they normally get paid in little bags of salt (honest again!) it was no wonder they looked like Neets's cats feasting on a vat of cream.

"So why *did* you bring us down here then?" Neets

asked, as she poked around in the bottom of one of the chests to make sure there wasn't a stray coin waiting to be found. "We're just two girls up from the country and not used to your city ways…" This girl was getting good, and what's more she hadn't mentioned Bryn once since we'd left Camelot. Well, maybe once, or twice under her breath, but that didn't count, "…even though we are world-class and vastly experienced at detecting crimes."

"I believed there may be more to you than meets the eye. You also have the same strange accent as the visitor I showed around the treasury two days ago, just before the coins went missing. Though I doubt you're working with him, because you wouldn't be hanging around here if you were."

"Lucky we're detectives then, isn't it. What did this man look like," I asked, although I was pretty sure I already knew. I just wanted to be certain.

"He was tall, good-looking, clean-shaven, had long dark hair. Oh, and he looked as though he could be very useful with a sword. Ring any bells?"

Neets and I looked at each other. It sounded like our Leading Man, though why he'd come all the way back to ancient Rome, steal two thousand gold coins that belonged to Caesar and then bring them back to Camelot – only to give them away to strangers – was a mystery. On the other hand, the Temporal Detective Agency loves mysteries like a starving man loves food, and this had the promise of a five-course gourmet meal with chocolate mints to finish.

"He sounds familiar," I said. "Could be from our village, or thereabouts, but he's not someone I know. What about you, Neets?" My cousin shrugged, pursed her lips, then gave a sweetly innocent smile. She's always been good at innocence and the boys love it. If I do the same thing they run a mile. "We might know him, but if you showed him the treasury and he was alone, how come he managed to walk up those stairs carrying two thousand gold coins in loose change without you seeing him?"

The man looked embarrassed as he pushed the head of a small stone statue hidden in a wall niche. "The back door," he said as a small part of the circular wall swung out with hardly a sound. "It's a secret passageway leading to the cellars of the Senate House, known only to me and a very few people in the Senate. I use it occasionally and it's how we got the chests in here in the first place. My name's Cicero, by the way, Senator of Rome and poet. You may have heard of me?" We shook hands like old friends, while Neets and I made *Wow, not THE Cicero? Gosh,* noises as we mentally shrugged our shoulders, *Who?*

"You're saying the chests weren't brought from upstairs, but along there and you inspected them when they arrived here."

"That's right, more or less."

"So no one up top and outside the treasury even knew the chests were down here?" puzzled Neets.

Good question.

"What do you mean by *more or less*?" I asked.

Cicero looked embarrassed for a second time. "I didn't actually count the coins in the treasury. I checked the chests in the Senate and everything was fine, so I knew they were intact after the men carried them along the passage and left them here." He looked uncertain. "I'm sure."

"Were the chests ever out of your sight once you checked and signed for them?"

"Of course not. I locked the chests in the Senate and I was with them until after they were carried here."

"Who carried them?"

"Four slaves owned by senators Brutus and Cassius. Good friends of mine. I don't mean the slaves obviously." Cicero giggled and gave a genteel cough. "Once I'd closed and locked the chests, Brutus, Cassius and I toasted the success of our birthday project with a goblet of wine or two. Then I gave the go-ahead for the slaves to pick up the coin chests and take them along the passage."

"And you reckon there's no way anyone could have stolen the coins once they arrived in the treasury?" I was beginning to get an idea.

"Even if they could have opened the chests, they'd have been seen upstairs by the guards, so they'd have had to have gone back along the passage to the Senate cellars and that would have been silly."

"And you're sure the chests were full when they arrived here?" Neets was on the ball and I had a feeling it was the same ball I was on.

"Oh yes. The slaves were struggling under the weight of the coins. There's no doubt."

"So the chests were never out of your sight after you sealed them, except when you had a drink with your friends." It seemed a good time to summarise things. "Then your friend's slaves picked them up and carried them here with obvious difficulty, where the chests remained until you unlocked them and discovered the coins were missing. Oh, and of course you had the visitor who wanted to be shown round the treasury. Is that about right?"

Cicero stared up at the ceiling for a moment, deep in thought. "Yes," he said at last. I knew then what had happened to the coins and if I was right the treasury basement was not the place to be found hanging around in. "So what do you think happened to the coins, then?" Cicero asked, but there was no way I was going to tell him. As far as I knew he could have been behind the whole thing, though I doubted it, but at the very least he'd probably want to compose an epic poem and a book about it all.

I shook my head. "The coins were stolen, that's for sure, and I reckon whoever stole them is going to try to get someone else to take the blame." I was sure I could hear the sound of footsteps echoing along the passageway and they sounded more *left-right* military to me than civilian. "Right now that looks like Neets and me, or at the very least you, Mister Cicero, so if you don't mind we'll go and do some sightseeing and grab some food, 'cos personally I'm starving and Neets wants to buy a handbag."

As I talked I was moving towards the stairs and by the time Cicero realised we were off, I'd already reached the top with Neets close behind. Below us I heard Cicero yelp in surprise as the basement treasury room filled with soldiers from the Senate. The last thing we heard as we raced into sunlight was, "Right you three, you're nicked … hang on, where are the girls? Blimey, someone's not going to be happy about this!"

We'd been set up and the treasury was no place to hang around.

This was more than a little bit of nastiness by the Leading Man to stop us saving Arthur. Somehow this involved Caesar, the Roman Senate, a fortune in missing gold coins and now us. Neets and I needed to sit down and think this through, but first we needed to run.

We ran.

Chapter Eight

The Olé Grill-Pizzeria and a Trip to the Roman Senate

Actually it was more of a jostling shuffle through the crowded Forum, dodging arguing orators, stall-holders and Romans who didn't take kindly to being shoved aside by two foreign girls wrapped in bed linen.

I stopped to get our bearings, because we seemed to be jostling round in circles and whoever was chasing us couldn't be that far behind, or that dumb not to notice us. At one end of the Forum was an imposing building with large columns at its front and the word *CURIA* above its main archway. It also had lots of soldiers, none of whom looked as though they were there to entertain tourists. At the other end of the Forum the road rose slightly, hiding the lower part of a massive circular stone building that made Shakespeare's Globe Theatre look silly. From drawings I'd seen of Rome, this was the famous Coliseum where massacres were staged almost on a daily basis. I had a feeling that if we went to the Senate we'd probably end up fighting lions and gladiators at the other end of the Forum before the day was out.

I looked up at the treasury and saw a small number of very efficient-looking soldiers emerge and scan the Forum, presumably trying to catch a glimpse of us. Cicero was in the middle of them, looking more like an indignant prisoner than a co-conspirator, and I reckoned I might have to change my ideas about the senator and would-be writer. I grabbed Neets's arm and dragged her towards one of the side streets that ran off from the Forum. I didn't care which one, just so long as it was away from the pursuing military and led away from the crowds.

Crowds are good things to get lost in if you keep your head down, but everyone in the Forum wanted to sell us something, have a philosophical argument, or question our politics, all of which made escape difficult. We were back into jostle mode and shoved our way into a wide alley flanked by three-storey-high buildings … something we never dreamed of in Camelot, where a second floor meant you were in the castle and the third floor meant you were on the roof.

At least it was quieter here. Neets and I stepped back into the shelter of a doorway, out of sight of any stray military, and relaxed. I looked up at a sign fixed above the doorway and burst out laughing as a hand grabbed my shoulder.

"I had a feeling you'd find your way to the best eatery in town." Galahad pulled us through the entrance into the *Olé Grill-Pizzeria* and locked the door. "So you got yourselves into a spot of trouble again. No change there then."

"We were set up," said Neets indignantly. "Anyway, what in blazes are you doing in Rome?"

Galahad guided us to a table in a far corner where we were surrounded by potted palms and wine bottles in wicker baskets suspended from the ceiling. Swords, spears and shields decorated the walls, competing for space with the odd legionnaire's uniform and horse brass. The whole place was a bit of a clutter really, just like any Italian restaurant. We sat down and picked up menus without thinking.

"Something to drink first?" inquired the knight in his best *Olé Grill* voice. "I wouldn't recommend the water – I've seen where it comes from – but the local wine isn't bad. A small glass each?" We nodded enthusiastically. "And then a large stuff-crust pizza. Speciality of the house!"

At least he didn't try the accent, though he did kiss the tips of his fingers like any good Italian foodie. He shouted the order towards a hatchway, which presumably hid the kitchens, and a voice we knew only too well called back, "I've only got one pair of hands." There was a pause. "One-and-a-half hands." Lancelot poked his head through the hatch and froze, his mouth wide open and the colour draining from his face. I was nearly as surprised as the old knight, but I wasn't lost for words. Never am!

"Galahad, I wouldn't put anything past you, but what in Merl's teeth is Lancelot doing here cooking up fast food? Is Guinevere waiting on tables?" I pretended to look under the table and behind a potted palm for Arthur's old queen.

"No," replied Galahad indignantly. "It's her day off."

"Galahad, I was kidding!" At least I think I was. "But more to the point, why are you here and how come out of all the places you could have been in Rome, you just happen to be behind the very doorway we sheltered in. Oh, and Guinevere I can understand as a waitress. She's youngish and not too bad looking, but Lancelot, I mean he's a hundred if he's a day and gaga most of the time. Before you answer let's have those drinks. I'm parched and Neets is too, but she's too ladylike to tell you. Put your tongue back in, Neets, what would Bryn think?"

We sipped the weak wine and were so thirsty that the purest mountain-cool spring water couldn't have tasted better. Though in fact what we drank was probably the vilest gut-rot imaginable from the sludge at the bottom of the municipal wine vats. Galahad always knew how to turn a good profit.

"Skip the food, Galahad, and tell us what scam you're up to. Everyone knows the Temporal Detective Agency doesn't believe in coincidences." I turned to the hatch. "And, Lancelot, we'll have some nuts over here." I don't know why I asked for peanuts because they wouldn't be around for another couple of thousand years and yet a shower of peanuts landed on our table and skittered onto the floor, followed by some highly inventive verbal abuse from Lancelot as he slammed the hatch closed.

"Never mind him," Galahad said cheerfully. "He's a moody old fool at the best of times. He insisted on coming along with Guinevere and I didn't have the heart to stop him. Besides, I've got loads more nuts if you want them. I brought several boxes with me from the twenty-first century, just in case the Romans liked them. They don't and I'm prepared to let you have a box at trade price." Galahad never lost the opportunity to unload slow-moving goods, but I ignored his offer.

"And you?" I asked. "Why are you here? All your *Olé Grill* places are in Merl's old cave up and down the centuries and this is definitely not her cave. It's not even in the same country."

Galahad sat down next to me, picked up a stray peanut, flicked it into the air and caught it in his mouth. Smooth. "I wanted to do something different.

To be honest, the *Olé Grills* run themselves and wearing a tuxedo every night up and down the centuries is beginning to get boring. So I thought I'd invent the ancient Roman pizza and maybe have a go at creating the Caesar Salad while I was at it."

Neets was appalled. "You can't come back in time and pretend to invent something that already exists."

"I'm beginning to think you're right. Business has been disastrous since we opened." Galahad absent-mindedly picked up Neets's wine glass and drained it. "Amazingly, the Romans don't seem to like their own food and yet the new Southern Fried Chicken place next door is doing a great trade. There's no accounting for taste! I even thought I'd try snails as a topping, but Lancelot refused to cook them on the grounds some of them were friends of his. Actually, between you and me," he went all conspiratorial and whispered, "I reckon the Green Knight started the fried chicken place. The fool was always boasting what a great chef he was and about doing different things with bits of chicken. What's more he kept hinting he was going into business miles away from Camelot." He paused. "By the way, what does *Viridis Eques* mean? It's on a sign above the door." Realisation grew over him and he groaned.

"Stop wittering, Galahad." I gave him a warning Tertia *look*. "None of that explains how come you just happened to launch a restaurant exactly where we chose to hide, hundreds of years and a couple of thousand miles from Camelot."

"Okay, but don't tell Merlin, or she'll probably stop me using her cave and the Time Portal." Galahad made a face. "In which case no more *Olé Grill*."

"Tell!" I made an equally scrunched-up face and poked out my tongue for good measure. Neets gathered together most of the peanuts remaining on the table and started munching as though she was watching a movie – probably sitting in the back row with Bryn.

"After you went through the Portal and came to Rome," said Galahad, "Marlene, Merlin and I watched you in the thing's PortalVision and made sure you arrived safely. But we soon lost sight of you when you disappeared into the crowd and Marlene asked me to come to Rome and make sure you were still okay, ideally without either of you seeing me."

Neets looked puzzled. "So, how come you've already got a restaurant and everything, when you arrived in Rome after us?" Good question.

"Because when I got here I saw you go up the steps to the treasury building, but what you didn't notice was that the crowd was guiding you. It was inevitable where you'd ended up and that the Roman military would surround you. When you started throwing those gold coins around, you told anyone who cared exactly who you were and that's when the fun started."

"That's crazy. How could the crowd have known we

were coming here?" I said. "Come to that, how could anyone? It was almost a spur of the moment thing."

"The same person who knew you'd have the coins, of course. The same person that wants to eliminate Arthur ... your Leading Man. He organised it all. He had his men in the crowd make sure you went up to the treasury. He had the soldiers waiting and made sure Cicero would take you down to the basement so you could be caught and imprisoned for the theft of Caesar's gold."

"But we didn't get caught," said Neets, stating the obvious.

"No, you didn't," replied Galahad, "but the fact remains it was a trap. You came here because the Leading Man wanted you away from Camelot and in Rome where he could get rid of you and stop you interfering in his plans for Arthur."

"So he's here in Rome?"

"I think so. No, I'm sure he is."

"Galahad, none of that explains how come you have a pizza restaurant in Rome, when you came here after we did." I suspected I knew, and Merl was not going to be pleased with the knight. "You messed about with history, didn't you?"

Galahad hesitated as he flicked a stray peanut into the far corner of the empty restaurant. "Only a bit, and if I don't sell some pizzas soon with my special Camelot toppings, I'll close the place down and nobody'll know we were ever here. Anyway, I found out that Roman farmers already eat something like pizza, but they just don't call it anything in particular. So no harm done."

"That's not what I'm talking about and you know it!"

"Yes," admitted the knight. "Okay, after I saw what happened to you and especially when I saw you run across the Forum and into this side street, I went back to Camelot and gave my report to Marlene and Merlin. They told me to get back here and do what I could to help, but I couldn't see what help I could be by turning up after the event as it were, so I changed the Portal coordinates when no one was looking and arrived back in Rome about six months ago. I managed to rent this building and started up the *Olé Grill-Pizzeria* with on-off help from Lancelot. Mostly off, but then these days he tends to forget where he is, let alone what century he's in." Galahad got up and brought a carafe of weak red wine back to the table, along with a glass for himself. He filled our glasses and sipped from his, making a sour face, because the wine wasn't that good, no matter what he said. "We had a few Romans who came in just after we opened, probably for the novelty of the thing, but it's been slow to stationary since then. Anyway, I employed a couple of Romans to look after the place while I was running the real *Olé Grill* chain, then came back today so I could bring you in here when you ran into my side street. It worked a treat and now you're perfectly safe."

"From what?" asked Neets. She was right, of course. A chasing mob and a few soldiers was the least of our worries.

"Who from?" I asked, because that would probably also tell us what we were fighting. "And don't tell me it's our Leading Man. He may be stirring up trouble for us here, but he isn't the one we have to watch. You've been here six months on and off, so what have you found out?"

"There's a conspiracy to kill Caesar." Galahad looked from me to Neets and back at me again as though his news was earth-shattering instead of old history. He looked disappointed at our lack or reaction.

"Galahad, we know there was a conspiracy to kill Caesar," I said, "and it worked after he went to Egypt and then conquered Britain. Any book could have told you that."

"*This* conspiracy is going on right now and his Egypt trip isn't due to start for another week or two."

"You make it sound like a holiday," Neets said through a mouthful of peanuts.

"Compared to what they've got planned for him here, it will be. It looks like your Leading Man is stirring things up for Caesar a few years ahead of time and messing around with history far more than I could have done by opening my pizza restaurant."

I saw what he was getting at, but so far Galahad

was only telling us a story that fitted the facts and even Neets could have done that … given a bit of prompting and a good script. If we were going to stop Caesar being assassinated and save Arthur I needed to see the facts and get proof. Which is pretty much what I told Galahad, give or take a word or two, and it was why five minutes later the three of us walked up the steps of the Senate building, past the very efficient-looking soldier guards and into the thick of the conspiracy.

"I thought the guards would have stopped us," said Neets.

"I'm surprised they didn't," replied Galahad. "Only senators wear bed sheet togas, but all other Romans hate them because they're so difficult to move around in. They wear tunics, so they probably think you're making fun of their ruling class, which no one will worry about … except the ruling class. Of course they may just think you can't afford tunics and have to wear your sheets, but either way, we're in, so let's explore."

The building wasn't particularly impressive once we got past the columns. In fact considering this was where the most powerful men in the Roman Empire met to run everything it was decidedly down-market. The inside was one large and very high room lit by three large shuttered openings near the roof. Oil lamps gave an artificial glow, though the whole place could only be described as gloomy. What struck me most was the total lack of chairs. For all their sophistication, Romans didn't seem to have mastered the art of sitting down and everything was done by standing round in groups, chatting.

Galahad pointed at a small cluster at the far end of the building. "That's Julius Caesar and Mark Anthony with their supporters." He pointed at another group. "That's Brutus, Cassius and Caesar's opposition. They're the ones who'll assassinate Caesar after he becomes Emperor in a few years time. At least that's the way history has it planned at the moment, which would be fine, because Arthur's ancestor will still be born."

"So where's the problem then?" I asked.

"The *problem* is the man talking to Brutus and calling himself Perducendum. Roughly translated that means *Leading Man*. Somehow he's got people believing he's a senator and I've seen him in here before talking to Brutus and his friends."

"But what do you think he's doing?" asked Neets.

Sometimes my cousin can be very slow. "Trying to convince the conspirators to assassinate Caesar now, rather than wait. He has no choice either. He knows we're in Rome and he must know by now that his plan with the coins backfired and we're still free. He'll act soon. Besides, look at the date, it's the Ides of March, the same date Caesar was assassinated on, just a few years earlier. He won't be able to resist it."

"Are you armed?" asked Galahad, as he showed us a

small arsenal of kitchen knives hidden beneath his tunic. "I can let you borrow something sharp if you want. Even a pizza cutter can be pretty useful in a close quarter fight."

I looked scornfully at Galahad. "We're founder members of the Temporal Detective Agency, not a bleedin' army. You're the knight, so you sort it." I had a feeling that being found with a knife of any sort was probably not going to be a good idea after what we figured might be about to happen. "And I'd keep that lot out of sight too."

We watched the Leading Man talking urgently to Brutus, Cassius and a small number of their followers, using all his acting skills as he nodded in the direction of Caesar. Neets and I kept our heads down and our faces covered as we edged closer to the actor and his friends so we could at least hear what was being planned. Galahad's pizza slice was tucked in the folds of my sheet and felt reassuringly solid and sharp, while Neets had grabbed a possibly lethal ladle from the knightly chef who had sensibly stayed back near the entrance. The conspirators looked to me as though they were somewhat reluctant to conspire, although the actor was slowly manoeuvring the group towards Caesar. Eventually Neets and I were within earshot.

"Brutus," said the Leading Man, "it was all agreed. Caesar poses a threat to you all and I told you how he intends having you arrested on trumped-up charges of theft."

"But, Perducendum," replied Brutus in a voice made for whining, "we did steal it, or more to the point we've kept it for ourselves."

"And it was ours anyway," said Cassius, not to be out-whined by Brutus. "Caesar knows nothing about it."

"And besides," added Brutus, "you said you were going to get those two girls to take the blame. But they got away."

"All part of the plan," our Leading Man said smoothly. "It diverts the attention away from you, my friends, and be assured the two brats will be far away by now."

"But what if they talk and word gets back to Caesar?" Cassius was obviously far from convinced.

"There are witnesses who will confirm the girls had the gold coins in their possession outside the treasury and were handing them out to soldiers as bribes."

"But how does that help us if we assassinate Caesar?" asked Cassius. "Even though killing him might be good for the Roman Empire, we'll still get arrested and they'll probably..." he gulped, "hurt us."

"Nonsense. You will have rescued Rome from a tyrant and be heralded as the heroes you truly are." The Leading Man paused meaningfully. "As we all agreed."

Neither Brutus, nor Cassius, really struck me as conspirator material, which was most likely why the

Leading Man had chosen them. I got the impression they'd do whatever he told them to do, even kill Caesar … just for a quiet life. What bugged me was that Neets and I had been played for suckers by the Leading Man right from the time we first saw him in Shakespeare's Globe Theatre. He'd tempted us into Rome with the fake gold coins that turned out to be real, and set us up to take the rap for stealing them, when most of them hadn't left Rome at all. He wanted us well and truly out of the way. I suppose I should have felt flattered that the TDA was held in such high esteem by the man who wanted to destroy Arthur and us, but I didn't.

I could tell that Brutus and Cassius were wavering and that their senator followers were being carried forward on the crest of the Leading Man's silver tongue. I noticed a few of them had slipped their hands into their togas and I caught the odd glimpse of steel as we drew nearer to Caesar, who from the look of things was nearing the end of a joke. I couldn't help thinking he'd better hurry up, or he'd never get to the punch line.

The Leading Man was moving into the background as he urged the conspirators to act, and before we could move away he was standing between Neets and me, pushing us towards the action.

"Are you armed?" He asked us enthusiastically. We both nodded, taking care not to uncover our faces and showed him the ladle and pizza slicer. "Good, then rescue Rome and kill Caesar. Be heroes!" He shouted the last words as he slipped through a side door, leaving us once again to face the music. At least this time he didn't know it was us, though I have to say, that wasn't much of a comfort.

Caesar was surrounded by the conspirators, each of whom looked as though they were encouraging their fellow senators to strike, while trying not to be seen to be involved in case things didn't work out. Brutus and Cassius were leading from the rear. The general was smiling and trying to shake hands like any good politician, causing one or two of the conspirators to drop their ill-concealed weapons and change sides with a whimper. Others were made of sterner stuff and drew daggers as they advanced on Caesar, who looked as though he was beginning to realise something was wrong. I decided it was time for Neets and me to take action. I started screaming and waved my pizza slicer like a maniac, while Neets thumped one of the conspirators over the head with her ladle – she'll make someone a lovely cook one day – but all we succeeded in doing was make the more determined of the assassins press home their attack with cries along the lines of *death to the traitor*. Probably made them feel better. It looked pretty final for Caesar and it didn't look too good for us either.

Brutus and Cassius looked as though they could have been on either side and were hedging their bets trying to be more onlookers than participants. Caesar looked at his belt where his sword should have been, but all weapons had to be handed into safe-keeping on entering the Senate building. Only conspirators and girls carrying kitchen utensils were seemingly exempt. He swore, quite understandably, because most of his trusted senate supporters had moved backwards, leaving him alone to face the conspirators and with barely enough time to complete his unfinished joke.

Neets and I charged screaming through the armed senators and cannoned into two members of the elite Praetorian Guard who had appeared out of nowhere and stood between us and the general like two parts of an immovable brick wall. I closed my eyes expecting a quick military sword strike, but when nothing happened I opened my eyes again. One of the soldiers looked at me and smiled.

"Hello, Tertia." My Welsh David was grinning like a cat. "Got yourselves into a spot of bother again, is it?"

"Hi, Uni…" was as far as Bryn got before Neets launched herself at him and hung onto his neck like a tie. Then she slapped him.

"Why didn't you let us know you were here?" she shouted. "We could have been killed, you fool. We were prepared to put ourselves between the assassins and Caesar and you'd have let us! I hate you. I hate you!" I knew then from the way she hit him again that my cousin was truly in love, poor cow, whereas

David and I were just jolly good friends. He and I shook hands.

Bryn managed to grab Neets's arms before she did him any real harm and to my amazement they both burst out laughing. "Unita, I've come to rescue you, yet again," he said a little bit pompously to my mind. "Merlin and Marlene sent us here a few moments ago and David and I managed to grab Praetorian Guard uniforms from a couple of unsuspecting soldiers. And here we are, like your Camelot knights in shining armour … well, skirts anyway."

I looked around.

The attacking senators, armed with a variety of sharp objects, were trying to surround Caesar and the few followers who stayed by his side. Bryn and David had drawn their swords and growled their defiance, looking more menacing in their Roman uniforms than I ever remembered them back home. Neets and I tried to help as much as we could by brandishing our kitchen utensils, but the conspiring senators at the back were pushing the ones who had surprisingly found themselves at the front. Pure weight of numbers meant we would lose the fight and Rome would lose its best general and future emperor. Right at the very back, like all good leaders, I spotted Brutus and Cassius, whose sneeringly nervous shout of *Surprise! Happy Birthday* was an inspired piece of irony. The Leading Man had gone, presumably believing Caesar was as good as dead and Arthur well on the way to being eliminated, but Bryn and David were taking no chances and for Arthur's sake were ready to defend the general with their lives – I like to think they felt the same way about Neets and me – as well as point him in the direction of Egypt. Luckily Egypt happened to be in the same direction as the main doors.

We broke and ran, almost carrying the bewildered Caesar into the warm Roman sunlight and straight into the arms of the Leading Man.

Chapter Nine

The End of Roman Pizzas and the Start of Holidays

Cicero raised his hands as though he was conducting a choir and led the Praetorian Guard in a rousing chorus of *Happy Birthday To You*. A few of the braver senators joined in, while the Leading Man looked daggers and strained at the ropes that for the moment kept him securely away from Caesar. Personally, I didn't trust any of them and as far as I was concerned they were a lot of smiling knives.

"Boys, we need to get Caesar away from here fast."

I tried to separate Bryn from the clutching Neets, but her grip was too determined and I decided they were probably better as a team anyway. I told David to get the general back to the *Olé Grill-Pizzeria* because it was the only place I knew in Rome where he'd be safe while the military rounded up the conspirators. Mind you, I didn't think that would take long. Suddenly everyone seemed to be the general's friend.

Caesar was enjoying himself, walking up and down the line of singing senators and pumping hands like any good politician. Plus, of course, I knew he'd been promised a special birthday present of two thousand gold coins minted in his honour, which would make anyone cheerful, though I doubted he was actually going to get them. We needed a diversion.

"General Caesar," I whispered repeatedly in his ear until I got his attention. "It's party time!" I yelled the words as I formed the head of a conga line. Bryn grabbed my waist and Neets made sure nobody other than she grabbed his. David manoeuvred Caesar so he was next in line and Galahad brought up the rear behind my David. I say *my* David, because everyone belongs to someone sometime and besides I quite liked the boy, even though his stepfather was a murderous ship wrecker.

We conga-danced and sang our way through the Forum, weaving in and out of the cheering crowds, who at least recognised the Birthday Boy and some of whom even joined the end of the snaking line. By the direct route, it should have taken two minutes to get to Galahad's restaurant, but it took us nearly half an hour thanks to the enthusiastic Romans who either wanted to join us, argue philosophy or sell Neets and me an Italian leather handbag. Caesar didn't help. He kept stopping to shake hands, as though he'd totally forgotten we'd just saved his life in the Senate, but that's politicians for you, especially when they're incredibly famous generals. My other thought was that this was Arthur's ancestor, but then you couldn't have everything.

Not for the first time, I remembered that if Caesar didn't meet Cleopatra then Arthur's ancestor wouldn't be born, meaning that Arthur wouldn't exist, or at least as we knew him, and Merl and Marlene had already had a sort of future vision of what our king might become. Ugh! Even worse, Merlin wouldn't become the world's best wizard, and Neets and I would be ignorant farm girls with no future and no Temporal Detective Agency.

I shuddered and led the lengthening conga to the safety of the pizza restaurant and the comfort of our recently vacated table. We gratefully sat down, because nearly being killed in a Roman conspiracy and leading a conga dance is a tiring mix.

"Lancelot!" Galahad shouted at the closed hatch. "If you're in there, get a large carafe of wine and six glasses," he looked around, "and make that *cheap* wine, out here now." He waited, but there was no reply. "If you're not in there ... forget the tip!" The hatch remained firmly closed and Galahad muttered something about not being able to get good help these days, before marching into the kitchen and returning with a loaded tray. He may have owned the place, but he hadn't forgotten how to water down the wine.

Caesar was still in a party mood and I had the feeling he was expecting half of Rome to jump out from under the tables, over screens and out of the kitchens shouting *Surprise!* before dancing round the room carrying presents. I poured him a glass of wine as consolation.

"To General Caesar," I raised my glass in a birthday toast and everyone did the same. "Right, to business. First of all introductions, then we'll do our best to explain what's going on."

Without mentioning Camelot, South Wales, time travel, wizards and the like, I explained to Caesar who Neets and I were, where the boys fitted in without being too specific and how come we'd ended up in a pizza restaurant owned by Galahad. I explained we were from out of town, which was why we all had such funny names. He didn't seem all that fussed and I reckoned he was still expecting the surprise guests. Besides, we had a much more difficult job now we'd saved his life. We had to persuade Caesar to go to Egypt.

"Been on holiday yet this year, Julius?" was Neets's

best attempt. "You don't mind if I call you Julius, do you?" Bryn didn't look amused, but Caesar nodded with a smile.

"I don't take holidays," he said.

"But you must go abroad sometimes," said Galahad. "I mean, as a general you go to other countries, surely."

"Only to invade them and after that I might look around a bit if there's anything left worth seeing." Caesar turned to Bryn and David. "You two soldiers know what it's like. You go to foreign places, meet exotic people and end up cutting them into little pieces." He laughed. "By the way, my thanks for protecting me in the Senate, but shouldn't you be back on duty now, or at least standing guard at the door to this place? What's a pizza anyway?"

The boys sensibly didn't answer and I explained to the general once again that Bryn and David were in disguise and not part of his military elite. Actually, I began to wonder if we'd rescued the right man, but a quick look at the one gold coin I had left convinced me that this was the real Julius Caesar.

"You need a break, Julius," I said. "Neets is right; a holiday would do you a world of good, especially after what you've been through today. It wouldn't be a bad idea to get away from Rome for a bit, while your supporters and the military round up the conspirators. Then you can come back as the hero, Julius, with no worries."

"It has its attractions," admitted Caesar. "You have somewhere in mind?"

"Well now that you mention it," said Neets as she leaned back in her chair, "I hear that Egypt is nice at this time of year."

"Excellent food, I hear," added Galahad. "Well, very good figs and yoghurt."

"And it's just across the sea." I finished off the travelogue. "Only a few days travel by road and boat. You'll love it. In fact I wish we were coming with you."

Julius looked at each of us in turn. "Are you serious? You think I should run away, just because a few senators don't like me?" He pushed his chair back and leapt to his feet. He felt for his sword, but he was still in his senator's toga, so he borrowed David's just so he could wave it round and make a point. "I need to stay in Rome and show everyone I'm not afraid. The Roman people must see that their favourite general is in charge and not going overseas to get a tan at the slightest threat of an insurrection."

"You silly man." I thumped the table. "You need to leave Rome and stay alive. Most people don't care whether you're as brave as a lion, or scared witless. Most people just want to have bread on their table and live for tomorrow. Only the conspirators care and that's because they want you dead so they can take over and stop you from becoming emperor."

"I have no ambitions towards becoming emperor of

Rome," Caesar said rather pompously, which told us all that he wanted the job *really* badly. Then he paused. "Is it true that most people don't care what I do?" He sounded shocked.

"I'm afraid so, Julius. On the other hand, you have a significant part to play in history and I rather expect you'll be remembered for many centuries as the greatest Roman of them all."

Caesar struck a heroic pose and preened. "I always knew I had a greater destiny than just being a Roman soldier, or come to that, even a senator." He sat down and pushed his glass towards Galahad for a refill, which amazingly he got. "A holiday. I will of course have to take my army with me. Just for safe keeping, you understand."

I gritted my teeth. "What do you think you're going to do on this holiday?"

"I'll lead my armies into Egypt, lay waste to the countryside, set siege to the towns, kill as many people as possible and turn the whole place into a Roman province. The normal routine, relaxing stuff."

"Hmm," I said thoughtfully, "it really seems a shame to do all that to little Egypt. All you'll have to show for your trouble will be loads of dead bodies and vast piles of sand. You can get those anywhere, Julius. It's nice if that's all you want, of course, but why not arrange to see the Egyptian leaders, make friends with them and agree to sell things to each other?"

"Things?"

"Yeah, like gold, trinkets, farming implements, grain and wine," said Neets.

"And figs and yoghurt," added Galahad.

Caesar considered the option. "I see," he said after a pause. "So you're saying lull them into a false sense of security and *then* kill them?"

"No, you stupid man!" I felt that talking to Caesar was like walking through treacle. "Try to benefit from their knowledge and let them benefit from yours. It's called international trade and it's all the rage where we come from. Besides, you might find some very nice people there worth getting to know. Well, hopefully *one* anyway."

"In which case why should I bother to take my army?" Caesar asked with just a hint of sarcasm. "Why don't I just send in some old men to negotiate a deal with Egypt, while I go off to invade Britannica right now, instead of in a few years time when I had it scheduled in my diary?"

"What's Britannica, Neets?" I whispered.

"That's us, Tersh. That's where we live."

"Blimey! Then he's got to go to Egypt!"

"He also has to come to Britain," Neets replied, "but only after he and Cleopatra have had a son. Definitely not before, or there'll be no Arthur."

"Or us, or Merlin or the TDA."

I knew we had to think about this very carefully, because Caesar had a point about his own. We needed him to believe it was ultimately his own brilliant idea to meet Cleopatra and trade with Egypt and, most important, that his reputation would be greatly enhanced if he walked out with a fortune instead of the usual pile of heads and a couple of empty legions. We conferred while Julius sipped his wine.

"You know, Caesar," I said at last, as though the idea had just occurred to me, "with your charisma, wit and charm you could conquer a kingdom just with the strength of your personality." Neets nodded vigorously while Galahad and the boys grimaced. "The world would know that you, Julius Caesar, had overcome Egypt without the loss of a single life and your reputation would be … phew, phenomenal!"

Caesar stroked his chin and looked thoughtful, because for a Roman he was also surprisingly intelligent. "I want to attack Gaul and Britain in a couple of years and a complete army would be a definite advantage," he said. "Otherwise it means having to go to Rome to beg the Senate for more costly recruits and they get very annoyed when I do that. The trouble is I'm not much good at the diplomatic stuff." He lied easily, like a born politician. "So I may need you to help me in an advisory capacity, you understand. Unpaid, of course," he added quickly.

"A holiday's a holiday, Julius," I said, "and we wouldn't expect to get paid for joining you. In fact it would be an honour." *And necessary to make sure you and Cleopatra don't kill each other*, I mentally added. "I'd also suggest that you take David and Bryn with you as your honour guard and maybe a small legion, just for the looks of the thing."

"Aren't you coming with us?" asked Bryn in surprise. David's face was a picture.

"Neets and I will join you in Egypt. We have one or two things to sort out back in C—" I stopped myself just in time, not that Camelot would have meant anything to Julius, "back in our village first."

"Right," Caesar leapt to his feet and rubbed his hands together in obvious anticipation. "There's lots of organising to be done before we go. You two come with me," the general was so good at giving commands that the boys almost saluted. "You can prepare my parade uniforms and take my orders to the legion commanders."

The looks Bryn and David gave us were almost spaniel-like ... without the ears, of course. But they didn't complain and followed Caesar out of the restaurant. It was a minute or two before we realised they should have gone first, in case an escaped conspiracy member had been waiting outside.

Neets, Galahad and I were ridiculously sad because we'd only been back together with the boys for an hour or so and they were already off on holiday. Typical!

The hatch crashed open and we all jumped out of our chairs, making the decorative hanging wine bottles clang against each other, some of the armoury hung by a thread and threatened to fall, as a couple of dribbly candles rolled across the floor.

"So you're back then," said Lancelot with a sneer. "Leave old Lancelot in the lurch in a strange town and wander off, why don't you. Have some more peanuts." A gloved hand shot out and a fistful of shells pattered randomly round the restaurant. The hatch slammed shut.

"Lancelot," yelled Galahad, staring at the debris in his not-very-successful restaurant, "I want you out here now. This is not acceptable behaviour … even if the place is empty."

The kitchen door opened and Lancelot's ancient face peered round, before the knight himself entered looking slightly sheepish. "Sorry," he muttered, "been that sort of a day. Guinevere spent all my money buying clothes in the market and I got knocked over by a bunch of idiots doing some sort of snake dance through the Forum. Then to cap it all, just outside the Senate I saw the tall man from Camelot and he was flashing round those fake gold coins."

"Well, at least he's still a prisoner," said Neets.

"No, he isn't," replied Lancelot with what I was sure was a leering grin. "He cut his bonds with some sword or other he'd hidden in his robes, knocked out his guards and escaped into the crowd."

"And we've just sent Julius outside with Bryn and David," I moaned. "Caesar's as good as dead meat." I hit the table for good measure.

Neets was less pessimistic. "My Bryn will look after him," she said proudly, "and your David will probably be able to help a bit," she added, a wee bit too smugly for my liking.

"He's not *my David*, as I keep telling you. We're jolly good friends and he could hold his own with Bryn any day."

Galahad laughed. "Girls, stop it. This is becoming *my dad's better than your dad*. We're a team, not a family, and certainly not in a competition." He may have been laughing, but I knew he was deadly serious, and he was right. "Lancelot, which way did the man go?"

"*I* don't know," the old knight sounded almost indignant. "He just melted into the crowd and could have gone anywhere. He's good, you know!" He gave a little cackle. "Anyway, where's Julius Caesar off to with your fancy boys?"

It was my turn to sound indignant. "David is *not* my fancy boy. He's ... he's David." I wondered why I was so careful to leave out the *my*, but I did. "He and Bryn are getting Caesar ready to visit Egypt, not that it's any business of yours. Besides, you're supposed to be back in Camelot with Guinevere, not cooking up pizzas for Galahad in Rome." I'd always considered old Lancelot to be one of my friends and yet just lately the knight was becoming a bit sneery, but I put it down to his extreme age.

"Suit yourselves. I'm off to find Guinevere." With that, Lancelot turned unsteadily on his heel and disappeared back into the kitchen, slamming the door as he did so.

I was sure I could hear hushed voices through the hatch, but I couldn't make out any words, although one of the voices sounded like a woman's. Either Guinevere had come back unexpectedly, or she'd been there all the time, in which case the man I considered an old friend had been lying. The voices stopped and another door slammed shut.

Galahad shook his head sadly. "He's not improving with age," he said as he gathered up the glasses and carafe before taking them into the empty kitchen. "He's gone," he shouted through the hatch, "and left the place in a right state. I suppose I'll have to do the washing up."

"Forget that, Galahad," I said. "In fact, forget Rome for the time being. We need to get back to Camelot now that the boys are looking after Julius and find out what Merl and Marlene want us to do. Are you staying here, or coming back with us?"

Galahad looked wistfully around the *Olé Grill-Pizzeria* and sighed. "I would have liked to have made a go of this place. I even had thoughts of buying out the Southern Fried Chicken takeaway next door, but I suppose I'll have to concentrate on my original restaurant back in Merlin's cave." He shrugged his shoulders. "Let's go."

As we left the restaurant I thought I heard an inside door open and after a few seconds

close again, but I didn't say anything because I was probably mistaken and it was just the wind or something. So much for being a detective.

The Forum was still full of people, even though the sun had almost gone down, and many of the stall holders had lit oil lamps so they could take the last possible coins from the Roman shoppers. We tried to remain as inconspicuous as possible by pretending to chat among ourselves until we reached a quiet spot where we could open up the portable Time Portal without too many prying eyes seeing us ... at least half-intelligent ones. It was time to get back to Camelot.

Zzzzp. Zzzzp. Zzzzp.

When we arrived, the castle's kitchens were working on double-shift overtime to keep pace with the *Olé Grill* demand up and down the centuries. Galahad immediately took charge, while Neets and I dodged trays of food destined for the distant future and ran up the steps to the archive room above Merl's old laboratory. The two wizards were still standing over the vast book, trying to decipher the faded writing from another era and almost without looking up, Marlene motioned us to two of the chairs they'd presumably had brought up by one of the servants that hadn't left the castle. We sat and waited while they talked.

Then we talked while they waited, because they were only doing it for effect.

"So you two came back then," Merl said eventually, "minus one Roman general as I understand it, and two Welsh boys." She crossed her arms and tapped a foot, which is normally a very bad sign. "I sent Bryn and David back to help you, not to have a sunshine holiday on the Mediterranean, so you'd better tell me everything that happened in Rome and make it quick."

Neets and I took turns to bring the wizard sisters up to date, though I admit we left out the bit about Galahad's pizza venture and made only a passing reference to Lancelot. After all we did promise Galahad we wouldn't say a word to Merl, and Lancelot just seemed irrelevant without the Pizzeria.

"So the gold coins were real," said Marlene, "and our Leading Man used a few of them to entice you to Rome. He must have known you'd flash them around when you got there and hoped you'd be arrested as thieves. As the coins were all destined for Caesar, of course, any punishment would have been very severe, even for a first offence."

"How severe, Merlin?" asked Neets.

"There definitely wouldn't have been a second offence."

Neets looked at me in horror and I couldn't help thinking that ancient Rome's cruelty was on a par with the Black Knight's in South Wales. Still, at least we beat him.

"I suspect Brutus and Cassius were behind the theft," Merl continued, "and they probably wouldn't have cared whether you got the blame, or Cicero. They'd be considerably richer either way, and doubtless the Leading Man took his share."

"What about the boys and Caesar?" asked Marlene. "How come you're here and they're on their way to Egypt, That's if they haven't been killed by now." Marlene never crossed her arms, or tapped feet, which in many ways was even more scary. "Why didn't you bring them back here so we could have sent you all off to Egypt in safety?"

"I think I know the answer to that," said Merl, putting a calming hand on her smaller sister's shoulder. "Correct me if I'm wrong, girls, but you were absolutely right in thinking that bringing Caesar back to Camelot would only have confused the poor man and might even have caused one of Unita's temporal anemones. Besides, our villainous Leading Man would be expecting you to take him through the Time Portal, either to Egypt, or to here. So sending him by land and sea guarded by Bryn and David was inspired thinking, and no more than I would have expected from my Merl's Girls."

Merl may be a wizard rather than a conjuror, but she certainly pulls the rabbit out of the hat when needed. Marlene stood with her mouth open and eventually chose to side with us by claiming the credit was due to the Temporal Detective Agency, of which she was senior partner and therefore due any good fortune that came along. Fair shares and honour satisfied all round!

There was one question I'd forgotten to ask the boys before we left Rome and, while Merl's sister was on the back foot, now was as good a time as any to get an answer. "Marlene, where did you send Bryn and David and why was it so urgent? They didn't tell us a thing in Rome. Mind you we were a bit busy with assassinations and stuff and there wasn't really time to ask them before we came back here without Caesar getting interested for the wrong reasons. I'm sure Neets would like to know why you sent the beloved Bryn on a case without her and I know she would have liked to have shown him to Merl." I mumbled something about how Merl might also have quite liked David.

Marlene smiled. "Merlin will have plenty of opportunities to meet the lads, but her priority right now is to save Arthur, not meet your boyfriends."

I spluttered a protest, which was more than Neets did, but Marlene waved me into silence.

"As to why I sent them away, someone called me about the *Mary Celeste* at just the right time and as I knew the boys would be just a distraction in Rome, I decided to send them on a rescue mission. Besides, the Leading Man and the conspirators were only expecting the two of you and to have had Bryn and

David turn up with you might have frightened them off. We couldn't have that, so I sent them to help the crew and passengers of the *Mary Celeste* until I – sorry, I mean the Temporal Detective Agency – needed their muscle in the Senate to stop the assassination. It all worked well, I think." Marlene pushed her hands through her fright-wig of orange frizz hair, which I'd learned to recognise as a *don't make waves, please* message.

"Are you saying you sent them somewhere you knew nothing about," Neets said with a dangerous glint in her eye, "just so you could use them in Rome on a whim?" She hadn't recognised the hair-tugging message.

"Far from a whim." Marlene had an equally dangerous glint in her eye. "Have you never heard of the *Mary Celeste*? She was found in 1872 drifting in the Atlantic. There was no sign of the passengers and crew and no visible reason why they'd left the ship, though there's lots of theories as to what happened to them. I rather think the boys will know and I gave them instructions as to what they should do when they arrived on board. They went where I told them to go and carried out my instructions to the letter, so please don't criticise me, or them. On the contrary, by letting Caesar make his own way to Egypt you've probably put his life in danger, whatever Merlin says. Let's just hope Bryn and David use their abilities to protect him and keep Arthur alive." I saw her turn to

Merl and give a wink that said *I showed them!* Neets just looked sullen. I just looked, because Marlene normally treated us as equals and right now she was pulling her Senior Partner weight for the first time in ages.

"Don't think about the boys and Caesar," continued Marlene and I noticed she didn't say *worry*. "I want you two to go back to Shakespeare's Globe Theatre and talk to the three witches. I have a feeling we're going to need their help again before all this is over."

"What do you want us to tell them?" muttered Neets. She still looked rebellious … at least for her.

"Tell them to be ready to travel to Rome and give them this letter." She handed Neets an envelope. "It's got the date and location coordinates. And no peeking, young lady. That's why it's sealed."

As if we would, I thought. At least, not without a steaming kettle.

"Why are we being kept in the dark again, Marlene?" I asked. "It's beginning to look as though you've got me and Neets doing one thing, Bryn and David doing another, and now the lovely witches doing something else. And only you and Merl know what we're all doing and why."

"I'm sorry, Tertia," Merl took over from her sister. "The less you know, the safer you'll be and that goes for the boys and the three hags as well. Our priority is to stop the Leading Man – stupid name, I know, but it's the only one we have for him – from eliminating my Arthur by changing history. He's crazy enough to do it without thinking of the consequences, although right now we know Arthur lives and that he and I are still going to have a little prince. But Caesar has to meet Cleopatra, or we lose everything and the Leading Man will do all he can to stop the Egyptian queen from giving birth to Arthur's ancestor."

Merl hadn't really told us anything new, like why the boys went to the *Mary Celeste*, like what happened to the crew, and like why the witches had to get involved in Rome at some point. We were still racing round time, meeting people like Galahad, old Lancelot and the two boys when we least expected it, but I had to admit they only appeared when we needed them to be there. Maybe it was best not to know when something was going to help in case we got too dependent, and then for some reason it didn't happen.

"I think I see what you're getting at, Merl," I said, as much for Neets's benefit as the wizard sisters'. "The whole thing's down to us to get right and you'll arrange help when we need it. But we're in charge and if it all goes pear-shaped then it's sort of down to us."

"In a nutshell," agreed Merl, and Marlene nodded. "And now please take the message to the witches and then carry on to Egypt."

"Anything else you want to tell us," I asked.

"Er … good luck?" said Marlene.

"That'll do for starters, but I was thinking more of the coordinates for Egypt."

"Or are you going to keep those a secret too?" Neets was obviously still feeling miffed.

"Sorry, girls," said Marlene. "Don't know what I was thinking about." She handed me a slip of paper and shooed us out of the room as though we were ten-year-olds rather than equal partners in the Temporal Detective Agency. The door slammed after us.

As we ran down to the kitchens I was tempted to swap our piece of paper for the witches' envelope out of sheer devilment, mostly because where they were going might prove more interesting than our destination. I didn't though. We'd never been to Egypt and we had a bit of a reputation in Rome. But first of all we had to go back to the Globe Theatre and the three witches.

Zzzzzp.

Chapter Ten

Witches, a Knight, a Queen and Lots and Lots of Sand

When we arrived at Shakespeare's Globe Theatre, Macbeth was in full swing and the three witches had just finished their offer to help the hero become King of Scotland. Not much of an offer to my mind. Arthur told me it's a barren, cold place full of mountains and shivering sheep and he only went there by mistake.

There was no sign of Shakespeare, or of the Leading Man, and the main part of Macbeth was being played by somebody reading the words from a book … and reading them very badly. Neets and I stood in the middle of the crowd and cheered with the rest of them as Rosie, Petal and Jennie took a prolonged bow and disappeared off the stage into the wings. Being the pretty one, Petal blew the fans a kiss, dodging the flowers, but caught the fruit. When we arrived at the rear of the stage she was nibbling away at an apple with her one tooth, while the other two sucked busily on what looked like rotten peaches.

"You came back then?" said Petal, spraying bits of apple everywhere, mostly over Neets and me. "Sorry."

"We've not got long, girls." said Rosie. "We're due back on stage in a few minutes. What do you want?"

"We wondered when we five would meet again," said Jennie before I could reply. "Personally I hoped we'd seen the last of you. There's always trouble when you two turn up, and last time we lost our main actor and the best Macbeth ever. Not only that, Shakespeare's disappeared and his cousin has had to take over from him as front man. He scribbles away at what he can, but his new play *Porklet* isn't a patch on William's stuff. Never mind, at least the fool didn't put any witches in it."

"What do you want?" repeated Rosie. "Did you give that parcel to Merlin?"

"Yes," said Neets as she peeled an orange and popped a segment in her mouth. I grabbed half of what was left because neither of us had eaten since ancient Rome. "She seemed pleased enough with what was in it and read out the rhyme you sent. She seemed quite pleased with that too."

"She understood it then?" said Rosie. "Good. So she knows what 'as to be done and why Caesar and Cleopatra 'ave to be brought together. You'd better make it 'appen too because the new Mister Shakespeare's already writing 'is *Julius Caesar* play and I want a 'appy ending." The three witches gave a well-practiced cackle, spraying more bits of fruit over us, and went back on stage to great cheers for an unscripted encore.

"Blimey, Neets, you forgot to give them Merl's message." I grabbed the envelope from my cousin's hand and ran on stage to even greater applause. I bowed and held out the envelope to Rosie. "A message, O great lady," cheers erupted, "from the King of…"

"Scotland," hissed Petal.

"That's the place," I said. "Merl, I mean the king sends you greetings and bids you go to … er, wherever and whenever it says in here." I thrust the envelope into Rosie's outstretched hand and gave the audience a self-conscious grin, not sure whether to run off stage, or wait for a cue. Actually, I have to admit I froze.

Neets dashed on stage and dragged me into the wings, waving wildly to the cheering audience and shouted "see you in Rome, or wherever…" to the witches.

We'd completed our Shakespearean mission and now it was time for us to go to Egypt and save Arthur.

Zzzzzp.

In the few seconds it took to travel from London's Globe Theatre to ancient Egypt, we had another go at puzzling through the witches' rhyme...

If Cleo and her Jules meet up
They may produce a charming pup;
Then Arthur's future is secure
But if they don't, he's dead for sure.

...but before we even got past the first two lines we tumbled out of the Portal into blistering heat and high rolling sand dunes.

"Any idea where we are?" I shielded my eyes from the glare of the searing sun, but still couldn't make out much of the landscape. "Even roughly?" The shimmering heat was so fierce, the sky so intensely blue and everywhere between the horizons was so full of sand that an educated guess suggested a desert. At least that's what I presumed never having seen one before, except in a photo back in the twenty-first century. Neets was no help at all. She was too busy working on her tan.

"Outside the North Gate of Alexandria," the voice from behind us just oozed authority, "or so I believe." Sir Gawain looked every bit the powerful Camelot knight we remembered and was wearing full armour. He stood, feet slightly apart, with one hand on the pommel of his sword and looked totally in control.

"Gawain!" mouthed Neets. The knight's good looks were at their best in the desert heat while the sun picked out the gold and silver decorations on his armour to perfection. His scarlet cloak completed the effect and Neets was definitely more than mildly impressed. "Wow! What a hunk!" she said throatily.

"Neets," I whispered, "close your mouth. You look silly and remember he's getting on for being your father-in-law."

I looked at Gawain and wondered how much was Camelot knight and how much was Mr Lewis, the squire of Port Eynon. "What in the name of Arthur are you doing here? And you might find this question silly, but are you Sir Gawain before you went to Wales, or have you come back as Mr Lewis dressed up as Gawain."

"I'm here to help my son." The knight turned towards us with a smile. He was Lewis dressed up as Gawain. "I'm sure that answers your question, but call me Gawain because this is all about Camelot. Merlin asked me to join you in order to help where I can and she thought wearing my knight's armour might be less conspicuous. Unfortunately, as you know I burned my own, so I borrowed this from Galahad. Fits quite well, don't you think?" As he talked he climbed the nearest sand dune closely followed by Neets and me for whom sand on this scale was a complete novelty. So was trying to climb it.

From the top we had a great view of the Alexandrian countryside stretching out in front of us for mile after sandy mile. Worryingly, every inch of the desert seemed to be covered by Roman soldiers, tents, horses, siege engines, equipment and forage wagons, plus the normal hangers-on that any army gathers. This didn't look good for what was supposed to be the love match of the millennium.

"How on earth are we going to stop Caesar using this lot?" I said as I scanned the vast army below us.

"I rather suspect it's mostly for show." Gawain's voice was full of nostalgia as he surveyed the troops. "After all, a great general can't just wander into a country armed with a couple of suitcases and a beach towel. He has to lead his armies in a display of power, then when he's made his point he can have a nice little holiday and do as he pleases. Though in this case he must do as *we* please."

"Hmm," I said thoughtfully, "it really seems a shame to make poor little Egypt think it's going to be smashed, but I suppose it's all down to empire credibility. Mind you, all the Romans normally have to show for their troubles is a lot of dead bodies and vast piles of sand and you can get those anywhere."

"It's nice if that's all they want," said Gawain, "but not only are we going to get Caesar to meet Cleopatra, but we will also give them the opportunity to talk to the Egyptian leaders, make friends with them and sell things to each other."

"Things like gold, trinkets, farming implements, grain and wine?" said Neets. "I told Caesar that in Rome."

"So long as he still doesn't think you were telling him to lull them into a false sense of security," I said, "and then kill them."

"I don't think he's a stupid man." replied Gawain. "With luck he'll benefit from the Egyptians' knowledge and let them benefit from his."

"In which case I wonder why he brought his army all this way?" I said with just a hint of sarcasm and a nod in the direction of the vast numbers of legions. "There's far too many, even for a show-off. At least he didn't just send in some old men to negotiate a deal and go off on holiday, or worse, save time and invade our Britannica."

I paused, because I couldn't help thinking we'd already had most of this conversation with Caesar in Rome and I knew we had to think about this very carefully. We needed Caesar to believe it was ultimately his own brilliant idea to meet Cleopatra and trade with Egypt and, most important, that his reputation would be greatly enhanced.

"From what I know of Caesar," Gawain said at last, "he prefers slaughter to politics and that's why we have to watch him carefully, no matter what he may have agreed with you back in Rome." Neets nodded vigorously, smiling at her possible future father-in-law, while I grimaced.

Gawain stroked his chin and looked thoughtful, because for a Camelot knight he was also surprisingly intelligent. "History says Caesar has to attack Gaul and Britain in a few years and he must take his son with him," he said. "I believe we'll have to act as match-makers here and I may need you to help me once more."

"No problem, Gawain," Neets said. "We're used to it. Let me just have a little chat with Tersh and I'll be right back."

We went into a huddle far enough away from Gawain not to be overheard, although we needn't have worried, because he was too preoccupied with studying the Roman army to worry about our idle chatter. We knew we needed a better game plan because convincing only one of the prospective parents of Arthur's ancestor to use diplomacy instead of extreme violence would be useless unless the other one did the same.

"I reckon the two of us will have to find a way into the city," I said, "and get a meeting with this Cleopatra."

"Good idea," said Neets, "but what about Gawain? He can't just turn up in Alexandria dressed in full knight armour."

I glanced at the famous Gawain. He was still engrossed in Caesar's progress. "I think if we sort out

Cleopatra, then the best place for our friend is down there with Caesar. He won't look too out of place and he can keep an eye on David and Bryn, as well as the general.

"Okay," I said, "we'll go to Alexandria and sort out the Egyptian Queen and while we do that, Gawain can make sure Caesar doesn't suddenly feel the need for some invigorating Siege and Pillage therapy. Let's go and tell him the good news."

I hadn't seen Gawain resplendent in Camelot armour for some time and had forgotten just how well it suited him. Actually he'd have looked good in a potato sack and I began to realise that Neets wasn't only taken with what Bryn looked like, but that if he took after his father he was going to be an incredible specimen. Poor cow, as I think I've said already. We rejoined Gawain and looked down at the massed Roman legions.

"You know, Mr Lewis, or whatever you want us to call you here," I prepared to lie a bit, "now that we think about it, you're dead right. Someone needs to make sure the boys are okay and help them keep Caesar in line, or there's no saying what he might get up to. Neets and I would have loved to have done it, but we're just girlies and we'd only get sand in our shoes and have to keep stopping to do our makeup. So Neets and I reckon there's only one man for the job, and that's you. It'll be dangerous, it'll need a quick thinker and someone whose charisma and ability to lead is without question in the most difficult of situations. The question is, Gawain, if we go to Alexandria and suffer all the temptations Cleopatra will try to throw at us, will you help Caesar make the right decisions?" I looked at the knight who I had to admit wouldn't have looked out of place at the head of anyone's army.

Gawain turned and smiled. "I'm sorry, I wasn't listening, Tertia. What did you say?"

All that carefully planned speech-making and the guy was daydreaming. "I said we'll go to Alexandria, while you go down to the Romans. Think you could manage that?"

"I think so, and it'll be nice to see my son again, though David may have to keep out of my way." David had been the adopted son of the Black Knight and had been passing information about Gawain to his enemy. To a large extent he'd made up for things since he joined the TDA with Bryn, but Gawain would never totally trust him. "It looks as though the Romans are making camp for the night, so that would seem a good time for me to join them and make myself known to Caesar." He looked at the brilliant blue sky. "There's probably three to four hours of sunlight left, so what will you do?"

"We'll walk to Alexandria," said Neets, "knock on the gates and ask to see Queen Cleopatra." She said it with such certainty that even I believed her.

"You really think it'll work?" asked Gawain.

"Amazingly enough, it never seems to fail," I replied, glancing at Neets. "People don't expect girls to ask to see their leader and look as though they mean it *and* expect it to happen. It worked against the Black Knight when he was Schwartz, so there's no reason why it won't work here."

"I can't argue with that," laughed Gawain. "Now if I tried it, I'd probably end up in a mess of gore and blood ... the other guy's, of course! After that they might not let me in."

Job done, I thought. Gawain was taken care of and not for the last time I wondered how come Marie, his wife, had let him leave their home in Port Eynon in the year 1734.

"So you'll go to the Romans," I said, "and we'll start off to Alexandria. Give us a day," I added, "and then bring Caesar into the city, but make sure he's got no more than a small honour guard. Oh, and watch out for traps," I added, "there's no saying what little surprises our Leading Man may have put here and I expect it won't be too long before he finds out we've brought Caesar to Egypt. He won't be happy!"

Gawain smiled and gave us a perfunctory salute, before strolling down the hill, slipping and sliding on the sand as he went, but somehow managing to keep his feet and his charisma. When he was half way towards the Roman camp and we were sure he had attracted the guards' attention, Neets and I picked our way slowly among the dunes and moved towards the city, taking care not to be seen by the vast Roman army and its scavenger scouts. Even when we were in the deep sandy valleys we both knew the way to Alexandria by heading for the population heat haze and the smell of foreign cooking. The city was still about a mile and a half away, but it was already making its presence felt.

"Shush! Look over there." I put a hand on Neets's shoulder and pointed to the top of the next dune. A group of soldiers dressed in uniforms much more colourful than those the Romans wore was lying on their stomachs and trying to see as much of the opposing army as possible without being spotted. Unfortunately their ornate costumes and plumed helmets meant anything more than a crouch was out of the question, while the decorative metal that glinted in the sun was a dead giveaway to anyone looking in their direction.

"Egyptians, I reckon," whispered Neets. "Probably scouts of some kind, but there's loads more down below not wearing uniforms. I'd guess they're civilians and most likely important ones too, because they've all got somebody holding umbrellas over their heads. And it's not even raining."

Before I could answer, a beautiful voice crammed with a sense of fun filled our ears. "You're absolutely right, young lady." We froze listening for the hint of a Roman accent, but there wasn't one. "These are my advisors, while my generals are up there spying on the enemy's army. And you are…?"

Neets and I spun round ready to run, but ended up staring at the most drop-dead beautiful woman either of us had ever seen. Her hair was the colour of a raven's wing, her eyes were the deepest emerald green and the tiny laughter lines radiating either side of them were reflected in the humour of her smile. Her dress was made of the most delicate silks in various shades of crimson and was held together by broaches mounted with what I hoped were the rarest precious stones, because that would have been appropriate. Pearls and strands of silver cascaded from her hair, framing the perfect oval of her face, and what little makeup she wore was expertly applied and almost undetectable. The woman was the sort of person you instantly liked so much that you trusted her with all your secrets and if you didn't have any secrets you'd make up a few just to please her. What was more she was obviously extremely important, because she had *two* umbrellas.

"I'm Tertia and this is Unita," Neets spluttered. "Sorry, I mean the other way round."

"Well, whichever way round it is I'm pleased to meet both of you. I take it you're not Romans, or you wouldn't be wandering around trying to avoid their army, but you certainly don't look like Egyptians either."

"We're from Britain, Miss, Ma'am, your Highness, Honour … whatever." I stared at the woman,

166

wondering what her beauty secret was. I decided it was probably money.

"Wonderful!" exclaimed the stranger clapping her hands. "Tourists! I've always tried to encourage visitors to the Nile Valley and I've always felt we have so much to offer the enquiring mind. By the way, I'm Cleopatra, Queen of the Nile and of all Upper Egypt, but please call me Cleo, all my best friends do."

"You're Cleopatra?" I asked. I knew now why the Portal had thrown us out where it had. We'd almost landed right on top of the Queen of the Nile.

Cleo smiled and nodded. "Don't I look like Cleopatra?" she laughed. "Not enough jewellery? Clothes not fancy enough? Not pretty enough, is that it?"

"Too sandy," I answered with an embarrassed grin that became a blush. "If you're Cleopatra why are you out in the desert spying on the Romans when you should be sitting on your throne in Alexandria munching on a grape?" I certainly would have been, given the chance.

"Ah, good question. As to the sand, it's good sand," Cleopatra bent down and picked up a handful of fine yellow grains letting them slowly run through her fingers, "and more to the point it's my sand. However, I do like to see for myself what sort of people are invading my country and it helps me to understand them better. Now tell me what *you're* doing here and please call me Cleo."

Obviously we could never tell Cleopatra the whole truth, but a cut down version leaving out Arthur, Merlin, Marlene, Camelot, the Leading Man and time-travel was possible. Best of all it would be very, very short.

Cleopatra waited patiently until we finished our story. "You're saying you rescued the famous Julius Caesar from assassins in Rome?" We knew it sounded farfetched, but it was true and we nodded. "Then you persuaded him to come to Egypt and to negotiate with me rather than blindly invade my country?" We nodded again, while Cleopatra stared searchingly at each of us in turn looking for untruths. She found none. "You probably saved my country from obliteration, or, at least conquest by Rome. As a result, right now I must go to the North Gate of Alexandria, ascend the throne of my Nile Kingdom and prepare to meet the great Julius Caesar." The warmth of her smile put the heat of the day into a cloudy shade. "And if it's not too inconvenient, I also rather think I'd like you to join me in my palace for some refreshment."

"Sounds great, Cleo!" Neets said enthusiastically, shielding her eyes against the searing sun as it beat down with almost unbearable intensity. I agreed because we hadn't eaten for several centuries and a glass of something cool would do wonders for the sand in my mouth. We followed Cleopatra at a steady uphill scramble taking two sliding steps to each of her steady ones until we joined the queen's soldier scouts at the top of the dune. From there, Neets and I caught our first sight of both the royal city of Alexandria and the Roman army's camp. Riding in his chariot on a tour of inspection, resplendent in his general's armour and flowing scarlet cloak was Julius Caesar, looking every bit the potential ruler of the known world. Riding with him was a tall armoured figure whose glossy hair blew in the breeze like a lion's mane. One hand held onto the chariot's guardrail while the other gripped a raised sword and he was definitely laughing.

"Nice one, Gawain." I couldn't help grinning and at the same time wondering how he'd managed to hitch a lift in Caesar's chariot. David and Bryn rode horses on either side of Caesar and still wore their Praetorian Guard uniforms. The general was in good hands.

"Quick," said Cleopatra as she scrambled down the dune preceded by two sand-surfing Merl's Girls and pursued at a distance by her flagging sunshade carriers, "we have to get into Alexandria before the Romans get to the gate, but if what you said is true then I don't think they're here to fight, or they'd have already besieged the city. Either way I still need to do some preparation work with my ministers before Julius Caesar makes his move." She summoned her generals and courtiers, leading them through the sandy maze of dunes back to her capital city.

Neets and I followed Cleopatra as she hurried

under the ornately carved North Gate archway, through the crowded streets of shops and temples and up to the imposing royal palace. We looked back and stared at the massive stone buildings on either side of the wide bustling streets that put early London and even twenty-first century Salisbury to shame. Not to mention the shambles of Camelot housing. As we passed, the Alexandrians seemed only slightly surprised to see their queen covered in dust and sand, her hair in a comparative mess, without an honour guard and accompanied by two young foreigners in weird clothes. But then Cleo was not your run-of-the-mill queen.

When we reached the main palace courtyard Cleopatra clapped her hands for attention and was immediately surrounded by a horde of grovelling servants. She talked as she walked. "Fetch food and drink for my friends, whatever they want, and get them new clothes. We all need baths, so run three hot tubs ... and water this time, not asses' milk!" She smiled at us. "I don't want to smell like a bowl of yoghurt when Caesar arrives, now do I?" We could see the sense in that, although I was far more concerned with admiring the wonders of Cleopatra's palace than the liquid content of her baths.

Large flowers of red, yellow, purple and white grew from every crevice, as trees, shrubs, creepers and climbers sent cascades of colour over every stone, making the palace look like a giant, but tastefully put together bouquet. The overall effect was stunning as we sniffed the intoxicating smell of blossom and listened to the tinkling sound of running water coming from hundreds of fountains and artificial streams. We were both so hungry we could have eaten all the freely available tree fruit in one sitting and drunk the palace water supply dry in one great big glug. And in Neets's case it was a close thing.

The Queen of the Nile led her entourage into the palace antechambers, past grovelling servants and sycophantic courtiers who were excellent at looking in mirrors and checking their hair. Somebody has to do it. "We need to talk in an hour," she said quietly to her chief adviser as he walked beside her. "Julius Caesar will be in the city tomorrow to negotiate an alliance between Egypt and Rome and he'll expect to get the upper hand. I want him to make the mistake of thinking he's got it." She turned to us. "And now we eat, drink and get refreshed."

Cleo insisted we bathed before we ate and she may well have had a point because baths in Camelot were taken only when necessary, which usually coincided with important festivals and holidays, even though most were considered unimportant. Eventually we got round to the food and it was worth the wait, because it looked and tasted fabulous. Neets and I didn't know so many types of meat existed, and the selection of exotic fruit, most of which we'd never seen before let alone tasted, was incredible. To stop the juices spilling on the clothes we'd borrowed, Cleo insisted I put on a bib, while Neets put on about a stone in weight. It was a great evening and the Queen of the Nile talked about little else except her upcoming meeting with Caesar, but I wanted to make sure the other part of our plan was working. I wanted to check on Gawain and the boys.

I made an excuse and left Neets and Cleo telling dirty jokes, as they threw grapes into each other's mouths and lounged on what were at the end of the day great big uncomfortable beds. The palace was full of people milling around, but I was only challenged a couple of times and even then mostly by men with strangely high voices. I managed to talk my way out, which was just as well because I found out later that kneeing them in the particulars, as Marlene called it, would almost certainly have had no effect. Getting out of the city was also a lot easier than I'd expected, but then I'd always been told that getting out of a castle is always a lot easier than convincing guards to let you back in.

Beyond the city an avenue of giant stone pharaohs and sphinxes, each one larger than the last, led up to the entrance of Alexandria's even more ornate East Gate. The overall effect was designed to increase the awe of anyone approaching, making them feel smaller as the statues got larger until by the time anyone entered the city they were just as the Alexandrians wanted them … awe inspired, gaping tourists with open wallets. It worked a treat.

I didn't have to walk more than half a mile before I heard the noise of the Roman camp and saw the glow from their oil lamps. The soldiers were still sorting out their tents and had stopped far enough from Alexandria for the city guards not to mistake the delegation as a night-time invasion. I moved behind the nearest hiding place, a small stone lion on a plinth, and watched and listened.

As soon as the Roman tents were pitched, Caesar was ordering food and wine to be served to him, his guests of honour, and the more important of his generals. Trays of food overflowing with cheeses, figs and cold meats together with freshly baked fruit bread and wines were taken into his tent and, true to form, David stuffed his pockets when Caesar wasn't looking just in case he and Bryn needed a nibble during the night. David told me later it was the best food he'd ever tasted, but I hadn't the heart to tell him what Cleo had served up to Neets and me, mostly because I couldn't remember what half of it was called.

Everything looked fine and I was tired, but as I was about to walk back to the city, Gawain emerged from Caesar's tent holding a goblet of wine. He smiled and walked over to my hiding place, gnawing on a chicken leg and holding another as a spare, which being a generously charismatic man, he offered to me.

I didn't want Bryn and David to know I was checking up on them, so Gawain and I remained behind the sphinx munching on chicken bones while I gave him the low-down on Cleo and he brought me up to date on Caesar. I punched the air because it was beginning to look as though we were winning and this time without any interference from Merl and Marlene. Gawain laughed and told me Caesar was looking forward to meeting the queen although he reckoned the stories about her beauty and brains were probably just marketing hype from the Egyptian Tourist Board, but that he'd draw his own conclusions when they met. The general was equally sure Cleopatra would do the same about him because he knew the Rome Tourist Board also had a habit of not mentioning his receding hairline, let alone his hook nose.

Gawain threw the chicken leg over his shoulder and gave a gentlemanly burp. I did the same and belched, but then I was brought up on a farm and I also had to admit it was the best chicken I'd ever eaten. It had a light batter coating with a slight herb and lemony taste and I suspected it probably came from the Southern Fried Chicken takeaway shop next to Galahad's *Olé Grill-Pizzeria*.

"The Romans have a new chef," admitted Gawain, "and his food is to die for … though not literally, I hope." He laughed, but I didn't, because a fat Caesar with a potential coronary condition was not to my mind Cleo marriage material. "Tomorrow, we've been promised a breakfast we won't forget in a hurry and in preparation I intend to get a good night's sleep."

Gawain made no attempt to hide a gigantic yawn then walked back to his tent with a muffled *good night*. A minute or so later I belched again in a most unladylike way and wandered down the line of statues back to the city.

Tomorrow would either end up in the love match of the millennium, or a bloodbath, in which case Arthur's ancestor would never be born and neither would Arthur.

And Caesar being Caesar, it could go either way.

Chapter Eleven

*A Roman Invitation, a Royal Meeting
and a Dynasty*

When I got back to the palace, Neets and Cleo were laughing like old friends and, having run out of grapes, had started throwing sliced apple chunks at each other. Grapefruits would probably be next and then whole melons. I sat down, peeled a banana and watched the show.

I was amazed how easy it had been to get inside the city again. The guards both on the gate and at the palace must have seen me, but took no notice. Even when I opened a small door set in the massive East Gate no one paid the slightest attention, so either her soldiers were stupid and blind, or had been briefed exceptionally well by a very observant queen.

Neets and I slept until just before dawn, grateful for our first good night's sleep for what seemed like centuries. We watched the sun climb above the cloudless horizon as it did every day in Alexandria splashing everything in molten gold, while the clear sky was a deep holiday blue. The three witches had told us the full heat of the morning would come later, but for the moment the air was fresh and pleasantly warm, while the marble and sandstone buildings were still cool to the touch and the stone benches not yet bottom-blisteringly hot to sit on. We walked across a marble courtyard and up to a terrace overlooking the palace gardens where the scent of hibiscus and orange filled the air as it had the night before. We still only recognised it as being a pleasant pong, never having seen either the fruit or the flower before the previous evening, but the palace servants filled in the horticultural gaps for us.

I had more than gardening on my mind and wondered whether the Leading Man was in Egypt, and if so what mischief he was planning. Somehow I doubted he'd slink off with his tail between his legs and admit defeat before the game had really started. His kind are like wasps and never know when to stop trying to sting you, until after the final swat with a newspaper.

"This is all too easy," I said to Neets with a far more serious look than the beautiful morning deserved. "Either we're losing it, or the Leading Man's got a few surprises in store for us."

"Yes," said Neets as she scanned the terraces and courtyards for any sign of breakfast, "but I don't think we're losing, or that our enemy's particularly winning. I reckon Time's fitting everything into place because we're so near to the central part of all this time manipulation vortex stuff and it's like the last few pieces of a jigsaw. Time's trying to make its own bed as it were and it's sorting out the right sheets."

"Blimey! Deep or what!" I must admit I didn't understand a word, but it sounded bloody good even if it was a load of rubbish. I walked round the corner at the end of the terrace looking for a quick distraction and saw two rather neat ones in the shape of the Queen of the Nile and a table laden with fruits of every colour. "There's Cleo," I said innocently as I grabbed Neets's arm. "Don't know if you fancy joining her for breakfast?" Frequently the reason for my cousin's silent moments was either because she was thinking of Bryn, or her mouth was full of food, though on this occasion an empty mouthed nod was enough of a reply.

The queen was as immaculately beautiful as she had been the previous evening and looked as though the threat of an attack by the all-powerful Roman army probably came about ninth on her agenda for the day. She was sitting at a table nibbling her way through a bowl of fruit and reading a number of papyrus scrolls that lay stacked in a small basket. She smiled as she motioned us to join her and seemingly at random handed one of the scrolls to Neets who took it without thinking.

"This one just arrived from the Roman camp," said Cleo. "Julius Caesar is officially requesting permission to enter my city so we can talk about an alliance, just as you said he would." She popped another grape into her mouth and offered a small bunch to each of us. "What do you think, should I invite him in?"

Neets looked at Cleopatra. "Are you serious? You want my advice?" I knew she didn't dare admit that her reading skills were less than basic, especially when it came to Latin and Egyptian hieroglyphs.

"But of course I do!" Cleo touched her on the arm. "I may miss something obvious by trying to be too subtle and I would greatly value your opinion on what I should do." This was a once in a lifetime opportunity to advise the leader of one of the greatest empires and it had been given to my cousin. Blimey!

"Well," Neets began with a blush and a squeak. She coughed and lowered her voice an octave. "Well, you could always go out to Caesar, although that would give him the upper hand of course." She glanced at me for encouragement, but I was far too busy demolishing grapes to help. "Looking at it the other way, his army's big enough to fight its way into Alexandria any time it wants to, so it's probably best to invite him to enter while he's being friendly and have him on your territory as a potential ally."

Cleopatra carefully considered what Neets said, then looked at me to see what I thought. I shrugged and nodded in silent agreement because my mouth was still too full to say anything without spraying food everywhere.

"My thoughts exactly," smiled Cleo, "so let's write a reply along those lines and see how long it takes him to accept my invitation."

She started writing on a blank papyrus scroll while we looked on in awe. Neets grinned while I tried unsuccessfully to read Cleopatra's squiggle-writing upside down. Amazingly it looked as though our plan was working and with any luck by the end of the day Caesar and Cleopatra would become the happy *Jules and Cleo* of the witches' rhyme. The *pup* could come later.

Cleo rolled the papyrus into a scroll, then sealed it with a blob of wax and the coiled asp snake imprint of her signet ring. She looked up and smiled at both of us before handing me the scroll as though it was the most natural thing in the world to do, and I have to admit I took it without thinking, but then it began to dawn on me what the Queen intended. She laughed and I knew I was right when she winked, tapped the side of her nose and signalled to the captain of her palace guard. She knew I'd left the city the previous night, which explained why it had all been so easy and my reward was to do it all over again today, but this time as an official messenger with my own honour guard. My mum and dad would have been so proud, if just a bit worried, because they never really trusted foreigners.

The Roman camp was still yawning when I arrived and even the guards were rubbing the sleep out of their eyes. I spotted David, Bryn and Gawain wandering round with a look of horror on their faces, because they told me later that the toilet facilities were miles worse than even Camelot's and that privacy was a matter of finding your own sand dune and whistling loudly. The promised breakfast hadn't started yet and I must admit I was famished. After all, a bunch of grapes is no substitute for bacon and eggs with a couple of slices of toast and a glass of fresh orange juice.

The general's mess tent was already getting packed when we entered, but Caesar had saved the four of us seats at his high table, while my Egyptian soldiers stood guard outside the tent munching on their favourite fruit. The delicious smell of cooking wafted from the kitchen, giving us a pretty good idea why this was going to be such a special meal. Soon each table was laden with piping hot food and must have included the best breakfasts from pretty well every country Rome had conquered. At a signal from

Caesar, the military might of Rome grabbed platefuls of whatever was nearest, even if that meant their neighbour's food, and gorged themselves silly. The whole thing didn't last more than five minutes and the total lack of conversation was replaced by munching, chewing, lots of swallowing and satisfied belching. I have to say that the Temporal Detective Agency ate more than its fair share, but then we'd been brought up to respect food, especially when it's free.

As Caesar reluctantly stood up to declare the meal at an end, I noticed that a number of belts were let out a notch or two and several uniforms were loosened. This was definitely not an army preparing itself for an all-out attack, unless it was of the heart variety, and I couldn't see the march into Alexandria being any more than a pleasant stroll.

Gawain, Bryn, David and I walked either side of Caesar while my six Egyptian soldiers strutted ahead of me like well-armed peacocks. Caesar's handpicked men marched in perfect time behind us in four ranks as we made our way along the avenue of towering East Gate sculptures. There was something almost scary about the statues and I noticed the soldiers stared with grim determination at the sandals of the soldier in front because none of them wanted to glimpse the stone pharaohs in case they glimpsed back. I knew they had the same sort of stuff back in Rome, but nothing on this scale and there was something sinister about the way the statues looked at us all, with the sort of eyes that follow you round the desert.

At the column's head I listened to the noise of sand whispering in the wind and the accompanying army feet tramping in time to a lone drumbeat, but goose bumps told me something was wrong. I cocked my head and heard another sound getting louder and deeper until it drowned out everything, not because of its volume but because of what it suggested was happening. The low rumbling thunder of heavy stone slabs grinding together made the ground shake and my hair stand on end in sympathy, while men who would have happily stood up to a barbarian horde dropped to their knees, covered their ears and whimpered because Romans were no strangers to earthquakes.

I turned and stared at the ancient stone pharaohs as they rose from their plinths and stamped their feet making spider web cracks race across the hardened roadway. Mineral muscles that had never been intended for use jerked into creaking action, spilling marble and sandstone dust like dandruff. Massive heads swivelled, turning sightless eyes on the cowering pride of the Roman army, a large part of which was already trying to bury its head in the sand as the ancient giants formed a surrounding circle of crushing stone. A triumphant howl from a hundred rocky throats echoed like a distant mineshaft explosion, causing hardened centurions to be glad they had a change of underwear and a return ticket home. Even Julius Caesar nearly had an accident when he was thumped on the back hard enough to make his eyes bulge. Maybe I shouldn't have hit him so hard.

"Sorry, Julius." I sank to my knees and shook with uncontrollable laughter as Caesar stared at me in astonishment. "Sorry, I can't help it. Look at them all. Grovelling in the dirt like terrified kids." I walked over to the nearest legionnaire and kicked his trembling bum so hard he fell on his face in terror. "There's nothing to be afraid of. If there was, I tell you'd I'd be the first out of here." Caesar stared in horror as I walked up to one of the bellowing statues made a face and went "Boo!" before running over to another pharaoh and kicking it on the shins. A cowering soldier hid his face behind trembling hands and I have to admit I sympathised. I'd always been one to take risks, but at face value this was a risk too great even for me.

To everyone's amazement, except my own, the stone giant took no notice, but Caesar was awake enough to see that my foot had sunk into the pharaoh's knee right up to my ankle and yet I was still happily skipping around laughing at his soldiers. I also began to throw stones at the bellowing monsters even though every stone seemed to miss its target and go bouncing off into the desert. Caesar took hold of my arm and though he didn't understand what he'd seen he realised that for some reason he was in no danger. Gawain and the boys were slightly slower on the uptake, but only by a few seconds.

"They're not real," I shouted as I pranced in front of the largest giant of all. "They're not really there. We just think they are. Look." I stood to attention, gave a mocking salute then pirouetted up to each of the pharaohs in turn and blew a raspberry. None of the statues paid me any attention even when I walked right through them. I turned back to a speechless Caesar and took a bow. "See? It's all in the mind, mine as well. And unfortunately your men obviously have very weak minds," I glanced around, "and bladders too some of them."

I took Caesar's sword from his unresisting hand and after a short run-up gave each of the trembling legionnaires a forehand thwack on the backside. I wanted to give them something to concentrate on other than non-existent giant pharaohs and besides it was too good an opportunity to miss.

"Tell them to close their eyes and sing as loud as they can, Julius." I yelled.

"Any particular song?"

I hefted the sword and nearly took a swipe at Caesar, but stopped just in time. "Just get them to sing, you Roman dork, anything to take their minds off these stone monsters ... that aren't there." I strode up and down the line of bemused soldiers, sword smacking those who still had their eyes open and singing dirty songs at the top of my voice. Caesar joined in as best he could though some of the words I used were new to him and were probably rather questionable in any language. Still, he got the idea.

"Sing, you sons of galley slaves," he shouted. "Close your eyes and think of Rome. Make a noise!"

Several different songs rang across the desert, rising in volume as the soldiers became more confident, especially as obviously none of them had been squashed by a ton of carved stone. Caesar watched in amazement as the statues began to fade and then disappear one by one as his men's concentration focused on hitting the right notes and keeping time with my sword swiping.

"Told you so!" I shouted above the din. "Just a figment of their imagination. You can tell your men to stop now. We're quite safe."

That was easier said than done. The soldiers were enjoying themselves and I heard later that some decided to start a regular choir meeting back home, while five of the younger ones told me they reckoned they had a future as a Boy Band with top billing in the Coliseum. Eventually they shut up, opened their eyes and smiled at each other sheepishly, because of course none of them had *really* been scared. They formed a column and prepared to walk fearlessly down the avenue of silent stone pharaohs and into Alexandria.

"Okay, what was that all about and how come you knew it was all an illusion?"

I smiled at Caesar, tapped him on the arm with his own sword, before slipping it into its scabbard. "It's difficult to explain, Julius, but let's say that we've just found the little surprise the Leading Man left for us in Egypt. That's good news, because it probably means there may not be another one. As to how I knew, I looked at the Egyptian guards and fairly obviously none of them saw anything wrong and were looking at us as though we'd gone mad. It had to be an illusion."

"You're no fool," he said with a smile. "I take it you're talking about the leader of the assassins in the Roman Senate? How do you know he's not here?"

I looked around. "No ham acting! Talking of ham, that's probably how we must have been drugged. It was in the breakfast."

"Why do you think that?"

"Because my Egyptians ate their own fruit and haven't been affected."

"But he must have cooked our breakfast, so he'll still be back in the camp."

"I doubt it. He'll have drugged the food back in Rome and given instructions to the kitchen staff as to how they should cook it." I tweaked his arm. "Actually I rather think whatever it was he used wasn't supposed to have taken affect so quickly. I suspect the illusions should have started while you were in Alexandria with Cleopatra with all hell breaking loose."

"So how come it happened here?" asked Caesar.

"Because your men ate like pigs, Mr Roman … and so did we. Our friend didn't reckon on Roman appetites and everyone taking in so much of whatever drug he used so quickly." I punched him on the arm. "Come on. Now that your fearless elite soldiers have stopped peeing themselves let's get this show on the road and walk into Alexandria while it's still friendly. Your future awaits." *And hopefully so does Arthur's*, I added silently.

The Queen of Egypt's personal guard blew a horn fanfare as the country's first minister welcomed us all into the city as honoured guests. As soon as we were through the gates I avoided the excited crowds and ran along the backstreets up to the palace to rejoin Neets and Cleo, while Gawain and the boys thoroughly enjoyed themselves marching at the head of the Roman column with Julius Caesar.

High on a terrace in front of the royal apartments Cleopatra, Neets and I looked down as the elite Roman military marched into the main palace courtyard where the soldiers stared in wonder at the ornate fountains and exotic flowers that surrounded the pathways, just as we had done the day before.

"It would be difficult to mistake someone else for Caesar, wouldn't it?" Cleopatra tapped her chin with an elegant forefinger. "He's got so much presence and he's obviously more used to giving orders than taking them. I'll give my ministers a quarter of an hour with the general and then we'll go down and meet him."

I was intrigued. "So what are we going to do until then, Cleo?"

"Spy on him, of course. I want to understand everything about the actual man, not what people think I ought to be aware of just because I'm Queen. Follow me."

We walked back inside the palace, making our way through a mind-numbing series of corridors, terraces, gardens and audience chambers, making sure we kept as close as possible to Cleo. We'd have been lost in a second without her.

"So, no Significant Other then, Cleo?" I ventured at last just to be sure the stories about the Queen of the Nile were true. "No husband in the offing, or anything like that?"

"No such luck!" Cleopatra turned down another twisting maze of pillared corridors. "Oh, I've had the odd boyfriend, but either my parents thought they weren't good enough, or I scared them off. It's not easy when your dad's the pharaoh."

We came to a crossroads of seemingly identical terraces and even Cleopatra looked as though a map would have come in handy. She chose the terrace facing west, away from the rising sun.

"I tell you," she said, "being jaw-droppingly gorgeous and incredibly wealthy isn't all it's cracked up to be. Even grown men run a mile. And if I manage to trap one, as soon as I want a serious conversation they turn into babbling idiots and blush. Besides, if I wanted to marry it would have to be to a king and let's face it they don't grow on fig trees."

We came to another terrace intersection overlooking even more gardens and tumbling waterfalls, but this time Cleopatra had no hesitation in turning north.

"Maybe Julius Caesar might be worth looking at," I said as though the thought had only just occurred to me. It was worth a try.

"Caesar?" replied the queen as though also considering the thought for the first time. "But he's only a general and a fairly new one at that. Hardly royal marriage material."

"He's got potential, Cleo," I said, "and from what I hear he could well make Emperor if he plays his cards right, especially if he has the right person backing him, if you get my meaning."

Cleopatra stopped. "You mean help him up the promotion ladder so to speak and be the power behind the Roman throne? It's a thought, and he's not all that bad looking I suppose. At least, he's fairly passable from twenty-feet up even though he's going bald and has a hook nose. The Roman Tourist Board didn't mention that."

She laughed and started off again, eventually stepping onto a small balcony overlooking the royal throne room. From here we all had an excellent opportunity to observe Caesar without him realising, and more important, there were three well-cushioned couches set back far enough for no one below to be aware of our presence. Neets and I waited for Cleopatra to choose which couch she wanted before diving full length onto the other two, plumping up the cushions as we landed. This is definitely the life, I thought, as I lay back and stretched luxuriously.

"Peel me a grape, someone," sighed Neets, as she closed her eyes with a smile, "but do it quietly."

Below us the audience chamber doubled as a smaller throne room, though it was still larger than one of Arthur's football pitches. An ornate throne covered in jewels and gold leaf stood at one end of the room on a platform, raised slightly less than six inches from the rest of the floor. Brightly painted columns lined both sides of the chamber decreasing in size and diameter as they got nearer to the throne, giving the illusion that whoever was sitting at the far end was farther away and much larger than they really were. Everything was done to make any visitor feel truly humble in the presence of the great pharaoh. Just like the East Gate statues, and it worked too.

"Actually, I might just stay up here and watch." Cleopatra slowly stretched out her arms luxuriously. "My ministers are capable of handling the meeting on my behalf and besides I've told them what we'll agree to and what we won't."

"No, you mustn't!" I said it so quickly that Cleopatra sat bolt upright. "I mean you've got to go down there and meet him. You'll like him. Honest, he's a nice guy."

"Why? Surely as the absolute ruler I should remain aloof from haggling?"

"I think what she means, Cleo," explained Neets, "is that Caesar deals with ordinary male ministers every day of the week and eats them for breakfast. A beautiful Queen of the Nile with an incredible brain will absolutely blow him away. You'll have a fantastic advantage!"

Cleopatra thought about this as she picked up an apple from an ever-present bowl of fruit and took a delicate bite before placing the rest of it on a rosewood side table. She had to agree that what Neets said made total sense, because any negotiator looks for an advantage and being a drop-dead gorgeous queen with brains was a pretty good start. "What an excellent idea!" she said at length. "I shall let my ministers initiate the talks and then I'll make such a grand entrance that Caesar will agree to almost anything. Perhaps one of you has a suggestion for the grand entrance?"

"I've got one you might like," I said with a smile, as we watched the Romans file into the throne room and meet the Egyptian representatives.

Caesar and his team were getting into the really boring part of the negotiations to do with trade and taxes, but from the way he kept looking around he was more concerned with where the legendary

Cleopatra was than money. He picked a piece of fluff from his tunic and examined it in detail just for something to do. Gawain stood next to him, sword at the ready in case of another attack by the Leading Man.

Behind one of the larger pillars and hidden from everyone's view except ours, Bryn and David sat on three-legged stools waiting impatiently for something to happen. I saw Bryn take out the small knife he kept tucked in his belt and out of habit start to carve his name into the front leg of the stool, before realising it was made of solid gold and that the small *"B"* had probably cost thousands of … of whatever it was they used for money in Egypt. I decided they probably used gold. I watched him put the knife away and carefully place a bit of his uniform over the offending carved letter. David just laughed.

The words about grain and taxes, wheat and taxes, gold and taxes droned on and became background noises. I could see Caesar was slowly drifting off, lulled by the monotonous voices of the diplomats and negotiators and I decided it was time for us to help Cleopatra make her grand entrance before he started snoring. Neets and I took hold of the royal arms and pulled the queen to her feet.

Caesar came to with a start when the throne room doors burst open with a crash as Neets and I entered carrying a rolled up rug that looked as though it was considerably heavier than it should have been. He sprang to his feet and instinctively reached for his sword, which had been taken from him for security reasons, though not without a fight. As the general's bodyguard Gawain had been allowed to keep his, but was alert enough to realise this was no threat. Caesar relaxed and watched in fascination as we walked to the centre of the room, carefully put the rug on the floor and then with a flick slowly unrolled it before backing away. Caesar walked over and started to grin.

"Nice rug," he smiled, admiring the rich colours and ornate patterns. "Is this a gift, or was something supposed to be wrapped up inside it?"

"I believe," said a voice from behind him, "the original thought was that you would have found me, however, that wouldn't have been very dignified for a queen, now would it?"

"The history books said she was inside the rug," I whispered excitedly to Neets, "so we've changed history. Wow!" Bryn and David peeked round from behind their pillar and gave us the thumbs-up sign.

"We may have altered the facts," Neets whispered back, "but we haven't changed the legend. I bet you anything history will still say she was in the rug, but now it's probably added the word 'allegedly'! Look at Cleo. She looks stunning."

Cleopatra sat on her throne looking every inch the composed Queen of the Nile and the unopposed leader of her country. The diversionary tactic of the rug delivery had worked perfectly, allowing her to slip in through a side door without anyone noticing and take up her proper position as absolute ruler. Caesar turned towards the voice and bowed, looking as stunned as Cleopatra had intended him to be, but at least he didn't look as though he was about to run a Roman mile like most of Cleopatra's potential boyfriends. Instead he stared at her, unsure what to say, while she smiled sweetly back at him and was absolutely certain of her next lines.

"Although the question of trade is vital to our two countries, Caesar, I believe we both have people who are briefed on what we want. We have greater matters to discuss. You'll agree with me, I'm sure." Her smile made Neets's look like a scowl.

I rather suspected that no one had managed to make Caesar come out in goose bumps just by sitting in an ornate chair and saying a few carefully chosen words in a voice that sounded like warm honey spreading slowly over the smoothest of velvet.

"Aren't you going to say something, Caesar?" Cleopatra asked with a smile and an awesome wink that would have melted steel and turned mere mortal men into quivering wrecks. After another few seconds Julius Caesar burst out laughing and sat on a handy chair with tears in his eyes. Cleopatra raised her eyebrows, because from what I knew of her by reputation, this was one effect she normally didn't have on men – tears of sorrow frequently, but tears of laughter, never!

"I'm sorry," he managed finally. "That was a stunning entrance!"

She looked at him closely. "So you're the famous Julius Caesar."

"Indeed I am, Queen Cleopatra."

She looked him up and down, pausing for effect. "You're not as scary as people say, you know."

"And you're not as beautiful as everyone would have me believe," Caesar smiled broadly. "But you're still pretty good looking," he added hastily as he stood up. Then he blushed.

Cleopatra gracefully rose to her feet, took the general by his hand and led him without any protest past the negotiators towards the main door. As they passed Neets and me, Cleo winked and gave a playful little curtsey, small enough so that Caesar didn't notice, but obvious enough to say *thank you*.

"General, let me show you round my palace while the old men sort out the treaty. And by the way, call me Cleo, all my very best friends do."

Arm in arm, they strolled into the gardens, and history, hand in hand with Arthur's destiny, strolled with them. We watched them leave the Throne Room and it was obvious we were no longer required. "Job well done," I said with satisfaction, as Gawain and the two boys joined us.

"You sure?" asked Neets.

"Try the *Marlene and Merlin* test. Can you remember Arthur and everything we've been doing?" I asked her.

"Of course I can. Crystal clear," snorted Neets. "Oh, I see what you mean!"

"Then we've done it! Arthur's ancestor will be born and therefore so will Arthur in about five hundred years time," I explained. "If we'd failed we'd remember a warped version of Arthur, or probably absolutely nothing. Come to that we probably wouldn't be here at all."

Gawain brought us back to reality. "That's great, but your Leading Man is still very much alive and he'll want revenge for what we've just done. Let's get back to Merlin's cave. I have a feeling we may have a lot to do yet. I don't think he'll back down and admit defeat so easily. By the way, does anyone remember the way back to the Portal?"

"A few hundred yards from the city," I said, "and then third dune on the left."

"By the way I want to thank you," said Bryn as we approached the glowing archway. He was holding Neets, presumably in case she fell over.

"No problem," replied Neets. "Er … which thing are you thanking us for?"

"For not saying I came to Egypt to find my mummy again!" said Bryn.

Zzzzzp.

Chapter Twelve

Ideas, a Near-Capture and Another Trip to Rome

Galahad greeted his old friend Gawain with a steaming cup of Merl Grey tea and dragged him off to a table where the two knights were soon catching up on old times and new adventures. Neets, the boys and I left them to it and ran up the steps from the castle kitchens to the Archive room where we expected to be greeted like heroes with possibly a medal or two thrown in for good measure.

We burst through the door and were met with

complete silence; the sort of absolute quiet when two people are definitely not talking. Marlene had found another chair and the wizard sisters were sitting facing us, looking tight-lipped and very tense, though the sword point the Leading Man was holding to Merl's throat explained that away. A trickle of blood where she'd been nicked just below her chin had almost dried, which meant it must have been five minutes at least since our enemy had arrived. It also meant that he'd been waiting for us and that the two wizard sisters were probably intended as hostages, or they would already have been dead.

"Don't come any closer," said the Leading Man with a humourless smile. "Sit on the floor and put your hands where I can see them, and no tricks or I'll skewer the lovely Merlin and make a kebab of her dumpy little sister." Marlene bristled, but sensibly remained still, while we did as we were told, because there really wasn't a choice. "Good. So here we are all together again and I understand you've been to Egypt. You know, you two really are getting to be most annoying. Wherever I go, you're there causing trouble and disrupting my plans for that royal idiot Arthur Pendragon. Whether you're doing it by accident or design I really don't care, but it has to stop and as subtle persuasion hasn't worked I can but assume that the only argument you'll understand will be death … both yours and Arthur's."

He pushed the point of the sword against Merl's

throat and she grimaced as it threatened to break her skin, but that wasn't what had grabbed my attention and the Leading Man knew it.

"At long last!" He laughed. "One of you has realised you're all about to die on the point of Excalibur. How deliciously ironic. Of course, the sword is worthless now that the Camelot population believes you threw it into the lake, Merlin, so you'll die on a length of meaningless iron, which I shall destroy as soon as I've disposed of you all. And with Excalibur permanently gone, your so-called king can never return and I can kill him at my leisure."

To my amazement Bryn put up his hand like any school kid. "If Arthur has left Camelot and can't return as king because Excalibur doesn't exist anymore, why do you have to kill him? Come to that, why do you have to kill us?" Bloody good questions, I thought.

"Because I have to be sure," the Leading Man replied reasonably, "and because I want to." I thought that was a lot less reasonable.

"But if you kill us," said David, "you won't know where we've hidden Arthur."

"Rome," replied the Leading Man smugly. "He's in Rome. I have my sources, just as Galahad has his sauces." None of us laughed.

"Oh." David looked deflated and I sympathised with him, because ... well, because I liked the boy.

"But you don't know when," said Merl, careful not

to move her throat too much.

"That's true," said the Leading Man after a pause. "My informant only knew the location, so if I'm to complete the job one of you will have to tell me the year. And as I only need one of you to tell me, I can kill the rest of you one by one, starting with the lovely Merlin, until the one left alive spills the beans. After that I'll toss one of my gold coins to see whether the last one lives, or joins the rest of you in a pool of blood."

I was waiting for Merl to jump to her feet and cast a spell to end the Leading Man's evil once and for all, but for the first time I saw that she and Marlene were securely tied to their chairs, hand and foot. I closed my eyes for the second time, waiting for the sound of a sword whistling through the air and a head thumping onto the ground. I was sure the others were doing the same until David tapped me on the shoulder and told me to pull myself together. The nerve of it! After all I'd done for him in South Wales. I looked around and smiled.

"You and your kind always talk too much," said Gawain. "If you're going to kill, then get on with it. Don't discuss it like some bad actor, because bad actors never win." The knight had an arm round the Leading Man's neck and a long knife pressed to his heart. "Slowly take the sword away from Merlin's throat and drop it on the floor." There was a metallic *clang*. "Now sit down on your hands by the wall." The

Leading Man did as he was told and Gawain cut the ropes securing the two wizards.

"How on earth did you get in here, Gawain?" I asked, looking at the closed door before joining the others and helping Merl and Marlene to their feet.

"I sensed something might be wrong when the wizards weren't in the kitchens to welcome us," said Gawain, "so after I finished talking to Galahad I decided to come up to make sure you were okay. I listened at the door and heard a voice I didn't recognise and it sounded none too friendly, though I thought for a moment it reminded me of someone. I looked through a crack in the door and knew I couldn't get in that way, so went up the stairs to the very top of the tower and lowered myself from the turret to the Archive room window. Of course, as no windows in Camelot have glass, getting in was no problem and your Leading Man was too engrossed in his own importance to see me."

Gawain is charismatic and such a heroic story-teller that none of us noticed anything until the Leading Man launched himself across the room, grabbed Excalibur as he passed and shot through the door before any of us moved a muscle, or a wizard's wand. The words *too engrossed in his own importance* came to mind as Gawain swore and started the chase.

Seven of us all trying to get through the door at the same time caused a few seconds delay and the same problem going down the narrow spiral stairway probably gave the Leading Man about a couple of minutes start, but it wasn't until we reached the ground level that we heard the yells and the sound of crashing furniture coming from Merlin's old laboratory on the second floor. This time we let Gawain lead, after all he was the only qualified knight among us, although Bryn was fast becoming pretty useful with a sword.

The door to the laboratory was open and the room's floor covered in what had once probably been rather nice Swedish furniture collected from one of Merl's trips in time. Now it was mostly stylish matchwood. Twisted metal, ripped books and broken glass tubing littered the place to such a degree that at first we didn't see the body lying half covered by all the debris. A groan and an arm movement told us that whoever it was still lived, though probably only by a thread and was in need of urgent medical, if not wizarding attention. Merl and Marlene dashed forward, gently moved the man onto his back and put a rolled-up blanket under the groaning head. There was no blood that we could see, but a nasty lump was swelling up on his lined and balding forehead.

"Lancelot!" I said it rather loudly, but then as far as we all knew, the old knight was still pottering around in Rome with Guinevere. "How did you get here?" I suppose it was rather a silly question and one worthy of Neets really, because he could hardly have walked more than a thousand miles and five hundred years.

Not in his state of health anyway!

The knight's eyes flickered open and he muttered the question all people who recover from a bang on the head ask first, "Where am I?" Not *who am I?*—well occasionally I suppose—*not What am I?* or *When am I?*—which in this case would have been appropriate, or even *Why am I?*—which would have been a bit philosophical—but *Where am I?*

"You're in my old laboratory..." replied Merl as she gently bathed Lancelot's head with an old rag and what was probably water, or waterish, "...lying on the floor surrounded by the remains of some of my favourite experiments. What happened? Come to that, who smashed the place up, not you I hope?"

"I only saw him for a moment," moaned the old knight, "but he looked like that man who was handing out gold coins down in the village. I never got any. Bloody typical!"

"But what happened," Merl repeated, "and why on earth did he hit you?"

I must admit the same thought had been troubling me. Why hit an inoffensive old man like Lancelot? He wasn't known for his fighting skills and he certainly wasn't built for speed, so it must have been pure nastiness that made the Leading Man whack him.

Lancelot groaned and raised himself into a sitting position, carefully supported by the two wizards. He actually had a smile on his face, but then he now had two reasonably young and quite good-looking women tending to him. He may have been gaga, but he was no fool. "I tried to stop him," he said and groaned again, though I reckoned it was more for effect than anything else, "but he was too strong for me and after a struggle managed to escape by knocking me out." He brushed dust and bits of wood off his clothing and out of his hair. "And the next thing I knew, you two ladies were taking care of me." He was still smiling, but if anything it was now a wider and sillier smile.

"Two questions, Lancelot," said Gawain. "How did you get in here and how did the Leading Man get out when the door was closed?"

Marlene walked to the window and pointed to the rope dangling outside. She put her head through the window and looked up, then looked down. "I rather suspect," she said, "this may be the rope you used to lower yourself into the Archive room and if I'm right it looks as though it goes right down to the ground. That answers your questions as to how our lad got out." She paused, then walked back to Lancelot. "So, my old friend, how did you get here when as far as we all knew you were in Rome?"

Lancelot slowly got to his feet, moaning presumably because of his aching bones and the growing bump on his head. Merlin pushed a seat against the back of his legs and he sat down gratefully. He looked at each of us in turn, toying with a piece of twisted metal and tapping it on the table-top absent-mindedly. "I came back for Guinevere's bag," he muttered, "and I got lost. The old memory isn't what it was, you know."

Actually I couldn't remember Lancelot ever having a memory to speak of. Ever since he'd tottered up to Camelot from Cornwall he'd been old and doddery. Come to think of it he didn't seem to have aged one bit in all those years; he'd just always been old and I couldn't help thinking he'd probably been born that way.

"I came in here," he continued, "and the next thing I knew the door flew open and this man burst in, saw me and started smashing the place up. I tried to stop him but that just seemed to make him madder and he smashed it up some more before having a go at me. At least he only bopped me on the head. He had this great big sword in his hand and I wouldn't have stood a chance if he'd used it." Lancelot mopped his brow with his gloved left hand. "Has he gone? He's not here anymore is he?" For the first time he looked and sounded nervous.

"He got out through the window," said Marlene, "thanks to our Gawain here, and I should think he's miles away by now and out of our hair. He must have taken Excalibur with him. There's no sign of it here." She unconsciously ran her hands through her shock of orange-red tresses, which looked more like a Halloween wig on a colour-blind witch.

I wasn't so sure we were rid of the Leading Man. We might have stopped him killing Caesar in Rome and we certainly made sure the general and Cleopatra became an item in Egypt, but there was nothing to stop the man trying to kill any of Arthur's more recent ancestors, or even Arthur himself, if only he knew when and where we'd sent him. Not being one to keep my thoughts to myself, I told Marlene she was wrong and why. My TDA partner bristled, but Merl agreed with me to a large extent.

"You're right, Tertia," she said. "I can't see him giving up, now or any other time, but I don't think he'll try to eliminate any of Arthur's ancestors because quite frankly he won't know who they are. To be honest, even after knowing Arthur all this time and coupled with my researches in the Archive room, I've no idea who they were either."

"Start from Caesar's son and work on from there," said Gawain logically.

"That's the problem," Merl replied. "We know Caesar brought his son to Britain and left him here when he went back to Rome. We know that his son married a local girl in Cornwall and together they started the Pendragon dynasty. Pendragon by the way means *Son of the Dragon* in Cornish and the Dragon was of course Caesar. After that everything's a blank. There's no trace of what happened to Caesar's son or any of his descendants until Arthur's father, Uther, appeared and took the throne. He never really spoke about the past, because he always insisted the future was far more important."

I glanced across to where Neets and Bryn were holding hands, wrapped up in their own little world. They obviously thought the future was more important too and I suppose I couldn't blame them. I glanced at David, but he was concentrating on cleaning his sword on part of his Roman uniform and had paid little attention to me since we'd met in the Roman Senate. Oh well.

"So like I said, he can't do anything to Arthur now, even though he knows he's in Rome," said Marlene, "unless we actually tell him when in history we sent him and we're not about to do that!" She paused uncertainly. "Are we?"

"We may have to do just that," Merl replied. "Arthur has no idea the Leading Man is after him and if the man finds him and we're not there to help our king, he'll be killed. And so long as he's on the loose, the Leading Man will always be a very dangerous threat. We have to stop him and we have to protect Arthur."

"So we bring Arthur back to Camelot?" I asked.

"No, we can't do that. Without Excalibur Arthur would have no standing as King of the Britons and he'd be attacked and killed by all the rival warlords as soon as he came here. It was bad enough when the Black Knight was around and Arthur had the sword."

We all remembered the Black Knight. Gawain, the boys and the TDA had eventually fought and defeated him in South Wales, but not before he'd laid waste to large parts of Arthur's kingdom. He was now trapped in Time Limbo, a sort of no-man's land in the Time Portal and would stay there until someone replaced him.

"It might be better to force the Leading Man's hand," Merl continued, "and have a final showdown."

"Winner takes all?" said Gawain. "Sounds a bit risky."

"Less so than the Leading Man finding my Arthur while we sit around chatting about the good times in Camelot!"

"So we're off to Rome in the time of Ne…" Marlene didn't manage to finish her sentence.

"…in the time of no one in particular, dear." Merl stood up and looked around her shattered laboratory. It may have been old and long out of use, but it was still hers and must have had memories I suppose. "Let's get this place cleared up a bit first, though."

For the next thirty minutes the seven of us swept up whatever was broken beyond repair and put anything salvageable on one of the unbroken laboratory tables. Lancelot watched from his seat, holding his head and emitting the occasional moan if anyone came within earshot. One thing puzzled me. In my limited experience people who get knocked out usually ask for a mug of water when they come round. It seems to be a sort of natural reflex, but Lancelot hadn't asked for anything except female sympathy, so he was obviously made of sterner stuff than we all thought. Either that, or with his memory he'd just forgotten to ask for something to drink.

When we finished clearing up, the overall damage wasn't as bad as we'd thought and we found that some of the twisted metal was actually meant to be twisted in the first place. It just needed the skills of a jigsaw fanatic to put it all together again and Merl's wizardry to know why it looked that way. It was a job for a rainy Sunday afternoon and besides it was time for us all to go to Rome again, but this time to rescue Arthur and sort out the Leading Man.

Merl picked up odds and ends that looked like rejects from a rubbish dump and put them in one of her robe pockets. "I think it's time we left the castle," she said, "and went back to my cave. I'd rather use its Portal if only for the sake of privacy and there are a few things I'd like to take with us, and my staff is one of them."

We made our way down the spiral staircase to the ground floor and started walking towards the door to the courtyard, where with any luck our horses would be waiting faithfully for us. It was Marlene who remembered that Gawain, David, Bryn and Lancelot had all arrived through the kitchen Time Portal and not by nag, but it was Merl who about-marched us down to Galahad's inner sanctum of cookery and towards the glowing ultra-violet archway.

"Galahad," she called out as she pointed at the Time Portal, "you'll have to stop sending stuff to the

Olé Grill for a few minutes while we use it. Everybody grab something to eat for the journey. We won't have time to buy anything in Rome and there's nothing in the cave." As she passed a trestle table marked *T. Pratchett & Family February 7ᵗʰ 2002* she grabbed a medium rare fillet steak and some rolls, stuffing them in yet another voluminous pocket, and motioned us to do likewise. We hoped Mr Pratchett and his guests wouldn't mind the delay in being able to eat their food, but our need was greater than theirs and besides Galahad was quite capable of whipping up a replacement feast in minutes.

Zzzzzp.

The cave was exactly as we'd left it. Untidy, with clothes scattered in every corner and dust on all the shelves. It was fairly obvious that without us to look after her, Merl had let things go a bit, but then recently she'd mostly been on Avalon with her beloved Arthur. Neets and I looked around for nostalgia's sake more than anything else, because all our possessions, such as they were, had been moved to the twenty-first century ages ago and Merl's cave was now nothing more than just that … a cave.

Merl looked around to make sure we were all paying attention. "Is everyone ready?" We were. "Unita, have you put food and milk down for the cats? We could be away for some time, you know." Neets pointed out they were in the twenty-first century and well fed. The wizard was fussing

211

unnecessarily and we all knew it was purely nerves, so most of what she said was ignored. "We haven't forgotten anyone have we, Marlene?"

"We're all packed and waiting, dear," her sister replied patiently. "Not only that, but just for once we're all dressed for the part!" The younger wizard gave a twirl to show off the sheet draped over her body to its best advantage. "What do you think?"

"Nice toga." Merl stopped nervously picking things up and putting them down for no reason in a different place. Both wizards had also remembered to pick up their staffs. "Boys, you look fine in your uniforms, but girls, if you do the same with your sheets we'll merge perfectly with the Romans. Now remember, when in Rome…"

"Nick their purses?" It had to be me I suppose.

"Don't expect bed sheets, because they're already wearing them?" Logically it was Neets.

"Get a good suntan?" David and Bryn made a joint contribution.

"All very good ideas," laughed Marlene. "What Merlin's trying to say is behave like a Roman. Do what they do, say what they say and be as arrogant as they are."

"No problem there then," I laughed. "Arrogance and Merl's Girls go together hand in glove!"

"Very true!" Merl turned her attention to Lancelot. "Are you going to be okay to travel with us? It could be dangerous and at your age…" She didn't finish the

212

sentence.

The old knight tried to stand upright and tall, but his old bones wouldn't let him, so he sagged to his full height. "Don't you worry about me, I'll be fine, young Merlin," he said in his wobbly old voice. "Just one thing. I left Guinevere's bag at Camelot in all the rush, so if you'll wait for me I'll nip and get it. Shouldn't be more than a half-hour ... if I can just remember where I left it."

I could see Merl was more than impatient to get going and this last delay was making her angry. "You go back, Lancelot, get your stuff, then join us in Rome when you can. These are the coordinates." She handed the knight a slip of paper and almost pushed him into the Portal.

Zzzzzp.

It was Neets who then asked the best question of the day and I just wish I'd thought of it first. "Why are we going to the Roman Coliseum, Merlin? And how on earth do we know that's where Arthur's going to be. Come to that, how do we know that's where the Leading Man's going to be?"

"Because, Unita, as you may remember Arthur asked to go there." Merlin was talking very slowly as though Neets were a dim-witted kiddy, rather than a partner in the TDA and one of her old apprentices.

"No he didn't, Merl, be fair," I decided to stick up for my cousin, because the way Bryn was bristling he'd be getting physically angry if I didn't do something. Boyfriends, huh! "He asked to go to Rome in Domitian's time because they had great Saturday afternoon games. He didn't mention the Coliseum."

"He didn't need to, Tertia. My Arthur would do two things when he got to Rome. Firstly, being a king, he'd act like one, and another king turning up in Rome would soon come to the attention of Domitian. Secondly, he'd be attracted to the Coliseum like a moth to a flame, and Arthur hates being a spectator, so he'd want to take part in the games, whatever the risk. I don't think he really understands what happened there."

"What did happen?" asked Neets.

"Mostly it was the odd massacre and people fighting wild animals, from what I understand," said Gawain. "The animals usually won." He turned to Merl. "Arthur will be fine watching from the stands and cheering with the crowds."

"That's what worries me," replied the wizard. "I forgot what a fool he can be. He'll want to take part!"

Merl carefully set the dials on the Portal to Ancient Rome and a specific date in the time of Emperor Domitian, reputedly a totally nasty piece of work, though it was all relative and compared to some people we'd met recently he was probably an absolute saint. One by one we walked through the humming archway into the warmth and noise of a Roman Saturday afternoon, knowing that the Leading Man could be already waiting for us.

Merl and I were last to leave and I noticed she'd brought the parcel the witches had given me, but had left on the Round Table. She saw my gaze, shook her head and mouthed the words *for later*, then looked with sad fondness at the home she might never see again. She turned and walked with me into Rome.

Zzzzzp.

I imagined that inside the cave the Portal's ultraviolet glow dimmed and went out, then the hum that had been so much part of its background noise for so many years slowed and stopped. Merlin's cave must have been totally silent and very empty, except for the odd *"Meooooow,"* the occasional lapping sound and a purr echoing down from the twenty-first century.

Chapter Thirteen

Gladiators, Chariots and Lions

The Portal in Emperor Domitian's Rome was directly beneath one of the main archways of the famous Coliseum and tucked well out of sight of the local inhabitants. This was just as well, because we knew that Romans tended to be very inquisitive and had a nasty habit of grabbing first, using swords, then asking very awkwardly pointed questions afterwards, like, *I wonder who that was?*

Merl gathered us together in the shadowy depths of a neighbouring arch and after doing a final body count just to make doubly sure no one had been lost in transit gave us a last-minute briefing. "Right everybody, split into small groups, merge with the crowds and watch the show. I'm certain we'll catch sight of Arthur soon enough and whatever you do please look out for any sign of the Leading Man. Above all, remember to act like Romans."

David's hand shot up. "Question, Merlin. Bit of a dead giveaway, but none of us speaks a word of Latin."

"Good point," agreed the wizard, "and also a pretty dumb point too, young David. Think about it, you've spoken to Egyptians, Romans and lots of people in the distant past and future and you've never had a problem making yourself understood yet, have you?"

"Er … no," David admitted grudgingly. "No more than normal."

"Surely it must have occurred to you that there's a reason?" Merl was using sarcasm and David looked at me for support, but even though I felt a little pang of conscience I whistled an unrecognisable tune and admired the roof of the arch with a smile. "I programmed the Portal to translate everything you say into the language of just about every time and country. You must have realised that, surely." She turned to me. "It was actually a bit more complex than that, but now isn't the time to go into technicalities even if I understood them. Mind you," she said almost as an afterthought, "if that doesn't work then shout at the Romans very loudly. That always seems to do the trick."

"Right," said Marlene, bringing questions to a halt. "If there's nothing else, then let's get going. I'll be with Merlin and I would suggest, Gawain, that you take Bryn, David and Lancelot when he turns up, while Unita and Tertia go up to the highest seats to keep a lookout. Stay in sight of each other and watch for our signal to act because we probably won't have much time to warn you. Okay, let's go."

I could see that Neets and Bryn were on the point of saying they'd rather stay together, because let's be fair they *were* holding hands and it would mean they'd have to let go of each other. Vomit bag at the ready! David opened his mouth, but looked at me and wisely remained silent. I grabbed Neets spare hand and dragged her onto my team.

We all walked from under the archway into the hot Roman sunlight and merged into the excited crowd of Saturday afternoon fans. Neets and I watched the others disappear into the Coliseum stadium, then ran past the helpless ticket collectors like seasoned gatecrashers and up the wide stone stairs leading to the more expensive seats. We wanted to get the best possible vantage point so we could clearly see all our friends, while at the same time watch the Games for free. We weren't Merl's Girls for nothing. Well actually I suppose we were, because that's how much we usually got paid!

"Over there, Neets, quick." I pulled her forward. "There's a couple of spare places behind those two old guys." I jostled people out of the way and led my older cousin to two vacant seats that had little signs stuck on them saying *Reservatur*. Fortunately the writing was in Latin so being British, we quite rightly ignored it and the signs quickly disappeared under the seats. We eagerly sat down to watch.

"So what's the show about then, Tersh? Lots of dancing and singing and stuff?" Neets leaned forward in anticipation.

"I don't think so, not from what Gawain was saying," I replied, craning forward to see if the two wizards, Gawain and the boys from South Wales were in place and visible. "Plus from what Merl told me they also play lots of games and things, and apparently that's one of the reasons Arthur wanted to come here. You know how he loves to kick around an inflated pig's bladder. He's been trying for years to get Camelot Town to put together a team and challenge Cornwall."

"It still might be quite good fun then," Neets said cheerfully, trying to peer over the bald head of the man in front of her. She cupped her hands, shouted at him as loudly as she possibly could, which was pretty loud. He ducked down instinctively as if hit by a thunderbolt. "Hey, Merlin was right you know," Neets said with satisfaction, "shouting does work! I've got a great view now baldy's in a crouch."

"When in Rome, Neets," I agreed. "These two guys in front seem to know what they're doing so I suggest we go along with whatever they do, at least when yours has recovered. Sort of keep a low profile if you know what I mean."

The bald man turned to his friend and passed him a bag of candied locusts, carefully keeping it out of the reach of the two extremely annoying girls seated behind him, by which I mean Neets and me. We listened.

"Go on then, who are you putting your money on today, Agricola?"

I nudged my cousin. "They're betting, Neets," I whispered excitedly. "Maybe we ought to have a flutter, just to merge in with the crowd, you understand."

"No way," Neets replied emphatically. "You know Merlin doesn't hold with gambling."

"But this isn't gambling," I hissed earnestly. "This is a flutter and that's totally different!" The look on Neets's disgusted face convinced me otherwise and I concentrated on the conversation going on in front of me.

"If you must know, Septimus, I've put ten gold pieces on the Christians to win," Agricola said proudly apparently believing that if he said it with enough conviction it might actually happen.

His friend looked at him in amazement. "You're an idiot! They haven't beaten the Lions in nearly five years now. Not a good track record and the score's always the same. It's up to you, but you're throwing your money away."

"Yes I know," admitted Agricola, "but I've just got this feeling that today might be their lucky day. Besides, I got incredible odds on the Christians winning, five thousand to one! I was even offered two thousand to one for a draw!" I liked this guy. He was a risk taker.

"Who's on for the Christians today then?" asked Septimus.

Agricola opened his wax programme tablet and turned to the team page quickly scanning the names of the Christians. I craned over his shoulder, but couldn't make heads or tails of the squiggles. He passed the tablet to Septimus who turned to the team manager's article and read it out loud for everybody's benefit:

"Citizens and fellow Romans, Greetings!

You could have knocked me over with a sick parrot when I heard about good old Trident's transfer to Pompeii. I knew nothing about it, honest, and the new villa I've got at the foot of Mount Vesuvius is a total coincidence. Bung, indeed! May I be engulfed in molten lava if it's true!

Today's series of massacres should be right up everyone's alleyway. We've got gladiators with swords, tridents and nets, plus of course topping the bill we've got everyone's favourite ... the Lions versus the Christians!

So have a great family day out and remember that team colour togas are available in the stadium shops."

"Usual load of old tosh," Septimus said knowledgeably. "Come on, hand over the locusts while there's still a couple left." He popped the last two candies in his mouth, swallowing them in one gulp because I couldn't help thinking that if he didn't the wings on the little ones would get stuck between his teeth. Neets and I had eaten nothing since breakfast with Cleopatra in Egypt and we were ravenous, but strangely neither of us tried to dip into this particular sweetie bag.

Suddenly the crowd noise increased until it became a solid roar of approval as Emperor Domitian entered the royal box and sat down on his throne. He was surrounded by numerous slaves offering wines, exotic fruits and sweetmeats as though their lives depended on it, which in fact was probably true. He waved to the crowd and gestured to his cronies for them all to sit before slowly raising his hand, pausing for dramatic effect and then elegantly releasing a lace handkerchief specially laundered for the occasion. It fluttered into the stadium like a giant white butterfly and landed gracefully on the sand. Later, one of the gladiators used it for its proper purpose and blew his nose.

"Let the massacres begin!" cried the Master of Ceremonies and instantly multiple lines of trumpeters and drummers signalled the start of the Games with a rousing march tune that echoed round the stadium's lower seats and then spiralled up to stir the hearts of everyone in the more expensive upper tiers where we sat.

"Wow, this is great, Tersh," Neets shouted excitedly over the noise as she perched on the edge of her seat swinging her arms in time to the beat. "There's nothing like a good marching band to get the old blood going."

I looked at her with scorn, partly because I could, but mostly because I'm absolutely tone deaf.

The crowd rose to its feet and cheered as the gladiators entered the stadium to complete a lap of honour. They always did this before the fighting started, because I read in the cyclopaedia that afterwards there normally weren't enough of them left to even crawl round the arena. The top gladiators strutted their arrogance, flexed their muscles and waved to the masses as flowers and money rained down from all sides. To say that we were impressed would be an understatement. The newer and less experienced fighters stared in awe at the tiers of cheering humanity as they nervously followed their more seasoned colleagues and looked for a quick exit. I also noticed that the more experienced fighters picked up the money and left the flowers to the newcomers.

"A fine looking bunch of men, Agricola," Septimus

said knowledgeably and his friend nodded with only slight hesitation. Neets, on the other hand, agreed enthusiastically and with a huge grin gave me the thumbs-up sign in a way I suspected would have made Bryn grind his teeth.

"Fine indeed," agreed Agricola, "though the Retiarius nets look as though you could walk through them, a couple of the tridents have only got two prongs, and the Thracian's sword is definitely a cheap replica from Gaul. My money's on the Secutor. Big shield, long sword and virtually no armour so he can run faster." Agricola was showing even more detailed knowledge. "Christians and the Secutor as winners then. That'll do me for this afternoon!" He sat back with a smile.

Neets and I looked on in total fascination as the gladiators finished their circuit of the arena and arrived back in front of the royal box. Looking at them I couldn't help wondering how it was that Rome had built up such an incredible empire and yet let its best fighters kill each other every Saturday in the Coliseum. It may keep the citizens amused, I thought, but I was also sure the enemies of Rome were having a bloody good belly laugh about it too.

"Emperor Domitian," shouted the gladiators with one voice. "Those about to die salute you!" A few of the braver ones also mumbled, "and up yours, you blood-sucking parasite!" Domitian smiled, choosing to ignore the last bit though we heard it plain enough, and signalled for the games to commence.

The Master of Ceremonies climbed onto his podium and used a megaphone to start the day's events. "Emperor Domitian, my Lords, Ladies and Gentlemen!" As he shouted, rousing background music began to swell, adding to the already exciting atmosphere. "Today, Coliseum Productions is proud to present an all-star line-up of gladiatorial prowess. We offer you the finest fighters from all corners of the empire and the most savage animals known to Rome..."

"Not the man-eating tortoises of Germanica again, surely!" Septimus whispered to his friend. I shushed him, because even though I could barely make out a word of what was going on thanks to the noise, I didn't want to miss a thing. Neets just kicked him in the back, then got up and nicked a bag of frosted fruit sweets that looked lonely.

"...The chariots will be the fastest, most aerodynamic ever seen, and their hub knives will be the sharpest and longest ever to slice into an opponent. And, Ladies and Gentlemen, as our Grand Finale, we give you the Coliseum's famous Lions versus the Christians massacre! I thank you!"

The crowd cheered then hushed expectantly as the trumpeters and drummers reached an ear-splitting pitch and marched out of the arena, leaving the gladiators alone to kill each other. In total there were no more than forty fighters, though it seemed like many more as they moved quickly round the arena looking for the right opponent. I stared at the centre of the stadium, shielding my eyes against the sun.

"Arthur isn't down there is he?" I said, searching for one man in particular. "He's not one of those idiots trying to get killed, surely!" I craned forward, but could see no sign of our king. "If he was down there Merlin would be in the arena sorting them out by now, so my guess is he's not there. Mind you I wouldn't put it past the royal dummy to creep in when we're not looking, just for the fun of it."

The fighters squared up to each other in pairs, circling their opponents and looking for the important initial opening. When it came, the first swooping slash was greeted by a standing cheer from the massive crowd as the blood gushed from a Trident-and-Net man's shoulder. He grimaced with pain, but managed to sweep his net over the swordsman's head and blindly stab the two-pronged trident into his opponent's leg. Both men were now wounded and bleeding badly, but neither would yield as they threw down their weapons and grappled like a pair of wrestlers trying to go for a final submission with no holds barred.

Being a sophisticated person, Neets hid her face in her hands, but made sure she could still see what was going on between her fingers. I was less squeamish and cheered wildly, whirling my arms like twin windmills and kicking Septimus with my knees into several shades of black and blue as I bounced up and down in my seat. The crowd swayed and gasped as the gladiators' blood mixed with their sweat and poured in pools onto the ground where the sand absorbed it like a kitchen cloth. The same bloody sight was being repeated to a greater or lesser extent around the arena as a Thracian sword bit into a Retiarius net, and a Retiarius trident pronged into a Secutor shield. The clash of weaponry rang out through the stadium, mingling with the grunts of pain from the combatants and the cheers of delight from the Romans, but the grunts were getting fewer and the cheers were becoming more focused.

I looked round again for Arthur and noticed that one gladiator wasn't actually fighting, but was racing round like a madman, encouraging the fighters and giving them marks out of ten. As he came to each fighting couple he watched them with an expert's eye, then held up a card with a roman numeral on it which either got a roar of approval, or howls of disgust. We'd found our king, but there was nothing much we could do if he needed our help and besides, he looked to be having the time of his life.

The number of standing gladiators was slowly reducing, and I told Neets that I had a feeling it would reduce even further. Soon there would be only one left to acknowledge the crowd's cheers as *Victor Ludorum,* the Champion of Champions, and he would accept the laurel crown from the Emperor as

227

well as lots of money from grateful gamblers if he played his cards right. At last the winner's moment came and the emperor showed his disfavour of the losing finalist by signalling that he should die, a decision accepted by both of the gladiators and the order was carried out without hesitation. I explained to Neets that this was the prize for coming in second. Arthur shook the winner warmly by the hand and absent-mindedly patted the dead loser on the shoulder.

Neets swooned delicately, hitting Agricola a good wallop on the top of his head as she went down, while I excitedly slapped Septimus on the back and accidentally put my knee in his neck, shoulder, back and kidneys just for good measure.

"You enjoyed that, Tersh," Neets shrieked reproachfully once she'd fully recovered. "I'm ashamed of you. Bodies are everywhere and you're cheering like crazy." She stood up to get a better view of the winner.

"When in Rome, Neets," I giggled, standing on my seat and using Septimus as a support. "Anyway it's all fake. It's a put-up job, you'll see. They'll all get up and take a bow in a minute and Arthur'll lead them out of the arena." Nobody did of course, because that would have spoiled the entire effect.

"Ladies and Gentlemen," the Master of Ceremonies shouted through his megaphone as the losing gladiators were carried off, "Our Champion of

Champions." He pointed to the lone gladiator. "I give you the Secutor." Arthur held up the winner's hand and joined him on his victory lap, before disappearing through a tunnel.

I could see Merl and the rest milling around excitedly down at ground level in the stalls. They'd seen Arthur and like us had had no idea what to do. He hadn't seemed to be in any danger, so running into the arena would have been silly. Equally, if the Leading Man was here I suppose it was best we kept a low profile for the moment. Arthur was doing all the high profiling that was necessary.

Septimus and Agricola sat back fully satisfied with the afternoon's first event and were obviously looking forward to the chariot race, which was soon to follow. I had the strangest feeling, though, that if the two annoying girls behind them would stop shouting and keep still, or better still get thrown out, it would be a perfect day for them.

From what the two old men in front of us were saying, Emperor Domitian usually found the chariot races pretty boring, because as far as he was concerned everybody just went round and round in circles and there were always far too many survivors. I looked across at the emperor's box and he was leaning forward eagerly because this race was different. Just as promised the chariots were newer, sleeker, shinier, had much bigger hub knives, and looked as though they could slice each other to bits with tremendous efficiency. Neets was equally enthusiastic and was *whooping* like a mad thing.

The other difference was that one of the chariots was being driven by Arthur and he didn't stand a chance. The King of the Britons was wearing a green charioteer's tunic and held onto the reins controlling his four white horses like a professional, except that I knew Arthur couldn't drive a farm cart back in Camelot, let alone a lightweight racing machine pulled by highly-strung, thoroughbred gallopers. Even so I had to admit he looked the part and his confident laugh as he wished the other competitors good luck had the other charioteers joining in. The only trouble was, right now they were all standing still and that was the easy bit. Neets and I looked down to where Merl and the others were still trying to get onto the arena floor, but they were being held back for their own safety by the soldier guards and Arthur was on his own.

The starting flag dropped and the crowd leapt to its feet as the six chariots flew forward. By the look of it Arthur hadn't been expecting to go from a standing start to full speed in one second and he was nearly left at the starting line, but managed to use the reins and the side of the chariot to pull himself back on board. Amazingly he was in second place by the time they reached the first corner, right on the shoulder of the leading team, though Arthur looked more as though he was trying to pull his horses back rather than urge them forward. Behind him, two chariots collided, the long knives on their wheels cutting into the flimsy frames and scattering wood all over the arena floor. The horses were now free to run even faster and the two charioteers managed to stay on their feet like water skiers to the crowd's great pleasure. The next corner put an end to that as the horses sped round the bend and the two men flew through the air, landing on a small group of soldiers whose attention had been diverted by two wizards and a trio from South Wales who were trying to invade the arena.

It looked to me as though even Arthur had realised he wasn't cut out for the life of a charioteer and was looking for any opportunity to jump off the bouncing vehicle, but his horses were born to race and I reckon they sensed they were in charge this time and not the idiot holding the reins. They shot forward and came level on the inside of the track with the leading team and Neets jumped up and down, clapping her hands like a real girlie. I gave a genteel *whoop!* as Arthur took the lead for a couple of seconds.

It was inevitable they would come round to what was left of the two crashed chariots and the crowd hushed expectantly. Both charioteers must have known they had only five seconds at the most before they would hit the debris that still littered the racetrack, and as there were no brakes on a Roman racing chariot, I knew that saying *whoa there, horsey!* probably wasn't going to have much effect. It was time for evasive action and Arthur was the first to react. He climbed onto the side of his lurching chariot and leapt across the gap between him and his opponent, landing on the other charioteer's back and grabbing the reins the man had released at finding he had a passenger. One second later the other charioteer did an unrehearsed somersault and landed on the racetrack sand, rolling over several times before coming to a rest, remarkably unhurt. He got unsteadily to his feet and raised his arms soaking up the crowd's roar of approval, and was promptly run over by the following racer.

In his new chariot Arthur pulled hard on the reins and managed to divert the horses the few feet necessary to avoid the debris, but we all watched in horror as his original team of horses jumped the smashed chariots, managing to clear them by inches, but leaving the vehicle to disintegrate as it hit the growing pile of firewood. We all breathed a sigh of relief because no horses had been hurt and the people … well, they knew what they were in for when they entered the race.

The look on Arthur's face told Neets and me that his one piece of agile heroics had drained him. He was back to having the skills of a student driver again, but without any of the youthful confidence. He only had one lap to go, but was veering all over the place, causing chariots, soldiers and the odd fan to run for safety. The only competitor threatening Arthur's leading position slewed to one side and crashed through a barrier into the area where the next attraction was waiting. There was a jungle-type roar, but this time not from the crowd, followed by a short scream.

As Arthur came round the final bend Neets and I scattered what remained of the candied fruit sweets and pounded the air in our excitement, then pounded the two old men in front of us. Our king was hanging onto the reins for dear life as the chariot went onto one wheel and nearly tipped over. Arthur threw himself in the opposite direction, screaming words I can only describe as naughty, and brought the second wheel back to the ground as he crossed the finishing line.

"How's he going to stop, Tersh?" asked Neets, and I had to admit it was a darned good question and probably one that hadn't occurred to Arthur yet.

I tried to look on the positive side. "He got it started," I said, "so I expect he'll do the opposite to stop the thing."

"What is the opposite of *Help!*" Neets asked innocently.

I'd forgotten about Gawain. While the soldiers were busy keeping Merlin and Marlene off the track, the knight ran out and leapt onto an unseated horse and spurred it into a gallop after Arthur's fast disappearing chariot. It took nearly a whole circuit of the track before Gawain's fresh horse drew level and he managed to slow them to a canter that even Arthur could control.

Back at the finishing line the Master of Ceremonies announced that Arthur was disqualified because he hadn't actually finished the race in his own chariot, but because of his exceptional talents as a clown he would be awarded a special prize by Domitian. The Egyptian team was therefore declared the winner and even Arthur cheered as he was led off by the Roman soldiers through a large set of doors to receive his award. The doors slammed shut and the crowd waited impatiently for the next item on the afternoon's agenda.

Neets and I had mentally backed the Egyptian to win out of loyalty to Cleopatra and had mentally each won a lot of money, which we would pretend to spend later at an imaginary clothes shop.

After the excitement died down, I looked around. I could see the two wizards, Gawain and the boys far below and, true, we'd found Arthur, but far from being in danger he seemed to be having the time of his life and, other than the end of the chariot race, also seemed to have things pretty well in hand. With the absence of the Leading Man I was beginning to wonder if Merl had brought us here unnecessarily. I needn't have worried because at that moment the giant arena doors opened and ten men were pushed into the stadium at sword point. Nine of them looked terrified, but one was trotting from end to end of the

Coliseum waving to the crowd and doing push-ups to prove how fit he was. The crowd cheered and then cheered louder again when the lions entered. I recognised Arthur and I also recognised the sudden look of realisation and terror on his face. It wasn't fair because he wasn't even a Christian.

"I think it's time we went down and helped." I grabbed Neets by the elbow and we both got to our feet, managing to accidentally kick Agricola and Septimus several times in the back, neck and head for the last time as we did so.

"Sorry, guys." I ruffled the men's thinning hair. "Thanks for the company and all that. By the way, if I was you I'd put a couple of gold pieces on the guy doing the push-ups to win."

We jostled through the standing crowd, climbed over those who wouldn't move quickly enough and ran down the stairs to the stadium entrance past the stewards who made half-hearted attempts to stop us from entering the arena. Once on the ground floor we dashed through a series of linked back rooms marked 'Privata' trying to avoid the worst of the crush and bounced off numerous dead gladiators having their lunch before eagerly looking forward to rejoining our friends on the edge of the arena.

It was time to rescue Arthur, but first we had to save him from the lions.

Chapter Fourteen

Big Cats, a Big Surprise and Fireworks

"Get off my foot, you idiot!"

I recognised Merl's voice and dragged Neets through the final door onto the sand of the arena floor to join the two wizards, Galahad, David and Bryn. Neets and I could get a much better view of the lions from here and the one thing that struck me was that they were big!

"Sorry," Bryn shouted above the noise of the Coliseum crowd. "My fault!"

Merlin counted out loud. "I make that six lions against ten Christians including Arthur, plus Gawain, you two boys, Tertia, Unita, Marlene and myself. That's odds of three to one in favour of us humans." She sighed and added that we stood slightly less than a snowflake's chance in a blast furnace of rescuing her beloved warrior king. It seemed about right.

Gawain on the other hand was feeling ridiculously optimistic. After all, as he pointed out, there were nine Christians who had no wish to die and could probably run away quite fast if necessary, a heroic warlord king, a tremendously famous and powerful wizard and her equally capable sister. On top of that we also had two apprentice wizards, their boyfriends as well as a nourishing and vitamin enriched snack for halftime, courtesy of Galahad. How on earth could we lose! Personally I wasn't too sure about the *boyfriends* bit and gave David a warning glance.

The lions didn't seem to be in any hurry. They'd probably never been told not to play with their food, so they prowled around the cowering Christians and Arthur, occasionally pretending to spring with fangs wide open and a suitably bloodcurdling roar. At the last moment they'd hold back, sit down and lick a paw disdainfully. The crowd loved it, cheering their approval and if lions could have winked I reckon they would have done so.

"What's the game plan then, Merlin," asked Marlene rubbing her hands together enthusiastically.

"Frontal attack, or sneak up behind them?"

"Me? I don't know. You're the warrior wizard," Merl answered in exasperation, with just the merest hint of huffiness. "You're the one who's been belting round Time rescuing people from smugglers, wreckers and evil knights."

This was getting us nowhere and I could see poor old Arthur ending up as cat food if somebody didn't do something pretty quickly. I must have voiced my thoughts out loud, because David knelt on one knee in front of the wizard sisters and with the slightest of winks in my direction said, "I will happily lead the attack, O Wizard Ladies, to Death and to Honour! Follow me to Glory!"

"Good grief!" groaned Marlene. "That's all we need, a would-be hero with a death-wish! Still, it's a start I suppose."

David gave me a more open wink and even Gawain smiled, which was a massive improvement, considering he still hadn't really forgiven David for spying for his deadly enemy, the Black Knight, back in South Wales.

Gawain and the two boys drew their swords, giving the wizard sisters little choice but to follow them into the arena where I began to realise the increasing roar of approval from the crowd was aimed at us. The Christians were huddled together so tightly that the five heroes from Camelot were able to surround them with a protective human wall. Only Arthur was acting like a cheerleader, leaping in the air, then running up to one of the lions and pulling silly faces. It wasn't very kingly, but it certainly seemed to be confusing the big cats. Amazingly, the three swords and a couple of wizard staves wielded with all the force of five desperate Britons came as a complete shock to the six lions, even though the wizards' blows were softer than those of a Granny with a rolled up umbrella. But each wallop was a mind-numbing shock to the kings of the jungle.

To the crowd's delight there was an ultra-violet flash from a temporary Portal and Guinevere raced across from the other side of the arena, hitting the nearest lion a fearsome nose thwack with her fist in passing and joined the other five. Not to be outdone Neets and I joined in the fun throwing Neets's remaining sugared fruit sweets into the lions' mouths and then whacking them between the eyes as they caught them.

"Guinevere," Merl shouted, as she swiped at another lion with her staff, "nice of you to turn up, but where's Lancelot? He hasn't got lost again, has he?"

"He's on his way," replied the queen, punching another king of the jungle on the nose with a straight uppercut. "He wanted to pick up a couple of things first."

Arthur was now adding to the lions' confusion by repeatedly throwing his inflated pig's bladder in their faces, waving his arms frantically and shouting rubbish. Suddenly he stopped in mid-throw and stared at his rescuers with a look of stunned surprise. "Merlin? Is that you?" He looked at the wizard and a happy grin spread over his face. "Wonderful to see you, of course, but what on earth are you doing in Rome?" He looked closer. "And where's your false beard? People will notice you're a … you're a, er, you know … a woman." He whispered the last words. The king blushed without knowing why and came to a stammering halt.

Now was not the time for detailed explanations as the lions started to regroup for a counterattack.

Arthur looked closer at his rescuers and ignored most of us. "Gwendolyn? What on earth are you doing here? And Gawain, who are the two young knights dressed as Roman soldiers?"

The queen growled as she thwacked another confused lion on the nose and dodged behind Gawain when the big cat stupidly tried to retaliate. "Arthur, my name is Guinevere, not Gwendolyn and that probably says it all. It also explains why I feel like thumping you like I just thumped this lion."

"Yes, dear," Arthur said to his ex-queen before sneaking another look at Merlin as she zapped a lion with a lightning bolt from her staff. It was the first time I'd seen her use magic in years. "Sorry, dear!" said Arthur to the new lady in his life.

While Guinevere, Marlene and Merlin took care of

the cowering lions and became public heroines in the process, Galahad, Arthur, Neets and I herded the Christians back towards the closed arena gates and then sideways to a screen where we could all take shelter. The crowd went delirious, because even the Romans sometimes liked the underdog to win, especially at the expense of the overcat. Realising for once in his life which way public feeling was going, Domitian signalled for the handlers to capture the lions and declared the Christians the winners.

Providing they'd done what I told them to and put their money on Arthur, I could imagine Agricola and his friend would be quite happy. At odds of five thousand to one on the Christians to win they'd made more money in one afternoon than they could earn in a lifetime of working, which come to think of it was something that as Romans they very rarely did anyway.

When we got to the edge of the arena, Arthur told me that for the first couple of weeks his Roman hosts had treated him like royalty, which of course he was, giving him a small palace on the coast, slaves to answer his every whim, his own chef and even a personal trainer to help him keep fighting fit. Sun, sea and slaves … life couldn't have been better. Then the invitation arrived to join Emperor Domitian as a special guest for the following Saturday games in the Coliseum. The procession through Rome and the cheering crowds was a dream come true.

Not only was he to be a judge in the gladiator fight and a guest charioteer, but to his delight Arthur had also been selected to play for the Christians in their key game against the Lions team and in the two days leading up to the match he'd tried to get his teammates interested in tactics, but they just looked depressed and talked a load of nonsense about leaving a ship. It seemed to him they'd already accepted they were going to lose, but Arthur was made of sterner stuff and besides he'd never lost a game of pig's bladder kick-around yet and had no intention of starting now.

He also told me that beneath the Coliseum what he'd seen proved that I'd been right all along. Superb choreography and several bags of pigs' blood had meant that none of the gladiators had died and the Saturday Roman crowds were paying to see very fit, highly disciplined and well-trained actors. But Arthur hadn't been concerned about any of that. He'd just wanted to lead his team into the arena and get them face-to-face with their opponents, the Lions team. Sometimes, I thought, he could be so single-mindedly naive.

The main afternoon's entertainment was over and the crowd was beginning to shuffle and jostle as quickly as possible towards the exits as the band prepared to play the National Anthem. But before most had even remembered to go back for their new team togas everything went uncomfortably still and silence descended on the Coliseum like a heavy early morning mist hovering over the island of Avalon. The crowd slowed, sensing that something extraordinary was about to happen, then watched in amazement as six figures emerged from an ultra-violet archway that appeared seemingly from nowhere, then walked into the centre of the stadium where they were joined by a seventh.

The tallest of them was dressed in the grey robes of a druid wizard master and was flanked by two slightly shorter, but identically dressed men. All three had white beards that were so long they were tucked into their belts and carried staffs similar to the ones Merl and Marlene used. The fourth man was old and hunched as he held onto the arm of the woman who had just left us and I knew now why there were times when Lancelot had puzzled me. At last, he had arrived in Rome and Guinevere had shown her true allegiance by joining the man who had followed her to Wales when she left Arthur. We all recognised the last figure. His size, his bald head and his hate-filled features made him unmistakable as the man who we defeated in South Wales and trapped in the Limbo of the Time Portal. Somehow Schwartz, the Black Knight was free.

The tall druid raised his staff as the other two chanted and a mist slowly began to form with a glow that surrounded them all.

Lancelot shuffled forward then slowly straightened his back, adding a good foot to his height and taking several decades off his age. He looked at us as he took off his wig and grey beard, rubbing his face with an old cloth to remove the theatrical makeup that made him old and wizened. The Leading Man threw back his head and laughed as he drew the sword hanging from an ornate scabbard at his side and showed us Arthur's Excalibur. He handed it to the druid who tossed it in the air as though it was a feather and blasted it into a thousand pieces with a lightning bolt from his staff.

The Leading Man raised his arms. "Arthur of the Britons!" he yelled, his voice echoing round the stadium and causing immediate silence among the muttering crowd. "Your sword is destroyed and you dare not return to Camelot. Show yourself and come here to me, or will you continue to hide behind women and children like the coward you are?"

Lightning flashed from the tip of the druid's staff to all corners of the stadium leaving burn marks wherever it struck. The druid's breathtaking display of magical fireworks held the Romans spellbound as balls of coloured light swooped and wailed round the stadium. Even Merlin and Marlene who were used to magical tricks were impressed, while the rest of us were gobsmacked. The crowd cheered and sat down wherever they could, preparing to see the greatest unscheduled Coliseum spectacle ever. And it was all for free.

Showtime!

"Blimey, Tersh," spluttered Neets as the firework smoke slowly cleared leaving the crowd wanting more, "it's the Leading Man! How the heck did he find us?" We stared in disbelief as the actor strutted round the arena followed by three druids and a bewildered lion that soon slunk off to a secluded corner to lick its wounded pride. More fireworks flew from the druid's staff and exploded into the afternoon sky high above the Coliseum before cascading down as multi-coloured waterfalls of glowing fire.

"He found us because Merl gave him the coordinates, or at least she gave them to Lancelot who *is* the Leading Man." I paused before continuing. "Blimey, Neets, Lancelot never existed. He was just an act!"

As she popped the last of the nicked candied fruits in her mouth Neets nodded sadly, because we'd both liked the old Cornish knight. The Leading Man was a different matter all together. "He may have got here as Lancelot," she said, her mouth still full, "but there's no way he's going to get anywhere near Arthur as the Leading Man, not with us Merl's Girls around."

"No, dear, you're right he won't," Merl said from behind us, trying to sound confident, but there was a tremor in her voice. "Unfortunately this has got to be between the person you call the Leading Man, the druids, Marlene and myself. However, you could help Gawain and the boys protect the Christians and Arthur if you wouldn't mind."

Bryn and David looked embarrassed and Bryn shuffled his feet like a school kid caught smoking behind the bike sheds. David whistled tunelessly.

"They're not Christians, Merlin," said Bryn, talking to the ground. "They're the passengers and crew from the *Mary Celeste* ghost ship."

Merl and Marlene stared at the boys, then at the group of nine people whose clothes and sandals shouted out *I'm a Christian. Let me at those lions!* On the other hand the look and nod their leader gave our two wizards left us in no doubt who they really were, especially when he said "Captain Benjamin Briggs, Ma'am, of the *Mary Celeste* out of Boston. Rescued by these two brave lads and pleased to meet you." He saluted, then held out his hand. Merl shook it as an automatic reflex, but only for a fraction of a second.

"Bryn, David. Over here!" Merl grabbed the boys by an ear each and dragged them painfully to one side. "You rescued them by using the Portal's Time Limbo, didn't you?" The boys looked at each other, then nodded and nursed their ears. "By doing that you released the Black Knight, didn't you?" Again they nodded. "Which is why we now have to fight him all over again, as well as his new friends, the actor and three druids." The boys had enough sense not to nod this time. "I told you to see if you could help the ship and find out why everyone disappeared, so what on earth made you send them into the Portal?"

He may have been built like a quarterback, but

Bryn continued to scuff the ground like a naughty little boy and hold onto Neets's protective hand. David was made of sterner, if slightly smaller, stuff and faced up to the wizards like a quarterback should. I was warming to this boy.

"We had no choice, Merlin," David said, and I knew he was daring the wizard to contradict him. "The ship's cargo was highly likely to explode and because the boat was carrying barrels of alcohol, I knew from my stepdad's smuggling days that if alcohol leaks, as this lot had, the fumes can explode. All the lifeboats were securely tied to the ship, so there was no quick way off, and everyone was getting a bit hysterical, because the cargo could have exploded at any moment. Bryn and I decided the only way to save everyone was to take them through the Portal."

"Then why use the Time Limbo?" Merl asked quite logically. "Why didn't you bring them back to my cave?"

"Because the Portal coordinates were already set for ancient Rome," said David. "You must have given us the same remote Portal controller you used to send Arthur here, so when we sent the *Mary Celeste*'s people through the thing, they ended up here as well."

"Okay," Merl said grudgingly. "And Time Limbo?"

"Must have been our fault, Merlin," admitted Bryn. "You know my track record in operating the Portal isn't very good, so I probably hit the wrong button again. But the Black Knight didn't come out our way, so it looks as though he joined the crew and passengers here. They got herded up and were mistaken for Christians, but he must have escaped and joined up with the Leading Man."

"Something like that," agreed David. "But we had no idea they'd all come here and we certainly didn't know the Black Knight was free."

Marlene patted her sister on the shoulder. "Merlin, whether they're Christians or sailors makes no difference. They're brave, they're here, they're on our side and that's all that matters. As for the Black Knight, he was probably going to get free sometime anyway, so it might as well be now."

Neets was busy comforting Bryn and personally I really couldn't see why Merl was getting so heated. Okay, so now we also had to deal with the Black Knight, or Schwartz as everyone in South Wales knew him, as well as the Leading Man, but we'd beaten him once and I couldn't see any reason why we wouldn't do it again. I'm a positive little soul!

Then I noticed I wasn't the only person who was puzzled by our internal bickering.

"Merl!" I tried to get the wizard's attention. "I think our friends in the middle of the arena are getting confused and it's my guess they think we're supposed to be scared of *them*, not squabbling amongst ourselves. I could be wrong, of course."

The wizards, Gawain, Neets and the boys looked at me as though I'd flipped, then turned their attention on the Leading Man and his allies. The whole thing was becoming surreal. The crowd was treating us as a Saturday afternoon bonus feature and everything had gone beyond the rulebook of the Roman soldiers, so they did nothing to be on the safe side. The ticket collectors were still trying to get somebody, *anybody*, to pay our entrance fees and some of the *dead* gladiators had stopped snacking and come out to see what all the fuss was about. Meanwhile our enemies had stopped their magical firework display and had obviously realised they were losing control of events and that we'd lost control of ourselves.

"Merlin!" shouted the Leading Man. "If I could have your attention for a minute?" Presumably he'd decided on sarcasm as a weapon. "Get that wimp you call King Arthur over here and let me fight him man to man. The winner takes the kingdom. The loser takes … what's coming to them."

Arthur took a step forward and probably believed the Leading Man's promises of an honourable combat. After all if he closed his eyes this could have been Lancelot speaking and the king knew his trusted knight would never lie. Merl seized one arm and Marlene grabbed the other, stopping what we knew would have been a one-sided, but very heroic massacre of our king. Let's face it, Leading Men tend to cheat, which is how they become Leading Men in the first place, and Arthur had forgotten how he and Merl had cheated everyone to make him king in the second place. The Sword in the Stone scam had been a classic and The Leading Man had his answer.

"I see you're still ruled by females, Arthur, though the greatest woman in Camelot is now standing by my side and will rule Britain with me when I become king." He put an arm round Guinevere's shoulders and gave her a big kiss, which I reckon was designed to stir Arthur's blood to the boiling point and make him do something reckless. Unfortunately, though, Arthur's eyesight had never been brilliant at the best of times and with all the magical smoke still swirling around, coupled with the distance, he was peering at the kissing couple with a look of *who's that woman* on his face.

"You traitor!" Gawain had been silent up until now, but I could see he was seething. "I knew you as Lancelot of Cornwall and helped you become a Knight of the Round Table. When you stumbled, it was I that hid your mistakes from the eyes of younger and more ambitious knights and never asked for anything in return. I expected evil from the Black Knight and got it, but from you...! Do you have no shame?"

The Leading Man paused and cocked his head to one side as though considering the question. "No!" he said at last. "I don't think I do, but my thanks for asking."

"If you want to fight someone, fight me." Gawain was shouting now.

"No," replied the Leading Man without emotion and folded his arms with a smile. "I'll fight Arthur. Besides, I believe my friend the Black Knight may have plans for you."

"I'll fight you," shouted Bryn, "if you won't fight my father."

"Tempting, boy, but no."

I looked at David and shook my head, trying to tell him not to follow Bryn's dumb example and to my surprise he smiled back, nodded and blew me a kiss. This boy definitely needed watching, if only because he wasn't all that bad looking.

"Lancelot," Merl shouted, "or whatever you call yourself, you've failed. This is no longer about you and Arthur, it's about whether you'll be allowed to survive." This was the Merl I knew and we all loved, turning a pretty deadly situation to her advantage without anyone really noticing, especially on the other side. "You may wish to be destroyed, but there are those who may be tricked into following you. Allow them to leave and we will give each one safe passage back home."

Merl was so convincing that we were sure that at least the druids and Guinevere would join us, but when they all burst out laughing and the druids started their fireworks display again we knew we had a fight on our hands, or to be more exact … several fights.

"Merlin, I'm a fair man," the Leading Man said

quietly once the laughter and flashing explosions had died down, "let us talk together. We may still fight, but at least we will have tried negotiation."

Merl looked at the Leading Man. He was staring straight at her with his hypnotic eyes and although I knew he was smiling, his smile was less friendly than that of an angry skull. Merl tried to smile back, if only for effect, and managed a twitch.

I stared at her, horrified that our wizard thought she and Marlene had a chance of winning against the Leading Man, three obviously competent druid wizards and the most evil man I knew, and from the look on Gawain's face he wanted to make sure the man he also knew as Schwartz was taken care of ... permanently. Merl's no fool and she knew what I was thinking.

"I need help, Tertia, you're right," she said, "but I need the magical kind and you took care of that for me when you last went to the Globe Theatre in London." Dead on cue, because that's the way they do things, the three witches emerged from a temporary Portal and, dodging exasperated ticket collectors, cackled their way to stand next to Merl.

"I wondered when we..." Rosie paused to count and gave up when her fingers ran out, "would meet again. Well, I didn't actually, but it has to be said 'cos it's in the script, so best get it over and done with. Know what I mean?"

We did and knew it was one of the drawbacks of

being typecast as one of the must-have three witches. Merl looked the hags up and down as though inspecting a shoe after treading in something suspect and squishy. In Merl's defence, she hadn't seen the witches for some time and certainly not since they left Camelot through one of her portable Time Portals, unwittingly following the Leading Man. Rosie blushed and apologised in a tiny voice for what Merl was thinking. No witch will ever apologise in anything other than a tiny voice, and then only if confronted by someone better at magic than she is. Jennie and Petal followed suit.

"Good," said Merl, "now that's out of the way, let's get on with the matter in hand. Ladies." The witches looked around and eventually realised Merl was talking to them. "I allowed you to use my property, I allowed you to have fun with Mr Shakespeare and I allowed you to become rich in the process by playing yourselves. Now it's pay-back time."

The three witches all took a step back and made the sign against evil. After all this was nearly as bad as having money demanded with menaces, or as Galahad called it … taxation.

"Out there," Merl pointed at the Leading Man's group, "is as nasty a bunch of villains as I've met. You know their chief, just as you knew him when he was Lancelot, and of course you're familiar with Guinevere and the Black Knight. I won't bother introducing the rest, but they're the ones I need your help with."

The witches stared at the druids and took another step backwards, roughly in the direction of the Portal they'd just arrived through. Rosie gulped, because for the first time she was going to contradict Merl and had a distinctly rabbity future. "They're druids, Merlin. Ain't no way we're fighting druids, magic with magic like. They're real nasty that lot are!" Petal and Jennie nodded vigorously in mute agreement as their backwards progress was halted when they bumped into a determined line of the *Mary Celeste's* sailors.

"Ladies," said Marlene, trying a different angle. "Merlin and I realise your magical abilities are insignificant compared to ours," she knew how to ruffle feathers and the witches were indignantly ruffled, "so we'll understand if you want to chicken out and leave the real work to us ... and the two girls." Including Neets and me was the last straw.

"'oo said we wouldn't 'elp?" said Rosie, moving one foot forward.

"Our magic may be a bit rusty," added Jennie, keeping step with Rosie, "but we can mumble spells with the best of them." Petal nodded and the three witches were back on our team.

"A few mumbled spells is all I need of you," said Merl, "and you can leave the rest to us. It's a matter of strength in numbers and you'll make up the numbers quite nicely and we'll be the strength." The witches looked pleased and puzzled in equal measure. "Right, girls, I want you to join up with the others while

Marlene, our lovely witches and I sort out the nasties over there."

"You bet!" said Neets, presumably because she was going to be next to her beloved Bryn for the first time in days. She linked arms with me and we walked quickly over to where Gawain, David and Bryn were shielding Arthur. I looked over my shoulder and watched the two wizards exchange smiles and take a collective deep breath as they prepared to meet a combination of human evil and magic in mortal combat. The three witches followed them with obvious reluctance and I got the impression their mumblings probably weren't spells. I knew I had to be with Merl so gently released Neets's arm and walked back to the two wizards where I stood unnoticed behind them and the witches.

As we began the long walk out into the arena, I instinctively knew there would be no magic spared, or spells barred, especially when the stakes were our own lives and those of almost everyone we knew. We looked at the audience and I couldn't help feeling that most of Rome now seemed to be siding with the druids and their pyrotechnics rather than the earlier heroes of the Christians' defeat of the Lions. I had to admit their display of magical fireworks was brilliant and their leader had deliberately darkened the sky so that the adoring masses could fully appreciate the stunning colour effects.

"He's quite good, isn't he," Marlene said with just a

hint of grudging admiration in her voice as the three of us walked slowly towards the centre of the arena. "I mean for a druid of course. Anyway, I thought they weren't supposed to do magic."

I could see Merl was also reluctantly impressed, from the professional point of view. "It's sort of a grey area," she replied as they dodged a stray magical jet of flame. "The dividing line between a master druid with slight wizard tendencies and a powerful wizard who's also an associate druid is very thin. I'm a case in point. Besides you're a witch as well as a wizard."

"True!" Marlene stopped walking. "By the way, who *is* the druid?"

"If I'm right, he's Guinevere's father," replied Merl. "I know he's a welsh chieftain, verging on royalty, which would then make sense that he's also a high-ranking druid. Remember, we knew Lancelot followed Guinevere to her family home and he would have had plenty of time as the Leading Man to have recruited Guinevere's father to his cause."

I'm not going to repeat Marlene's answer, mostly because I didn't understand some of it, but what she said was pretty explicit.

With a series of theatrical gestures the druids produced a particularly spectacular mixture of explosions, cascading lights and whirring flashes that became known to the world as Roman Candles. The crowd rose to its feet and went delirious, and I sensed that from now on the organisers could keep the lions, because this was *real* theatre and Romans were so fickle. The wizards were obviously admiring the magical display from the professional point of view and I heard the occasional grudging *ooh* and *aah*.

"I think it's time we talked to the druid face to face," said Marlene taking charge, "Man to Man, if you'll excuse my Saxon!"

I hung back several feet behind the sisters as they walked nervously towards the druid like gunslingers, because I had no wish to be in the druid's direct firing line. Besides, I was never much good at the defensive spells Merlin taught us. The two women halted a few feet in front of the druids and I wondered who would be the quickest on the magical draw and, more to the point, who would be the first to die. The noise and coloured lights from the fireworks slowly died down and the crowd hushed in anticipation, looking forward to the almost certain gory deaths of the two upstart wizards and probably me.

"Good of you to join me, ladies," sneered the Leading Man. "Allow me to present my friends the Black Knight – but you've already met him of course – and Guinevere's father and his two assistants." He looked behind the two wizards. "I see you brought along your brats, Merlin. How very thoughtful, because now I can get rid of all of you in one go. So much more efficient."

I was gobsmacked by the sarcastic hatred in the actor's words and felt them like a slap, but the two wizards knew it was only the first salvo in a war of words and fired back.

"Why are you here?" asked Marlene. "You know you can't win."

We stared at the Leading Man and the pitiless hatred that filled his soul was there for all to see. "In the mood he's in I don't think that concerns him," Merl said quietly. "He's here to kill and he knows my Arthur's death would end everything once and for all in blood and gore. It's not exactly subtle, but he'll have achieved his goal regardless of whoever else he hurts in the process." She turned to the actor and her voice hardened. "The only thing is that I won't allow it to happen."

"Very good, Merlin!" the Leading Man said mockingly. "You're right though, I really don't care anymore. But I do like subtlety and you ruined an ingenious plan that would quite literally have brought history back onto its correct course when your interfering brats took Julius Caesar back to Egypt."

That's me and Neets, I thought. I was quite proud of being an interfering brat.

"There's one or two things I'm not sure of at all," said Marlene. "Like, who are you really? Who else are you? Where did you come from? And lastly, why are you such an arrogant swine that you think you have the right to kill our king and take over the throne of Britain?"

The Leading Man slowly smiled and I waited for

the screaming sword swipe that would end Marlene's life. It never came, as it hadn't on the road to Camelot when the Leading Man stripped Merl of her false beard. Instead, the actor nodded and said what I least expected. "I thought you'd never ask," he smiled as he spoke, although he did add, "because I want you to know why you and your Camelot rabble are going to die, each and every one of you."

Merl looked at him without returning his smile. "I knew you as old Lancelot from Cornwall and I liked you, I think we all did. I find little that's attractive about you now and I have little interest in hearing your life's story."

"Nevertheless, hear it you will," sneered the actor, though the Black Knight looked as though he'd rather get on with the business of wiping out Camelot's elite. "Generations back my family came from Cornwall where they were very rich landowners and highly respected among the community. Then a neighbouring ambitious family attacked our farms and estates, forcing my ancestors to leave the area. To make sure they never returned and to ruin them completely, they spread false rumours that my people had made their money through murder and ship wrecking. I was born in a small town in Warwickshire and being an actor by nature, as you may have noticed, I moved to London, took the name of William Shakespeare and started my own acting company. Before I left home, my father made sure I remembered the wrong that had been done to our family all those years earlier and made me promise to take revenge if I could."

"That's why we never saw you and Shakespeare together!" Rosie cackled. She, Petal and Jennie had joined us and I reckoned that just about evened out the magic fight with the druids.

"Obviously," said the Leading Man. "I found it great fun being both writer, producer and lead actor without anyone realising it. I'd almost forgotten about revenge on our Cornish enemies, when my friends the three witches arrived unexpectedly from Camelot and while they played in *Macbeth*, I started putting my plans together. By the way, I'm sure you must have realised by now that it was Arthur's ancestors led by Julius Caesar's son that robbed us of everything?"

"I guessed," muttered Merl.

"Plus," added Marlene, "she's not a fool, you arrogant … person!" She never had been very good at swearing in spite of living with Neets and me.

"But did you know that Caesar was called *The Dragon* by his troops and that his son was known as *Son of the Dragon*? In Cornish that becomes Pendragon, Arthur's family name. That gave me the idea of inventing old Lancelot, the Cornish knight, and getting myself accepted in Camelot."

"But if you wanted revenge on the people who took your family's lands," said Merl, "why only come back several hundred years to Arthur's time? Why not go all the way back and argue with Caesar's son?"

"The words *me and whose army?* come to mind," replied the actor, "and you know it. Caesar left his son with a small legion and when the boy married the daughter of a local Lord, he used that power base to make himself untouchable. That situation hadn't changed much until Arthur's father took over the throne of Britain, making the kingdom the prize instead of just a few acres of land in a desolate part of the country. His father's death made Arthur vulnerable and the destruction of Camelot was irresistible. That's when I decided to make sure Arthur never existed, or at least as the person you know, by stopping his ancestor's parents ever meeting ... Caesar and Cleopatra. That would have been such an elegant solution and one requiring little involvement on my part. Unfortunately, your two brats stopped my little conspiracy to have Caesar assassinated in Rome and then messed up my plan to have him and his army drugged so they would attack the Egyptians and probably kill Cleopatra."

"Excuse me," I interrupted, "as one of the interfering brats I suspected you and Lancelot were one and the same person when we briefly captured you in Camelot castle. You may be a bloody good actor, but you made mistakes." I had the Leading Man's attention and even my Camelot friends looked surprised. "You didn't ask for a mug of water when we found you unconscious in Merl's old laboratory.

Anybody else would have done so. There wasn't time for everything you said to have happened in the lab before we arrived. The Leading Man would have knocked Lancelot down and escaped through the window in seconds had he been a separate person. He certainly wouldn't have wasted time by smashing the place up. What would have been the point, unless it was to put us off the right track? How come Lancelot found it necessary to go to Rome after Galahad, unless it was because his real self, the Leading Man needed to be there too? How come Guinevere went off with an old gaga knight like Lancelot, unless, of course, he was really a young charismatic actor promising dreams? Shall I go on?"

The Leading Man looked at me and clapped. "Not bad, not bad at all … for an interfering brat. I may have to upgrade you to a little nuisance."

"The one thing that concerns me though," I continued, ignoring his *little* insult, "is that surely you must have realised that if you went back in time and changed history, then you'd probably be affected as well. Arthur would have changed, or not been born at all, but who knows what could have happened to you?" As I talked I watched Gawain out of the corner of my eye. He had been slowly moving round the edge of the arena until he was now almost directly behind the Leading Man and his followers.

"Of course I realised the consequences," laughed the actor, "which is why I went back to the time of

Caesar's son and made sure my ancestors would do what I needed them to if I managed to wipe out the Pendragon dynasty before it even started. I ensured that instead of me being born a humble playwright, my family would take on their rightful mantle as Lords of Cornwall and I would become the natural king of Britain."

"In which case Shakespeare would never have existed," Marlene said thoughtfully.

"You stupid woman," the Leading Man almost shouted. "Have you listened to nothing? He never did exist. I acted the part of Shakespeare, therefore there would have been nothing to have stopped me from being Shakespeare if I was king." He was getting annoyed now. "Has none of you made the link between the names … *Shakespeare* and *Lancelot*? Or to make it easier for you, *Spear* and *Lance*." He turned to the Black Knight. "I don't know, you go out of your way to provide little clues a ten–year-old could solve and they're ignored. You try to inject a bit of fun into the game and it goes right over their heads. What can you do?" He gave a theatrical sigh.

"Kill them." The Black Knight hadn't needed more than a second to think about it. "Kill them all. Let's get it over and done with. There's too much talking." The man we knew now as Schwartz drew his sword and for a moment it looked as though his sheer aggression might force the issue into a bloodbath.

The three druids seemed to agree as they unleashed

a massive volley of screaming lights and thunderous explosions that wheeled and echoed round the Coliseum, convincing those people in the audience who were getting bored to sit down again.

"Unfortunately, I believe you're right, my friend," replied the actor. "Shall we say to the death?" He drew his spare sword and we prepared to die.

Chapter Fifteen

A Showdown, Three Fights and an Illusion

I glanced to where Arthur had been standing with the sailor Christians and saw him following Gawain. Both now had their swords drawn and I couldn't see any way this was going to end in anything but the bonus feature in a typical Saturday afternoon Coliseum massacre. I looked at the Leading Man and the hate-filled Black Knight, then at the druids, and realised that we were pretty well matched. In fact, if the Master of Ceremonies had drawn up a program it probably would have said:

Arthur (King of the Britons) v. (a.k.a. Lancelot and Shakespeare)		The Leading Man
Sir Gawain (a.k.a. Lewis) v. (a.k.a. Schwartz)		The Black Knight
Merlin and Marlene v.		The three druids
The Three witches v. and anyone who gets in the way		The three druids
Bryn, David, Christians v. soldiers and ticket collectors		The gladiators,
Unita and Tertia v. anyone threatening the boys		Guinevere and

The druids shot another firework into the air to keep the crowd amused. It whizzed high above the stadium before exploding into a hundred spirals that whirled and screamed just above the heads of the spectators. Only the two wizards and I kept our eyes fixed on the Leading Man, because we knew that to look elsewhere and lose our concentration would probably have been fatal.

To give Gawain and Arthur a few extra seconds to get into position I asked the Leading Man how he'd managed to arrange everything in the Coliseum so cleverly. It was an ego question and I knew he wouldn't be able to ignore it.

"Simple. I made sure Merlin sent Arthur through her Time Portal after I stole Excalibur," replied the Leading Man. "You thought you were keeping him out of my way, but I wanted to eliminate him far away from Camelot and preferably in another time period. That way he wouldn't become a legend, or even worse a martyr. He'd just fade to nothing." The actor's voice trailed away dramatically. "When I was Lancelot, Merlin told me exactly where she'd sent him when I went back to Camelot to get Guinevere's handbag and actually gave me the coordinates. So of course when I arrived here just before the gladiator fight I knew the exact date when Arthur came to Rome. It was the work of moments to go back a couple of weeks in Roman time to fix it for your pathetic king to be a gladiator judge, so at least you'd know he was here. I then arranged for him to ride in the chariot race, which must have been a bit of a surprise for you and, of course, there was always the delightful possibility he might be killed. Then I made sure he was included in the Lions against the Christians massacre just to make sure he was finally going to be dead history."

The actor was highly gratified at the look on our faces as we realised we'd been his puppets and that we hadn't even seen the strings. "I may have gone back in Time for a few of my hours," he continued, "but I came back through the Portal only a fraction of a second after I left here. A blink and you'd have missed me, which you obviously did." He sighed theatrically, but then he wouldn't have known any other way. "But in spite of all that even the lions let me down and now I have no choice but to eliminate Arthur personally in the time-honoured way of assassins everywhere." He smiled and pulled his index finger slowly across his throat. "If you want something done right, best do it yourself I always say. Even my spy in Camelot was only of limited use."

"So we were right," Marlene said quietly. "You did have a spy in our camp. We know it wasn't Guinevere, so perhaps now that it doesn't matter anymore you'd like to tell us who it was?" The Leading Man's grim smile told us it would be pointless asking a second time. "I'll take that as a *no* then, shall I?"

I looked back towards the edge of the arena where the boys and Neets were shielding the Christian sailors who, fresh from defeating the Lions, were responding to the crowd's cheers by leaping up and down and punching the air. They looked ready to take on anybody and anything, which to me probably meant the poor idiots had no idea what they were letting themselves in for. I turned back to the actor, whereas Merl's gaze hadn't left him for a second.

"After all these years, Arthur's only just begun to find out who I really am," she said slowly, "and if you think I'll let you hurt a hair on his head you're crazier than we thought."

The Leading Man laughed at Merlin's show of bravado and turned to the three druids who up to this moment had been acting as a firework display. Guinevere's father looked ready to fight anybody and anything, whereas the other two who looked as though they'd come along expecting to make up the numbers as the actor's cheerleaders, were beginning to fear the worst.

"It's time for this to finish, gentlemen," shouted the actor with a distinct tone of death and finality as he slowly raised his arms into the air. "Prepare to cast your spells against these two, their witches and the brat." He vaguely gestured towards me and the wizards. The two assistant druids looked at the Leading Man in horror and I could understand why, because trying to hex Merl was a sure way to be turned into a Roman rabbit. Luckily the actor's attention was now concentrated elsewhere looking for Arthur and Gawain.

A beam of brilliant golden light sliced from the tall druid's staff and soared high into the pulsating air before spiralling down ever faster until it blurred into a painful stream of searing radiance. The crowd *oohed* and *aahed*. He hammered his staff on the ground making the beam change direction so that it zapped into the statues of old dead emperors dotted around the Coliseum, neatly knocking most of their heads off in the process. Domitian ducked, presumably because being the current emperor meant he might well be next on the druid's hit list.

"We could rush them," Marlene shouted above the magical din, because some sort of battle plan was called for, even a bad one, "and we might even get somewhere near the bearded wonder. Actually it's more likely he'd melt us with that power beam of his before we moved more than a couple of feet. I'm sorry to say that if we're going to beat him once and for all we'll have to play the game his way."

Merl nodded, though if I knew my wizard, this was the one fight she wanted to avoid at all costs. It had been some years since her last magic duel and she would be more than a little rusty at the more complex fighting spells, but for Arthur's sake I knew she'd give it her best. She began to put on a show of courage that proved her ability as an actress every bit as much as her pretended manhood had over the past twenty years. "What'll it be then, druid, magic at thirty paces?" she drawled.

In answer the druid raised his staff and muttered a few ancient words making a zap of lightning flash from its tip. The crowd rose to its feet and roared its approval as the bolt circled the stadium, arced down as if spotting its prey, and then seemed to pause for a second before burning a neat hole in each of the wizards' hats. Luckily it ignored me, especially as I wasn't wearing a hat and the five of us backed away a few feet to give ourselves room to operate.

The masses cheered and clapped at the wizards' humiliation and then became hushed as the atmosphere in the arena become thicker and the air more difficult to breathe. Guinevere's father mouthed more druidic incantations, some of which I recognised as intended to build up a feeling of depression and hopelessness in his enemies. It was working, too, especially on the wailing crowd who were hugging each other for comfort, but it just made the wizards sneeze as dust rose from the ground in swirling clouds. Standing only a few feet behind Merlin and Marlene, I was protected from the worst of the spell, but even there I felt like crying for no reason and the witches bawled uncontrollably.

"He definitely isn't supposed to use magic," shouted Merlin blowing her nose on her sleeve. "I was always taught that druids mustn't use it! It's that grey area I was telling you about."

"A case of *do as I say, not as I do*" replied Marlene. "Typical man. And I can say that, now that you're officially a woman again."

The air around us tingled with the smell of magic as the druids blitzed the five of us with a mixture of spells and explosions. The wizards deflected the druidic blows as best they could with their particular brand of defensive magic before adding their own thumping bangs and flashing lights to the show. The witches mumbled nervously and gave the odd cackle, while I did the best I could with the small amount of magic I'd learned, but I think my main contribution was in just being there as a morale boosting back-up. I was so nervous I got most of the words wrong anyway. Soon the ground was scorched for metres around and in places the sand melted, turning into dirty glass marbles that *pinged* and *tinkled* as they cooled.

The three witches muttered a few more spells, then looked as though they'd already decided to run away at the first opportunity, or if possible … immediately. When the magical fireworks started they had distanced themselves from the rest of us just slightly and were now shuffling even farther away while trying not to attract Merl's attention, or anyone else's for that matter.

"Sod this for a game of knights," growled Rosie above the crashing explosions. "We didn't sign up for this lark. Merlin must be raving mad!"

"As far as I'm concerned she got herself into this mess and she and Arthur can darned well get themselves out of it. Plus she bleedin' well conned us into doing most of the dirty work," snorted Jennie as loudly as she could. The other witches looked at her in surprise. "Well, I can't think of anything in particular, but I'm sure she would have done. So she can bleedin' well solve this pile of nastiness without our help."

"Besides, we're due to play in *Macbeth* on Broadway in a couple of thousand years and we don't want to miss our cue," added Petal logically.

"Good point!" said Jennie. "We've never missed a performance yet and it's our duty not to disappoint our fans."

"The show must go on," said Rosie, a thoroughbred *artiste*.

The witches were now a good fifty feet from the danger zone of magical warfare and saw their chance of escape. Almost without anyone noticing, they joined the Christian sailors and started looking for the Portal.

Merl, Marlene and I were beginning to feel distinctly uneasy about our chances of beating the druids and the way things looked of even surviving for the next few minutes. Marlene was leaping around catching incoming death bolts in an almost visible magical net, while Merlin was busy trying to preserve the defensive barrier she'd built around us like an umbrella, but it was becoming harder to stop the druids' demonic spells getting through and the two wizards were faltering as the druidic powers seemed to increase even further. We all knew it was time for the kill.

The Leading Man seemed to grow in size as he laughed at the two puny women standing before him. He ignored me again and pointed towards Arthur. "Merlin, let's see what Arthur will do to you, his dearest and oldest friend, shall we?" He nodded to the tall druid who raised his staff and shouted an obscure incantation known to very few and used by even fewer as he focused his gaze on the king. At the other end of the stadium we saw Arthur jerk as though hit between the eyes with a mallet and stand stock still as though waiting for instructions. Merl winced in sympathy. Then Arthur moved.

The King of the Britons began to tremble. His eyes closed as he clutched the sides of his head, shaking it like a dog to drive out whatever demons were eating into his brain. His face contorted into a silent scream and then froze as though he no longer had control of his body, let alone his mind. Like a robot, he walked haltingly towards the centre of the arena, drawing his short sword as he approached Merl, but then passing her without so much as a glance. The druid smiled as Arthur stood in front of him and he rested a hand on the king's shoulder as though welcoming an old and valued acquaintance, or more accurately a family pet.

"Thank you for joining us, my royal friend." Guinevere's druidic father smiled like a favourite uncle. "I wonder if you would do me a small favour?" Arthur nodded with difficulty. "Behind you there are two female wizards, which in itself is an abomination, who are frankly annoying me intensely and I would rather like you to kill them, please. Start with the taller one." The druid's eyes never left Arthur's for an instant and although the king nodded, his face showed no emotion as he turned towards Merl, his closest friend, ally of twenty years and now the mother of his unborn child.

I looked in horror as Arthur slowly raised his sword ready to chop down with all his strength, like a gardener getting rid of a troublesome and extremely tall weed. I willed him to stop, but although he hesitated it was only for an instant as he concentrated on where to slice into the wizard's neck. Merl stood and cried because she and Arthur would never truly get to know each other, let alone enjoy the birth of their young prince and in gut-wrenching despair she closed her eyes tight shut. I have to admit I did the same. I heard the sound of a weapon rushing through the air and waited for the crunching sword blow that would end Merl's life hundreds of years from home and any hope we had of defeating the Leading Man. I heard the blow land, then the sound of a body collapsing onto the sandy arena floor and hoped that Arthur had struck cleanly so that his poor Merlin had died quickly and without too much pain.

I opened my eyes and knew that she had never felt the blow.

"I always said Arthur was very impressionable," Marlene was chatting as though absolutely nothing out of the ordinary was going on. "Tell him to do something and he does it without question. Super bloke and all that, but he's not really my type at all. Not my cup of Merl Grey tea as it were."

Merl opened one eye and peeked, ready to dodge any late sword thrusts. She looked down at the unconscious figure of Arthur lying sprawled at her feet and then at her cheerful sister who was still holding her staff like a battle club. Marlene smiled happily at Merl and was obviously ready to give the king another thump if he showed any signs of movement beyond a groan.

"The druid forgot all about little me," Marlene explained with a triumphant grin, "and Arthur was too busy following his instructions about killing you, so I thought I'd take the opportunity to bop him while he wasn't looking." She demonstrated on thin air. "Pow! Not exactly magic I know, but very effective nevertheless." She looked across at me and winked. "The witches were a waste of space, but young Tertia was a good diversionary tactic. The druid wasn't sure why she was with us and whether to ignore her or not, so she was a very useful distraction." To be honest I wasn't sure whether to be pleased or not, but winked back anyway.

Merlin knelt down and cradled the groaning king in her arms. "You didn't hurt him, did you? My poor Arthur." She scooped together some sand, making a pillow and after gently laying his head on it she stood up, anger trembling through every part of her body. "Where's the druid, Marlene? He's not getting away with it, not this time."

Marlene pointed to one end of the stadium where the dazed druid was kneeling on the ground, holding his head and looking unsure of his invincibility. "I walloped him too!" she chuckled. "He's magic mad and it's the last thing he was expecting. I reckon he's gone off to lick his wounds while he tries to think up some new piece of nastiness. But we're going to strike first, Merlin," she added briskly, rubbing her hands in anticipation. "We're going to beat the druids and the

Leading Man at their own mind games, so do as I tell you and we'll be fine … probably."

Marlene grabbed her sister's hand and held onto it firmly. She held out her other hand to me and then signalled Unita to join us from the edge of the arena and do the same, forming a square of power. "Now everyone concentrate." Marlene closed her eyes. "Focus your minds, let your mental powers combine with mine and leave the rest to me."

I closed my eyes and knew the others had done the same when I felt the grip on my hands tighten. I tried to concentrate my thoughts so that they merged with Marlene's, and I realised with a shock I was looking out of the druid's eyes and that we were controlling what he and probably the Leading Man would be seeing and feeling.

As the druid, I looked at us through a dizzy fog and felt frustration verging on doubt. I knew that in his heart of hearts he felt he was far from beaten, he just needed time to think, then his enemies would die and he would win. I could feel him trying to concentrate on the crowd's cheering to boost his confidence and then I sensed how everything had gone strangely silent, as though the world was waiting for something to happen, but wasn't sure what. I knew that if I'd felt the shock of it, then it must have hit the druids and the Leading Man with the force of a lightning bolt.

Through the druid's eyes I saw a movement in the Coliseum galleries as a figure twice the size of a normal man stretched and climbed carefully off its pedestal. It looked around, focused on the Leading Man and his kneeling followers and walked jerkily across the arena trailing flakes of white stone as it came ponderously forward. A second statue woke and was soon joined by a third and a fourth, until a small army of silent stone giants was advancing purposefully towards the dumbstruck druids and the Leading Man like marble zombies.

I remembered that Caesar's men had seen the stone pharaohs come to life in Egypt after eating a drugged breakfast and I understood what was happening. This was all in our enemy's minds and therefore because of our mental link, it was in mine, too. I watched the statues walk past our square of four focused wizards towards the terrified druids and the actor. It was no time to lose concentration, but it occurred to me that the Black Knight wasn't part of our mental link. I risked opening one eye for no more than a couple of seconds and saw him staring slack-mouthed in disbelief at his allies as they knelt weeping on the ground for seemingly no reason. I thought he might attack us in his confusion, but he turned and broke into a screaming run when he saw Gawain. I shut my eyes and concentrated again.

I was sure the tall druid must have seen many strange things and done many more that were heart-stoppingly terrifying, but this time it wasn't him causing them, which must have made it infinitely worse. I reckon he could have handled any approaching hostile group easily with a minor spell, but this was different, this was a blood petrifying horror and probably for the first time in his life the druid was rooted to the ground, unable to move.

The statues were shouting although they made no noise and slowly surrounded our enemies, allowing no escape from the ring of human stone. The statues stopped and the tall druid screamed as the first marble giant came forward and slowly stretched out an arm to touch him. The second one moved forward and he screamed again, then curled into a trembling ball when the statues looked to the heavens, raised their arms and roared silently in triumph as their fists descended like sledgehammers to smash the life out of him.

We released each other's hands, breaking the mental link and the statues disappeared just as they had in Egypt. I'd have fallen to the ground if Marlene hadn't managed to support me as I once more looked out of my own eyes. Guinevere had seemingly been unaware of her father's visions and stared in amazement as the druid covered his face with his hands, screaming soundlessly, and crouched next to his two assistants and the Leading Man. She looked at Marlene for an explanation as she ran to her father and cradled his head.

"It's all in the mind, Guinevere," explained Marlene. "At least it's all in your father's mind, the poor mite. I'm not quite sure what he saw, though by the look of her I think Tertia might know, but it was his own worst nightmare—whatever that may be—and I just sort of let it appear, if you see what I mean."

Guinevere's look of hatred would have shattered marble and I wondered whether the once beautiful queen of Arthur's Britain was showing her true nature at last, or had she been warped into what we now saw by the Leading Man. Either way, it wasn't pretty.

Merl helped a groggy Arthur to his feet. "Never mind about Guinevere," she said. "She was happy to desert her king and would have helped the Leading Man kill us if necessary. Sympathy for her and the druid is the last thing you should have." She raised her staff once more and started mouthing the words that would launch a final killing blow to finish off the druid while he was defenceless. I gently pushed the wizard's staff down.

"It's over for the druid, Merl. He's beaten," I said quietly, "and if you kill him you'll be no better than a murderer, so let him be. We need to concentrate on saving Arthur and beating the rest of the Leading Man's gang."

Merl nodded slowly and defused the spell by banging her staff on the ground so that the magic earthed harmlessly away. Arthur was unsteadily getting to his feet and Merl quickly went to his side to nurse the lump on his head and use the gentle magic of a kiss to make it better. Ahh!

Not being the focus of our magical concentration, the visions seemingly hadn't affected the Leading Man as badly as they had the druid and he was shaking his head to rid his mind of whatever he had seen. It wouldn't be long before the actor was a threat again. The druid's two assistants had recovered enough to understand that their future lay as far away from us as possible, and were zigzagging their uncertain way towards the tunnel the lions had used earlier in the afternoon, which I thought was probably a bad mistake on their part.

Right now, though, I was more concerned about the Black Knight and Gawain.

Chapter Sixteen

A Knight Fight to the Finish

I'd first seen the two of them fight when the Black Knight tried to overthrow Arthur and seize the throne of Camelot. He hadn't cared how many people died, or whose life he destroyed, but Sir Gawain had eventually beaten him and his small army. He escaped while being taken to his execution and used one of Merl's portable Time Portals to reach South Wales in the year 1734. Gawain followed him and for seventeen years they battled using their aliases (squire Mr Lewis and the evil smuggler Schwartz). That is until Neets and I made the difference and the Black Knight was finally beaten.

Now they were clashing again and the Coliseum

audience loved every moment. This wasn't a well choreographed ballet with artificial blood between two gladiators; this was a street brawl between two men who hated each other and were determined to fight to the death. This was the real thing and I'm ashamed to say I didn't have enough confidence in Gawain to believe that without any doubt he would win, because I'd seen how the Black Knight fought and to say he sometimes used dirty tricks was like saying Merl had a nice line in party conjuring.

Still munching their tea, some of the real gladiators tried to restore order, because I suppose if any fighting was going to be done they weren't going to have amateurs doing it. A couple of soldiers even tried to arrest the two fighting knights, but they retreated before the adrenalin-fuelled Christian sailors and the three witches who could scare any man with a toothless leer. The arena was soon left to the two knights, much to the delight of the late-afternoon Coliseum crowd.

Gawain and the Black Knight were fighting like mad men, using anything to get an advantage. Throwing handfuls of dust, kicking, scratching and eye-gouging were some of the nicer things they did, but mostly they grunted and clashed swords, trying to kill each other through sheer brute strength. The rest of us might as well not have been there for all the notice they took of what was going on around them. This was a very personal battle and we weren't invited, so Neets and I sat down in the middle of the arena floor and had a chat.

"You and Bryn getting on okay?" I asked, as the clash of steel rang out through the Coliseum. "He's got no problem with you being fifteen hundred years older than him?"

Neets shook her head. "No, we're fine." She offered me one of the sandwiches she'd taken from the table marked *T Pratchett & Family* in the Camelot's kitchens. "He sometimes gets confused as to why I'm that much older than him and yet I live nearly four hundred years in his future, but he's coming to terms with it all. After all, his dad's even older than me."

"But not as pretty."

"As you say, Tersh, he's definitely not as pretty as me."

"Good legs though."

"Shut up, Tersh!"

Gawain and the Black Knight had left the floor of the arena and were continuing their fight in the Coliseum's stands, dodging those spectators who hadn't managed to get out of the way quickly enough. The panting and grunting, because of the ferocity of their sword blows, told us how hard they were trying to kill each other and yet neither knight looked to be winning, nor was there even the slightest wound as far as we could see. Lots of sweat, but no blood.

"What about you and David?" asked Neets after we finished the sandwiches and licked the crumbs off our fingers. Even the crumbs from Galahad's table were a taste to die for.

"I'm not sure," I replied after a moment's pause. "He's a nice lad and he makes the odd move..." I knew what I meant.

"And you keep warning him off, Tersh. I've watched you." Neets knew what she meant, too.

"Yes, but that's to sort of encourage him." I knew what I meant, but it didn't sound right to me either.

"He does everything you say," said Neets pointedly, and I nodded because that was part of the problem. "I want someone strong like Bryn who'll tell me what to do and think he's getting his way. But you're different, you want an equal and David isn't sure what you want. He'll work it out." I have to admit Neets was a far better judge of men than I, so I shut up.

The clash of swords from the stands was less regular now, but just as loud and the grunts just as fierce. For a moment what puzzled me was that all the noise from the two knights seemed to be coming in stereo, in front of us where it always had been and from behind us where the wizard sisters were looking after Arthur.

I twisted round and stared in horror at the Leading Man as he stood over Merl, Marlene and our king. His sword was raised ready for another blow and by the state of the two wizard staffs this wasn't his first strike, as Merl and Marlene desperately tried to protect Arthur who was still groggily trying to grab his sword. I took hold of Neets's arm, hauled her to her feet and launched myself at the crazed actor, while my cousin flew at the druid and Guinevere, who were shouting encouragement immediately behind him. Actually in Guinevere's case it was more a shriek of hate with a fleck of spittle, while her father still looked confused, but dangerous.

The Leading Man shrugged me off with a snarl, but at least those few seconds gave Arthur the chance to pick up his sword and stumble to his feet. The actor ignored me and swung his blade with both hands at the king's neck in a blow that should have taken his head off, but at the last moment Arthur lifted his sword and stopped the actor's slashing weapon inches from his throat. He countered with a forward thrust that made the actor jump back in surprise and for the first time the two men were fighting as equals.

Neets and I helped Merl and Marlene to their feet and the four of us acted as royal cheerleaders, because the last thing Arthur would have appreciated in this particular battle was interference from a bunch of women, unless it was to stop Guinevere from gouging his eyes out. I began to realise what Merl saw in our king as he countered every blow by the Leading Man with a sword strike of his own that made the actor stagger and forced him to retreat. The look on Arthur's face was calm and the slight smile said he wasn't letting his anger take control. The Leading Man was shouting his hatred as he tried to parry

Arthur's blows and from where I was standing his anger was giving way to surprise and desperation.

"Lancelot, or whatever you call yourself," shouted Arthur between strikes, "you stole my wife, though I admit that can't have been difficult, and tried to seize my throne." His last slash nearly got through, as the actor staggered back and nearly fell to his knees. "Why?"

"You know why, Arthur." The actor managed to get to his feet and made an unsuccessful lunge.

"Why didn't you come to me and explain your family's grievance?" said our king. "We could have talked and worked something out. You could have had your estates back in Cornwall for a start." I was pretty sure Arthur meant every word, but the sneer on the actor's face said that he didn't believe it. "Lancelot, these games and charades you've been playing with people's lives," each word was accompanied by a slashing sword blow, "have taken away any sympathy I might have had for you and now you'll have to pay the price for your stupid ambitions and misplaced revenge."

The fight was becoming more one-sided as Arthur beat down the Leading Man's defence, until the actor fell on his back and tried to crawl away from our king's constant attack. Guinevere tried to run to his side, but Merl and Marlene used their staffs to keep the screeching ex-queen back as Arthur knocked the Leading Man's weapon out of his hands. He raised his sword to deliver the killing blow then slowly placed its point against the actor's throat.

"I trusted you as Lancelot," said Arthur, "and in memory of that, I will spare your life and that of Guinevere. If you yield, your fate will be decided by Merlin and her sister, both of whom will be more merciful than I. Do you agree?" The point of Arthur's sword pressed harder against the actor's throat as the man nodded his defeat.

The fight was over and Arthur had shown us why he was King of the Britons and why the most powerful wizard in the world had fallen madly in love with him. Merl and Marlene tied the Leading Man's hands behind his back while Neets and I did the same to Guinevere, before marching them both to the arena's entrance and the tender mercies of the Christian sailors.

Gawain and the Black Knight were still fighting in the stands, though they were too far away for us to see them clearly, but the sound of their swords clashing gave us a pretty good idea of where they were, and the ripple in the audience—looking more like a Mexican Wave—showed us how the fight was progressing round the Coliseum. From the crowd's point of view it was getting boring, because there were still no injuries; just a lot of noise and growling with a complete absence of gladiator pig's blood to liven things up.

The crowd ripple moved towards the arena floor

and the two knights emerged in a grappling tumble that made the Romans in the opposite stands rise to their feet and cheer. After all it was the only fight left in the Coliseum and Domitian had left some minutes earlier, presumably because nobody was paying him any attention.

The Black Knight was the first to get to his feet and while he had the chance he kicked Gawain in the head. It wasn't a powerful kick because both knights were exhausted, but it was enough to stun our hero and the grin on the Black Knight's face was not pretty to see. He aimed a second kick that should have been fatal, but Gawain managed to catch the Black Knight's foot and twist it aside so it missed his head by inches, giving himself enough time to climb unsteadily to his feet. The two knights circled each other, looking for an opening and some way to end their bitter feud of Good versus Evil. I could see that both men were too tired to attack with any force and I told Neets that the winner would be the one that didn't fall over. In Camelot both men had armies backing them and in South Wales Gawain had the militia as well as the school kids and their catapults, but here in Rome they were evenly matched and only hatred kept them on their feet. It had to stop. We'd achieved what we came to do and anything more would be vengeance.

Only Bryn and David made any move towards the two fighters and Neets and I were certain Bryn would help his father Gawain, and I half thought David might go to the aid of the Black Knight, his adopted dad. In a way we were right, but both lads kept their swords sheathed and stood silently within easy striking distance of their respective fathers. The two knights stared at their sons, then hesitantly lowered their weapons in a sort of mutual truce.

Bryn put his hand on Gawain's arm. "It's over, Dad. No more killing, especially not to entertain the Romans." I could see the look of pride on Neets's face as Gawain eventually nodded.

David stood between Gawain and the Black Knight, facing his father. "For me, Dad, if for no one else, put your sword away. No more hatred. No more blood spilling. If you don't drop your sword I swear I'll make you do it by force." David paused and I realised he had drawn his sword and its point was pressed against the Black Knight's chest. "I have a future and I want you to be here to see it. I don't want the only father I've ever known to be dead and a bad memory." To my amazement the Black Knight dropped his sword and looked at David as though seeing him for the first time. Then he did something I'd never seen him do before, unless it was to kill someone … he put his arms round David and hugged him. Even though I couldn't see his face, I suspected there might be the odd tear or two. If Neets was proud of her Bryn, then my David was going the right way to getting an almighty hug from me as well.

My David? Blimey!

The skies cleared to a deep blue and the danger was gone, leaving the normal satisfying end to a Roman Coliseum Saturday afternoon massacre. The cheering Roman spectators rose to their feet and began the longest cry for an encore in the Coliseum's history, because sometimes even the most bloodthirsty crowd loves a happy ending.

"I think that if I'm right," said Marlene with satisfaction and considerable relief, "the Temporal Detective Agency has once again saved the day. We've beaten all the baddies, saved Arthur and sorted out the mystery of the *Mary Celeste*." She turned to her sister. "Actually, dear, that's one I'd like to talk to you about. Come on, let's join the others."

Neets and I watched as David and his adoptive father, followed by Bryn and Gawain, walked over to where we now stood with the Christian sailors. There was no sign of triumph on Gawain's face and the Black Knight just looked drained and tired, as though the centuries of fighting had been too much for both of them. I'd seen them fight over kingdoms, revenge for murders committed and wives presumed lost, but it had all come down to a one-on-one scrap in Rome and now they were oblivious to everything, even to the fact that the show was over and the Coliseum was nearly empty.

"I haven't heard anyone ask, Merl," I said as I checked that Guinevere's hands were securely tied.

Arthur had already made sure of the Leading Man. "Are you okay? The little prince, I mean."

She nodded. "I'm fine. And now that my Arthur's safe and those that would have killed him have been defeated, we can all go home." She paused. "Well, not quite all of us. The crew and passengers of the *Mary Celeste* will be staying here. They can't go back."

"Why, Merlin?" asked David in surprise. "Surely that's why you sent Bryn and me back to rescue them."

"I knew that everyone was supposed to have deserted the Mary Celeste in one of the life boats for some reason and were never seen again. As they were so far out to sea everyone presumed they all drowned, but one of their descendants contacted me through Marlene and asked me to solve the puzzle and see if I could somehow help."

"Who was that?" asked Bryn.

"An old friend of ours from South Wales, dear," replied Merl. "Chief Inspector Smollett."

"Yeah. He told me once he was into genealogy," explained Marlene, "and Tertia thought he meant he was a part-time doctor, when really he was tracing his family tree. He found that he was related to Volkert Lorenson, one of the crew of the *Mary Celeste* and asked me to talk to Merl."

"I sent you there for three reasons," Merl continued. "Firstly, because I wanted the girls to go alone to the Globe Theatre without any arguments or help from you boys. Secondly, I wanted to help Chief Inspector Smollett and you two were perfect for that. Lastly, I felt sorry for the Black Knight, because I knew he would probably never get released from Time Limbo as nobody would ever want to replace him. On the other hand, I was sure you'd find an excuse to get him out, David, for the best of reasons in the world, so when you took the *Mary Celeste*'s crew through the Portal to Rome I'd already arranged for the Black Knight's Time Prison to release him so he could join you."

"So why didn't we see him?" David asked.

"Because he went out of the Time Portal back door and travelled in parallel with you, but not on the same track if you like. I knew he and the Leading Man would link up. In fact, I was pretty sure they knew each other from the actor's days in Camelot when he was Lancelot, and I wanted all our enemies in one neutral place so with our little group we could defeat them once and for all. Mind you, I hadn't reckoned with the druids being involved, but then we had the witches as a magical backup of sorts. You can't have everything, I suppose."

"Especially the truth, I suspect," muttered Marlene. Then out loud she said, "So what are we going to do with this lot then, Merlin? We can't leave them here."

"The *Mary Celeste* crew will be staying. I've spoken to Captain Briggs and his wife and they realise they would be dead if the boys hadn't rescued them, and

293

putting them back on the boat would cause all sorts of temporal anomalies. Besides, they're all heroes now and if they play their cards right, they'll be the toast of Rome and life won't be so bad for them."

"Okay, so why were they fighting the lions in the first place?" asked Marlene.

"Someone asked Captain Briggs if they were Christians and of course he said they were. Next stop … the Coliseum Saturday afternoon show with Arthur as celebrity guest."

Arthur had been listening intently to everything that was being said and Merlin gave him a little cuddle. "Arthur," she stroked the bump on his head and smiled, "are you feeling better? So much has happened that you couldn't know about since you left my cave and I think I owe you an explanation." Before he could argue, Merl put her arm round Arthur's shoulder and talked as she walked him out of prying earshot. They talked for five minutes and then returned to the others.

The King of the Britons took a deep breath, looked at his Camelot friends and stared especially at the beardless Merl whose body shape was beginning to look mum-like in a curvy sort of way. He gave a start when he realised we were all waiting for him to speak and he let out the first deep breath a long sigh, before taking another one. "I know I've been in terrible danger, Merlin, and I've tried not to show how afraid I was by playing the fool at times." Arthur looked intently into Merl's eyes. "I know that you and so many people have kept me safe by risking your own lives, for which I'm eternally grateful. I'm so lucky to have such a wonderful woman to love and to have such loyal friends prepared to give their lives for me."

Neets and I looked at each other and shrugged, because he might have been right about the Merl bit, but the rest of us were pretty keen to carry on living. Neets, Marlene and I took the Christian sailors to the main forum outside the Coliseum where a crowd of new fans was patiently waiting. After all, no one had ever beaten the lions before and these guys were now heroes. Let's face it, Romans just loved heroes ... for a week or two at least.

Meanwhile, the witches concentrated on their cackling and croning because they needed the practice and their theatre audiences throughout the centuries demanded absolute perfection. Marlene tapped Rosie on the shoulder, stopping her in mid-cackle. The witch looked at the wizard with a sinking heart. "Oh, it's you! Why are Merlin and Arthur holding hands ... oh yes." Witches don't necessarily like a happy ending unless it's their own. "Come to take us back to Camelot as well have you, Marlene?" she asked with a distinct tone of depression. "Back to draughty caves, bloody awful food, cold dark nights and cow dung?"

Marlene smiled and ran a hand through her striking orange hair. "No, not unless you particularly want to go there, besides I've got a proposition you may be interested in. There's a new William Shakespeare back at the Globe Theatre replacing our Leading Man and he's going to need your help to fit in, if you wouldn't mind? I believe he might be the one everyone remembers as the Great Bard." Three happy cackles became three big grins, then three fast nods with not a single swear word. "Excellent! And thank you for the parcel you arranged for the girls to bring to Merlin," said Marlene. "Then I do believe at long last we can all go back home to Camelot and get on with our lives."

"What are we going to do about this bunch of villains?" I asked, because although we'd won the day no one had put forward any suggestion as to what happened next.

Marlene smiled. "Merlin will take care of that. Don't worry."

The Portal hidden under the Coliseum archway turned ultraviolet and pulsed into life as Gawain, Bryn, David, Unita, Marlene and the three witches pushed the Black Knight, the druid, the Leading Man and Guinevere through it and back to the wizard's cave.

As Arthur, Merlin and I were about to follow, the Master of Ceremonies came running up shouting and urgently waving his arms to attract our attention. "Stop, stop! I'll book you all for the rest of the season. Star billing, no nonsense and with your own dressing rooms."

Zzzzzp.

"Where'd they disappear to?"

Chapter Seventeen

The Original Scam and the Last Farewell

As soon as we got back to her cave, Merl asked Neets and me to go down to the village and check that the Leading Man's influence had definitely been broken and that it was safe for anyone who needed to go to the castle to do so. She also asked us to tell Galahad he could gear up Portal deliveries to the *Olé Grill* restaurants again, though I suspected he'd really never slowed them down.

The village was quiet and the few people we saw seemed friendly enough, but that could have been because they still had the odd pocketful of gold coins with Caesar's head, and of course because trouble hadn't been stirred up for at least twelve hours. People have very short memories. No one seemed particularly bothered that their king had been buried the day before, or that the castle was now one vast kitchen and most of Camelot's hierarchy had disappeared. Life goes on.

When we returned, Marlene had been right and Merl had disposed of our villainous enemies. There was no sign of the Black Knight, Guinevere, the druid or the Leading Man. Arthur still referred to him as Lancelot, which I supposed was understandable as he only met the actor as his true self once and that had been in Rome. Merl told me that she'd talked to the druid and was happy that Guinevere and the Leading Man had told him a pack of lies about Arthur. She felt he was no threat now he knew the truth and taking revenge on him would serve no useful purpose. She'd accepted his promise never to return to Camelot and sent him back to his settlement in Wales. I asked what had happened to the others, but she just smiled and refused to say anything except that none of them would pose a threat to any of us ever again. Even Marlene would only shrug her shoulders and change the subject.

I watched Marlene wander around Merlin's cave,

greeting each nook and cranny like an old friend, even though everything looked very bare and the words *"temporary"* and *"No Fixed Abode"* sprung to mind. Most of Merlin's mementoes had been wrapped in linen and packed away in chests before being slipped through the Portal to her new home, leaving shelves and display areas empty for dust to gather and mice to perch on.

"I thought none of us were ever going to see this place again," she said happily as she munched on a deliciously stale Galahad sandwich, "at least not in the Camelot era. Mind you, I've got used to the comforts of the cave in the twenty-first century and to taking lunch in the *Olé Grill*. I'd miss all that, so I'm glad we made it."

There had been one bit of excitement after we returned from Rome when Merl first lit the fire using an overly powerful spell and sent flames roaring up the chimney. A howl of painful surprise was followed by an urgent scrabbling from somewhere far above, which sent flakes of soot floating down into the cave.

"The Leading Man's spy, I do believe, dear," smiled Marlene as she sat down to enjoy what was going to happen next. "*Hot* on our trail."

"Probably *burning* to get back home, I'd say." Merl sat down next to her sister and listened to the sounds of desperate slipping and slithering coming from the chimney smoke hole. Neets and I became interested at this point and got up from our straw bales where we'd been enjoying a chat with Bryn and David to join the wizards.

"He'll have a *blazing* temper by now. By the way, Merlin, I hope you don't mind that I greased your chimney before we went to Rome?" said Marlene with a smile and a wink.

"Not at all. I'm sure it helps the smoke get out." A pair of legs appeared above them trying desperately to get a grip on the slippery rock. "Ah, at long last, I do believe our visitor has decided to meet us face to face."

With a final shriek of pain, presumably mixed with the fear of what may have been waiting below, a figure fell from the chimney hole high in the cave's ceiling and with a screech landed on the bale of hay Marlene had thoughtfully positioned to soften his fall. He sat up, rubbed various parts of his body to make sure he still had them, then with a series of smoky coughs glanced around for a quick way out. The look on the wizards' faces told him escape was not an immediate option.

"You could have killed me with that fire," he complained grumpily. "There was no call to go all vicious like that." He patted at his smouldering clothes and examined the more extensive burn marks. "Look, you've ruined them!" The once immaculate scarlet and yellow herald's uniform was almost certainly beyond repair, though the herald himself would be fine in a couple of days with a bit of magical help as Merl took great pains to point out.

"On the other hand," said Marlene, "if you have an attitude problem Merlin could always turn you into a bunny rabbit." She got up and walked to the kitchen spring to fetch a large mug of water. The look of hesitant *I don't believe you ... er, probably* became a certainty when the wizard added, "I suspect you've known lots of people who just disappeared one night, never to come back? Well now you know why there are so many rabbits near Camelot." She walked back to the trembling herald and handed him the mug. He gulped its contents in one massive swallow and handed it back with a nod of thanks. "I meant you to use it on your clothes, but I suppose you know best," sighed Marlene as she sat down and steepled her fingers. "Now to business. The question is, what on earth do we do with you?"

"Let me go," the herald suggested hopefully as he looked from wizard to wizard, "and we'll say no more about it, yes? No, I suppose not."

Merlin stared at the man and frowned. The herald was an institution in Camelot. Pretty well part of the furniture. He was well paid and except for reading out the odd proclamation he had very little to do. A cushy little number really. So what was he doing spying for the Leading Man, putting his king's life in mortal danger and jeopardising almost everything that existed in Camelot, past and future.

"You cheated," the herald said with a sulk and I

remembered that the Leading Man had used much the same excuse. "There are rules and you rode roughshod over them just so your man could become king and again when you buried him. You didn't care about the likes of me because I was just the funny little man with the scroll, and tradition counted for nothing against your ambition."

Merl was stunned. "And because of that, and I'm not saying you're right, you sold us all down the river and spied for the actor?"

"Yes." There was a long pause before the herald continued. "But I didn't know he wanted to kill King Arthur. Honest, I didn't know what he was going to do. He told me we were kindred spirits and that if I helped him by spying on you Camelot would return to normal and … and then things got out of hand. He kept wanting more and more information and he kept sending me back here. He told me about the smoke hole so I could listen in without being discovered, but I didn't understand half of what you said, although it seemed to make sense to him."

"But what were you doing up there just now?" asked Marlene. "It's all over. We've beaten the Leading Man so why are you still spying on us? And please don't tell me it's force of habit."

"I got stuck," mumbled the herald.

"You what?"

"I got stuck, all right? I climbed down the chimney just after you went off to wherever it was you went, but some fool had put animal fat all up the chimney and I couldn't get out again."

"But why didn't you call for help?" asked Merl. "I'm not a monster … most of the time."

The herald gave her a scornful *would you?* look and she gave an understanding nod, but that really solved nothing. The wizards knew they couldn't pat him on the head and send him on his way without some sort of punishment, but with the danger over, retribution didn't seem appropriate to any of us. Marlene took Merl by the arm and led her into the solitude of the kitchen area, but not out of earshot.

"Merlin, you might not like it, but the way out of this is to use the punishment reward scenario."

"I see what you mean, but would it work?"

"Don't know, but have you got a better idea?"

Twenty minutes later and after a thoroughly good verbal lashing from the sisters, the herald made his way back to Camelot having accepted his punishment with good grace plus, once he thought he was out of sight, a series of skips and the odd jump.

Merlin had refused to allow him to wear yellow and scarlet ever again and demanded that in future he would have to wear greens, browns and blues and have a large compulsory clothing allowance whether he liked it or not. Marlene had said that from now on he wouldn't be able to just make proclamations, he would have to do all the organising as well. He would be in charge of weddings, funerals, coronations, banquets and parties … whether he liked it or not. To top it all, both wizards told him there was to be no more blowing his own trumpet as they would provide two squires to do it for him on special occasions.

Problem solved, but even though it had been the previous day the smell of scorched clothing still hung in the air. Otherwise a sort of normality had been just around the corner, though even that was relative. Merl spent her time busying round the cave collecting her last remaining trinkets and wrapping them ready for storage. She picked up a small statuette and tried to remember where on earth it had come from, but the word *China* printed on the bottom gave no clue as I could see it was definitely made of metal.

Marlene decided that what the cave needed right now was someone to unpack the mugs Merlin had just packed up and make a cup of tea. She automatically looked for Neets as chief tea-maker, then remembered that this was going to be a DIY cuppa with an absence of fresh biscuits.

Merl stopped packing, because to be honest most of it had already gone through the Portal to the Isle of Avalon, and considered for a moment. I knew from what she'd told me it fitted in quite nicely with the plans she had for Arthur's future, most of which involved herself and the future little prince, somewhere far away from the minds and memories of Camelot. She picked up the cup her sister had left by the packing case and joined her at the Round Table.

The sisters moved even further out of Neets's earshot, sitting on their two favourite chairs facing each other either side of the fireplace. I stayed in my chair at the Round Table, but was still close enough to hear what was said. The fire wasn't lit, but with a flick of her staff Marlene conjured a very respectable blaze using a mixture of magic and bits of wood from a broken packing case.

Marlene ignored the last comment. "All this was about you and Arthur, so have you made any decisions as to what you're going to do yet?" She nodded towards the packing cases. "The witch part of me says it looks as though you've met a tall, blond stranger with a crown and plan to go on a long trip."

Merl sighed deeply. "What Arthur and I are going to do," she said at last, "has needed considerable thought. Arthur certainly won't want to live here. He's used to a little more comfort than this place can offer and to be honest I'd quite like to try getting used to a spot of luxury for a change, too. Arthur and I have decided to build a place on the Isle of Avalon where we won't be disturbed, but we'll spend most of our time touring Europe seeing the sights before we become parents. You see, Arthur has decided to remain 'dead' and he's given up being king for good. The legend will live on instead."

Against all the odds I could see that everything was falling into place for Merl and she threw back her head and laughed for sheer joy. I knew she would never be Arthur's queen and so did she, and everyone would always say Guinevere was the love of his life, but we both knew who Arthur really belonged to and the last obstacle had disappeared.

"I'm pleased for you, Merlin," Marlene said with total sincerity as she gave her sister a quick hug. Her sister hugged her back.

"Even though we'll all be leading new lives," replied Merl, "I don't want us to lose touch with one another."

"We won't," Neets and I promised. After all, our wizard was going out with a king and that sort of royal connection could be very good for the Temporal Detective Agency's business.

"One thing, Merl," I said, "I think I can count on the fingers of one hand the number of times I've actually seen you use magic, outside of Rome that is. What's the point of being a wizard if you don't make use of it?"

"That," explained Marlene, "is because my sister is such a great wizard that she doesn't need to use magic. Everyone knows she's the best in the world, so why should she spend valuable time and energy proving it to fools?"

"You're learning very quickly, sister," laughed Merl, "and I'm beginning to think you'll probably have to use magic even less than me. Now I must go. Arthur and I have one last task we need to complete before we go to Avalon." She got up and kissed Neets before giving her younger sister a hug. To my surprise she took me by the hand. "Tertia, I want you to come with me if you wouldn't mind. I want your help one last time." She picked up the long package wrapped in cloth I'd brought back from the witches and smiled, then with a final wave she and I walked through the Portal for the last time.

Zzzzzp.

When I opened my eyes, we were in the outskirts of Camelot village. The castle flag was flying at half mast and covered in the crest of Arthur's father, which told me we'd probably travelled back a good few years and were about to witness a new king being crowned.

"Did it all go okay?" Arthur asked from behind us, giving his beloved Merl a hug and a quick peck on the cheek.

"No problem." She smiled at her ex-king. "Give me a hand with these." Merlin carefully unwrapped the witches' parcel and held up three identical Excalibur swords. She handed one of them to Arthur, one to me and tucked the third into her belt. She put a finger to her lips for silence and motioned us to follow her into the village.

It was still early morning and the sun had barely climbed above the horizon when we entered Camelot's main square, which was in truth more of a village green. The last trails of a wispy mist drifted up from the lake and wafted over the grass, damping out sound and emphasising the near emptiness of the place. Perched on a tree stump was a very depressed looking young man holding what looked remarkably like a wizard's staff and a rather ornately pompous looking parchment scroll. Every so often he looked at the scroll, then at a nearby rock and each time he did so he let out a series of deep sighs.

"Just as I remember things," Merl whispered as she walked up to the young man. Arthur nodded because the scene was vaguely familiar to him too, as it was to me. The young man looked up as we approached and scrambled down from his perch ready to run. I recognised him now … or rather her.

"Don't go," said the wizard quickly, putting out a restraining hand. "We're here to help you. What's your name?"

The young man stood his ground studying the two newcomers. "I'm Merlin," he replied proudly, adjusting the fluffy beginnings of a false beard, "and I'm the greatest wizard in the world."

"Not yet, you aren't," Merl muttered and gave a half smile, "but one day you will be if we manage to get this right."

"Only I don't know how to make this work." The young man sighed again, held up the scroll and started to explain the rules for finding the new King of the Britons. "This time, though, they're making it really complicated. Not only has the new king got to pull a sword out of solid stone, but the organisers aren't even supplying the sword in the first place.

We've got to find our own sword and then get it into the stone somehow before we can even try to pull it out!"

"That's the trouble with swords," said Merl and just like any good wizard, which of course she was, she produced the first of the Excalibur swords and a tube of very quick-drying glue. "Stand back all of you," she ordered. With all her strength she raised the sword above her head and brought it down point first onto the top of the rock. The rest of us, including the younger Merl, shielded our eyes expecting either the sword or the stone to shatter and send off razor sharp shards in all directions, but to our amazement the sword sank into the stone a good two feet and stayed there quivering.

"Merlin, you're so strong!" Arthur whispered proudly, but I wondered if it was quite the right thing to say to his pregnant girlfriend.

Merl blushed and sensibly decided it was better to look beautiful and wise, rather than be known as a muscle-bound female hulk. "Not really, Arthur. Last night when I took the witches to the Globe Theatre I brought back a couple of the artificial rocks they leave around. This is one of them." As she spoke Merlin smeared glue all round the sword where it entered the stone and within seconds it had set rock hard ... no pun intended. "There you go," she said with satisfaction, "one Sword in the Stone."

"But it won't move," protested young Merlin after

giving the sword a tentative tug and watching it vibrate with a *twang*. "How is my Arthur ever going to pull it out now and become king?"

"Good point!" said Merl. "However, I suggest that this sword is for all the other knights to try and fail at, so it's a good job I brought a second rock from Hollywood. All you've got to do is swap the stones over when everybody's asleep and make sure Arthur is the first and preferably the only person to try to pull the sword out in the morning."

"But I haven't got a second sword!" wailed the young wizard. "It's got to be the same one, or everyone's going to notice and I'll need another identical stone too, or we'll end up with two swords in this one."

Merl took one of the spare Excaliburs from Arthur and handed it to her younger self, who looked at her in astonishment.

"You must have come here prepared for this, Lady," said young Merlin suspiciously. Nevertheless the junior wizard took the spare sword, tested it for weight then tucked it in her belt. "Can I really trust you?"

"With your life, I promise you. Right, you know what to do. Put this sword in the spare rock you'll find hidden behind those houses and swap the stones over tonight after everyone's given up and gone to bed. Oh, and one other thing," she pulled a small pouch out of her robes, "sprinkle some of this in the communal stew, but whatever you do, make sure Arthur doesn't eat any."

"It's not poison is it?" asked the younger Merlin suspiciously. "I don't want anyone to get hurt."

"No, it'll just inconvenience everyone long enough for Arthur to draw out the sword and be proclaimed King." Merl took Arthur's hand and turned to walk away.

"But I don't even know who you are, Lady."

"Just three friends who want to see Arthur become king and you become the greatest wizard in the world," replied Merl with a smile. On an impulse she gave her younger and very surprised self a quick hug before taking Arthur by the arm and walking him out of the village of Camelot hand in hand, leaving the youthful wizard a much happier lady.

Up until then I'd done almost nothing but when we reached the Portal, Merlin told me why she needed me to perform one last task for her. It was a small one and wouldn't take more than a few minutes, but unless I did it all our lives would be changed forever.

I waved to the royal pair as they walked to the Portal arm in arm on their way to their new life on Avalon and promised to let them know as soon as I'd succeeded in setting history on its correct course. Merl returned my wave, but Arthur only had eyes for his beautiful wizard.

"What was the third Excalibur for, Merlin?" I heard

Arthur ask. "I'm not complaining you understand, I like it, but why three identical swords?"

Merlin looked up at Arthur and kissed him on the cheek, while Arthur put his arm round her shoulder and gently touched his head to hers. They both smiled. "Technically you're no longer a king, Arthur, but you'll always be one to me and you should wear a sword fit for a King. That could only ever be Excalibur." Arthur almost purred with pleasure. "Besides, one day Britain might just need King Arthur to rise from his legendary deep sleep on the Isle of Avalon and if that ever happens I want you to be ready with a sword that proves to everyone that you're the real item."

They walked through the Portal to continue their honeymoon and start their new lives.

Zzzzzp.

The next morning I joined the crowds milling round Camelot village green, lapping up the atmosphere and relishing the excitement. I could see young Merlin and someone I presumed was the youthful Prince Arthur getting ready for their big moment, so I kept well out of their way in case one of them recognised me from the previous day. I saw the Leading Man's spy, the little herald, looking pompous in his multi-collared uniform, and eventually I saw the person I needed to meet, a young girl running round the standing stones with her friends playing tag. I'd have known her anywhere, because it was me.

I was only six then and convincing my younger self and elder cousin to stand still and watch a boring ceremony was always going to be tricky, but by pretending to join in the game of tag I managed to guide them towards the centre of the green and the all-important sword stuck in a fake stone. I told young Tertia and Unita about Merl and Arthur and how between them they could change the world and perform amazing magic. I told her with a sigh that I'd have given anything to have been one of Merl's apprentices, but that I was far too old to start now. Then I shut up and let a six year-old's imagination get to work.

Tertia and Unita would be Merl's Girls.

The sun shone down and life was good in Camelot.

I smiled, left the village to its celebrations and went through the Portal, forward those few years to Merl's old cave.

Zzzzzp.

There was no longer anything to keep us in the fifth century and it was time for us all to return to the *Olé Grill* and the storage room at the back of the restaurant that served as the Temporal Detective Agency offices. The kingdom was stable, Camelot was safe and one day the people would choose a new king who might, or might not be as good as Arthur. That was up to them. Meanwhile Arthur and Merlin had their lives before them, they would become legends and Marlene would soon be an auntie.

I had one final chore to do, one which I had always enjoyed, because I was quite attached to Merl's little furry friends. She'd left some lettuce in the cave and asked me to feed the rabbits before we went through the Portal.

David and I went to the entrance of the cave and made what seemed like pretty good rabbit noises, though come to think of it, I never heard a rabbit make any sound. It didn't matter, though, because we were soon surrounded by happy little bunnies that bobbed around us waiting for the tastiest iceberg lettuce morsels.

While they nibbled and munched, I noticed three rabbits that hadn't moved. They sat some twenty feet away and stared at me. I offered a lettuce leaf, but in return I got looks of pure hatred, if that's possible from a rabbit. I took a closer look. One was a pretty little thing with beautifully soft fur that shone in the morning sun. The second was a much larger specimen that for some reason had no fur on its head and looked as though it fought for fun, but obviously wasn't always the winner. The last was rather thin, but well-groomed and had an air of arrogance. It also had a mark on its left paw that looked remarkably like an *L*.

Merl had kept her word. She'd made sure our enemies were safely disposed of and had also proved once and for all that she was still the greatest wizard in the world.

David smiled. "My dad'll get used to it. They all will, and it'll be better than being in Time Limbo. Will Merlin turn them back, do you think?"

"She's not vindictive," I said. "It may take a year or two, but when she's happy they're no longer a threat she'll reverse the spell." I said that with certainty, because I knew my wizard. I got up and brushed bits of grass from my robes. "Time to go. They'll be fine." In fact, I reckoned the female rabbit would be the centre of attention, the large bald one would soon be organising raids on neighbouring colonies and the thin one would be putting on shows. Life goes on.

David looked nervous as we walked back to the cave. He was blushing a deeper red than Marlene's hair and the nearer we got to the cave the less likely it was he was going to say anything. I stopped, looked at him and smiled serenely. "Well?"

"There's something I've been meaning to ask you, Tertia," he said eventually. "I…"

He got no further. Marlene was calling for us to move ourselves *now* so we could all go back to the TDA offices. Galahad had already returned and was being deluged with calls that needed our attention. Actual cases, with actual money! Probably.

David looked so deflated that I gave him a quick kiss and held his hand as I pulled him into the cave.

I realised I was still holding his hand some minutes later as we walked through the Time Portal back to the TDA offices in the *Olé Grill*.

Such is life.
Zzzzzp.

THE END

Great Authors

Meet Authors Reach authors and discover our books:

- Detective thrillers
- Paranormal
- Horror
- ChicLit
- Fantasy
- Young Adult

Visit us at:
www.authorsreach.co.uk

Join us on facebook:
www.facebook.com/authorsreach

Lightning Source UK Ltd.
Milton Keynes UK
UKOW06f0851241215

265316UK00001B/2/P